TO THE BONE

J.R. JOHANSSON

First English Edition

Interior Layout and Cover Design by Melissa Williams Design, based on original designs by Marianela Acuna, OLIFANT–Valeria Miguel Villar, and Luis Tinoco
Cover Photos: Pavel Chagochkin/Shutterstock; Gergory/Shutterstock

Author photo by Brekke Felt

Summary: Seventeen-year-old Harley Martin has been obsessed with Paris for years, so when she gets a chance to visit her cousin Gretchen in Paris for the summer, she jumps at the chance. When a tour with Gretchen and her friends through the off-limits section of the Paris Catacombs goes awry and their guide is crushed in a cave-in, Harley must decide who she can trust among this group of strangers as she fights to escape alive from a place that only embraces death.

ISBN: 978-1-7340089-3-7 (paperback)
ISBN: 978-1-7340089-4-4 (eBook)

Don't Miss Out!

THE NIGHT WALKERS SERIES

Insomnia

Paranoia

Mania

OTHER NOVELS

Cut Me Free

The Row

RIVETING READS PODCAST

Available at jrjohansson.com
and other podcast media outlets

DON'T MISS OUT ON JENN'S TWITCH STREAM!

TO THE BONE

J.R. JOHANSSON

MIDNIGHT MEDIA

For My Readers—
You have held my words in your hands,
my worlds in your hearts and you've supported
me more than I ever expected. Thank you!

Chapter 1

Text from Chantal to Harley sent on June 10 at 6:14 p.m. –

Hi Harley! I'm so sorry. I know we were supposed to be there to pick you up at the airport, but some things came up and I can't make it. Don't worry though! I've set up a taxi to pick you up. He should be waiting outside the baggage claim for you and he knows where we live. Look for the sign with your name and you'll be fine! Love you and can't wait to see you! xoxoxo

—transmission successful

■ ■ ■

I stumble out of the cab on Boulevard Richard-Lenoir, tugging my tattered souvenir duffle bag from the School of the Art Institute of Chicago out behind me. Searching through my travel-frazzled brain, I try to remember anything from my one year of French class that will help me with the driver.

"Merci?" I say as my cabbie hauls my massive suitcase out of his trunk. He gives me a curt nod then rattles off a response in French that loses me completely. When he stops and waits for me to answer, I blink at him in helpless frustration.

Helpless. I hate that word. My parents have put me in a situation where I'm powerless. Now, thanks to them, I'm effectively futureless. I've been simmering with rage beneath my skin for over a month. It has changed me. It feels like anger is the thing I'm becoming, and I just wear a suit that looks like my old self. My parents have torn apart my life and all I can feel is furious.

Furious and destroyed, which is an exhausting combination to hold this tightly for this long.

The front door to the building opens and my aunt Chantal appears, breaking me from my spiraling thoughts and saving me from the annoyed glare of the driver. It's been five years since I've seen her and my cousin Gretchen, but my aunt doesn't look like a day has passed. Fluid French pours from her pink lips as she pays the driver. He flushes to the very top of his bald head and beams at her. Chantal always has that effect on men.

As soon as he drives off, she plants a barely-there kiss on each of my cheeks and furrows her meticulously shaped eyebrows. The wariness in her eyes tells me that she's been warned about me, but she doesn't need to worry. She's not the one I'm mad at.

"I'm sorry I couldn't pick you up from the airport, Harley."

"That's okay." I shrug and lower the duffle to the ground. Just looking at the worn initials on it brings me pain, but it's the only carry-on I have. I've wanted to attend the amazing architecture program at the SAIC since I was eight. "Thank you for bringing me out here."

She casually blows off the thousand-dollar flight with a wave of her long fingers. "Please. You know we've been wanting to have you visit since we moved. I'm just glad you finally agreed to come."

More like my parents finally agreed to let me.

I open my mouth to respond, but when I glance past her I lose the words. I can see the Bastille at the end of the street we're standing on. The Colonne de Juliet stands tall and bright against a sky of dark summer clouds, complete with the gilded angel on top: Génie de la Liberté, the Spirit of Freedom. I have a poster of it hanging in my bedroom back home. I remember sitting for hours while working on particularly difficult problems in Calculus and staring at it like it might unlock the answers I needed. But this is no poster. The mountain of stress I've been under for the last month of dealing with my parents' impending divorce finally cracks, easing its smothering grip on me. Tiny bubbles of joy sneak up through the crevices as where I am standing finally hits me.

I'm in *Paris*.

My hands are up and covering my mouth, like they're trying to stop me from "causing a scene," as Mom would say. I've always loved beautiful buildings, and Chicago has some that are spectacular, but Paris is ... *Paris*. The Gothic influence and limestone are everywhere. That stone was taken straight from the ground beneath Paris and then used to build up the city above. It's like Paris became an extension of the quarries beneath, and it is beautiful. I stare around us, trying to take in every little thing. If I could drink it in through my eyeballs, I would.

"*Bienvenue à Paris, ma chérie!*" Aunt Chantal laughs and lifts my duffel bag off the ground. Her nose wrinkles at the worn fabric and she holds it away from her so her perfectly-tailored lavender pantsuit won't come into direct contact with it. I hold back my laugh at her obvious disdain. On the surface, she almost exactly embodies the stuck-up model stereotype, but I remember her always being warm, kind, and generous, and bringing me here this summer goes above and beyond that.

I drag my gaze away from the city, and my nose from the tantalizing scent of fresh baked bread from the *boulangerie* on the corner, and follow her to the front door of her building.

The world tilts a bit and I slow down my breathing. Jet lag is already getting to me. I'm not really a fan of flying, but even strapping my body into a metal tube with wings and rocketing through the sky at nearly six hundred miles per hour over an ocean sounded good in comparison to dealing with the toxicity back home. Now that I'm here, I'm determined to soak up every bit of the city that I can. No matter what I have to face when I go back to my parents, I *will not* let it—or them—ruin this experience for me.

Chantal opens the door with an overly bright grin. "Gretchen is upstairs."

Tension pulls her smile tight and it squashes a bit of my optimism. My cousin and I were so close when they lived near us in Chicago, but then Chantal's modeling career took off and they had to move to New York. I thought we drifted apart then, but it's been even harder to keep in touch with her since they've been in Paris. I want to believe that she's still my hilarious cousin that I love so much, but what can I really know about her from a handful of emails a year?

Chantal hums softly as I follow her through a small lobby with bronze mailboxes along the left wall. She places a tiny card on her keychain against a black box next to the inner glass door and I hear a click before it opens.

"I heard from Milan this morning." The weight she gives the statement makes it sound like it was a call from the actual mayor. Knowing Chantal, maybe it was. I'm not sure what has to happen to bump you up to *supermodel* level, but I'm pretty sure she's somewhere around the *mega* level, if there is such a thing. Or . . . at least she used to be. I haven't seen her in nearly as many ads in the last year or so.

"Milan never returns my calls," I say with an exaggerated sigh, and Chantal looks at me funny. I move on. "Why did they call?"

"My agent is there this summer." She flutters her free hand at me. "He told me about a party in Paris tomorrow night that I simply can't miss. I'm meeting with my stylist tonight to figure out what I'll wear, but after that, we'll catch up."

"That's okay. I'm sure Gretchen and I will find something to keep us busy." In the modeling industry, parties are basically mandatory business meetings. I'm not surprised Chantal is ditching me because of one. I'm actually relieved. I love my aunt, but being around her always makes me feel like I should go fix my hair or put on some lipstick.

I follow her into a gorgeous marble entry with winding stairs that curve up, hugging the walls. My eyes follow the circular staircase in awe, but then I see the most hideous thing marring the center of this spectacular room.

"What is *that*?" I demand, wrinkling my nose at the towering metal shaft reaching several floors up to the roof.

Chantal seems confused. "You mean the elevator?"

I spot a bright red door at the bottom and shake my head in disgust. It looks like some sort of misshapen janitor's closet.

Next to all this marble it's ridiculously out of place. Like a grenade in a bowl of apples. When Chantal opens the door, I groan. It's the tiniest elevator I've ever seen. There won't be room for her, my suitcases, *and* me in this small space. It's simply not happening. I'm all for accessibility, but there has to be a better way to provide it than this.

"This is all wrong," I mutter. "It's so ugly and barely big enough to even be useful. If you're going to add an elevator, you should make sure it meets code and at least consider attaching it to the outside of the building instead of ruining a gorgeous room like this."

My aunt laughs and gestures for me to push my suitcase inside. She drops the duffel on top of it. "I agree. Maybe once you've finished school and you're a big fancy architect you can come back and fix it."

Her words slam into me like a fist to my gut, but I force out a pained laugh as I squeeze into the elevator next to my bags. "That's my plan. Fix Paris. The key to success is totally achievable goals."

"Absolutely." Chantal smiles as I turn to face her.

She reaches in and taps the button for the top floor with a finger tipped with pale pink polish. A metal bi-fold door closes, cutting us off and bumping me back into a sitting position on top of my suitcase. I take a deep breath and let the sting from her words fade away. Chantal doesn't know that the divorce makes my dream of attending SAIC close to impossible. How could she?

By the time I get to the top, I've gathered my composure again. When the elevator returns with Chantal, I give her a wry smile and grumble, "Next time I'll take the stairs. Whoever put in this elevator has a sick sense of humor . . . and design."

"You can if you like, but I promise there are more stairs than it looks like from the bottom." She leads the way to a large black door on the left. "By the time you get to the top the elevator looks a lot better."

With a few bumps, I manage to guide both of my bags in through the door after her. Chantal's flat is airy and open with plenty of light. The high ceilings are accented by metal beams and white drapes around every window. It's beautiful, modern, and elegant without losing the Parisian feel. It matches Chantal perfectly.

I spot Gretchen on the couch and grin. She, on the other hand, couldn't contrast more with the tone of this apartment if she tried—and from the looks of it, maybe she is trying.

Gretchen looks older than she did in the last photo I saw of her, but I'm sure I do too. Big silver cordless headphones press down purple hair that's cut in a pixie style. Her faded jeans are too long, tattered at the bottom and the knees. Her black tank top has a single sentence in hot pink block lettering: *I logged off for this?*

She didn't even look up when we entered, but when Chantal turns her back to help me with my bags, Gretchen shoots me a smile and an excited waggle of her fingers. By the time Chantal turns to face her, Gretchen's eyes are back on her laptop again. The tension in my aunt starts to make sense. My grin fades as memories of my parents arguing flash through my head. Did I escape their mess in Chicago only to be stuck in the middle of another mess with Gretchen and Chantal in Paris?

After a few seconds of silence, Chantal makes an attempt to relieve the tension. "She's really gotten into computers the last couple of years, and she dyed her hair, but I don't think she's turned into a serial killer or anything."

Gretchen doesn't look up or remove her headphones, but she responds in an utterly flat tone, "You really shouldn't make assumptions like that, Mom."

I barely contain my laughter and my smile is back full force. *That's* the cousin I remember. A little darker, maybe, but still her.

Chantal waves off Gretchen's statement as she heads toward the back of the flat. "Anyway, you two have fun. I'm going to make plans for tomorrow. Call for some take-out to be delivered if you're hungry."

The second that Chantal's bedroom door closes behind her, Gretchen's laptop snaps shut and she hurtles off the couch to pull me into a tight hug.

"You're here! I'm so glad you finally came!" She squeezes me until I can barely breathe through my laughter, and when she releases me I flop back on a white lounge chair.

"So . . ." I incline my head toward my aunt's closed door, wondering what has made things so strained, and Gretchen frowns.

"I don't want to talk about it."

"Right." I nod.

She sits back down on the couch and slips the headphones around her neck. Her face is even prettier than I remember, and her hair and dark eyeliner give her an edgy look that I wish I could pull off. I've never dyed my auburn curls, mostly because my mom tends to freak out about silly things, but I've always wanted to.

Gretchen scratches the bridge of her nose. "Has the jet-lag hit you yet?"

"I slept a bit on the plane, but I think it's starting to." I kick off my shoes and stretch my feet. Glancing at the ornate silver clock that hangs in the middle of two modern art paintings on the wall behind her, I see that it's already almost eight at night. I stifle a yawn.

"You should try to stay awake until at least ten. It will help you adjust faster."

I groan, but I know she's right. "In that case, I'm definitely going to need some caffeine." A quick search of the fridge turns up only juice, wine, and protein bars. "What, no soda?"

When I turn around, Gretchen is already on the phone ordering food in perfect French. I'm impressed. She barely knew any French when they moved here. She's learned a lot; I suppose she had to. She covers the mouthpiece and whispers, "You have to know that my mom wouldn't keep anything as unhealthy as that in her house."

She goes back to her phone conversation, and when I hear her say the words "Dr. Pepper" I give her two big thumbs up.

When she finishes the call, I realize that either I didn't know the French word, or I wasn't paying enough attention to hear what food would be arriving alongside my beverage of choice. "What did you order?"

"Pizza."

"The perfect Parisian food?" I chuckle.

"For tonight, it is."

Gretchen's phone starts ringing and it takes me a few seconds before I recognize "The Imperial March" from Star

Wars. Her ringtone is Darth Vader's theme song? Perfect. I give her a silent round of applause and she sticks her tongue out at me.

"*Salut?*" she answers it. "Yes, she's right here. I'll put her on." Gretchen hands me the phone. "It's your mom."

Everything in me retracts into a tight ball of anxiety. I haven't spoken to either of my parents in almost a month. Not since they dropped three bombs on me in one conversation: 1. "We're getting a divorce." 2. "We're both moving out of Chicago at the end of the summer." 3. "You have to pick which one of us you're going to live with by then."

I remember vividly the way the room seemed to spin when they told me. They took a flamethrower to my well-planned future without any hesitation, but I'm the unreasonable one for being upset about it.

We barely managed to save up enough for most of my tuition at SAIC. I planned to cover the rest by working while I attended school. I have seen enough people struggling with mountains of student debt to know that I don't want that.

But the whole plan depends on me still being able to live with one of my parents. There is no way I can afford tuition and housing without racking up the debt I've been trying so hard to avoid. I know my parents can't help any more than they have already agreed to, and with the divorce even that amount is in doubt.

I lost my family and my future in one conversation.

And I don't think my parents even considered any of that when they made their decision.

I walk out onto Chantal's balcony and the view of the Place de la Bastille at sunset nearly takes my breath away.

I grip the phone so tight that my knuckles ache, but I don't speak. I'm still too angry. I don't want to say something I'll regret. My breathing is the only clue to Mom that I'm here, but it's enough.

"Hi, Harley. How is Paris?" I hear the sound of her car in the background and try to calculate what time it is there. It's seven hours earlier. She's probably on her way to lunch.

I don't answer, but she seems to be expecting that. She doesn't wait long before she continues.

"I'm sure Gretchen and Chantal are so happy to have you there."

Shifting the phone to my shoulder, I scratch a bit of dirt off the railing with my fingernail.

"You should check into some architectural programs while you're visiting."

"*What*? Do you not think *at all* before you speak anymore?" I nearly drop the phone. I can't afford SAIC anymore and she thinks *Paris* might be a good alternative? Sure, one of the most expensive cities on the planet is a much better option.

Her shocked silence hangs between us for a moment. "Well, I guess anything is better than your stubborn silence."

My whole body trembles. It's like I've opened a floodgate and it's too late to shut it now. "You never think about anyone but yourself. You and Dad have *destroyed* my life. And you don't even spend enough time thinking about me to realize that!"

"Harley, calm down," Mom says, and even from across an ocean her tone sounds dismissive. By the reduction in background noise, I can tell that she's pulled over. "Sometimes parents have to make decisions that are right for them, too. We weren't happy anymore. You have to be as tired of the fighting as we are."

She has a point. Before they decided to get divorced it felt like all my parents knew how to do was tick each other off as much as humanly possible. And they used me to hurt each other all the time. They seemed to think I was a bomb they could arm and lob at each other whenever they felt like it. I really hated that. Since they announced their divorce, things have improved in that area.

But making me choose between them doesn't feel any less crappy.

"Everything doesn't have to change at once." I don't realize I'm yelling until a man on the street looks up at me. My emotions are like a wild animal. I've kept them caged, and now that they're free they've moved beyond my control.

"Harley, stop being so selfish," she says. I jerk away from the phone like it stung me.

Everything in me settles into a cold, still fury. I don't even bring the phone back to my ear as I say something I could never imagine saying to my mom.

"I hate you."

Then I click end and power off the phone.

I don't go back inside until I've calmed down enough that there's a small ball of icy regret in my stomach. Instead of turning the phone back on and calling Mom to apologize, I hand it over to Gretchen. My cousin realizes it's off and lifts one brow at me over her laptop.

"Parents, huh?" She smirks, but I see pain matching mine in her eyes. "Can't live with them, can't drop them off in a basket at the local fire department without having to answer embarrassing questions."

"Right?" I flop back on the lounge chair across from the couch she's sitting on.

Her focus drops back to her laptop and it's quiet for a moment. The silence isn't exactly awkward, but I'm definitely not as comfortable with her as I remember being before. We'll have half the summer to work on it though . . . starting right now.

"So I emailed you a list of what I want to do in Paris. Did you read it? Where should we start?" Relaxing on the lounge chair, I prop my head up on my elbow. "I'm so in love with the architecture and history here, I think I could walk down any street and be fascinated."

Gretchen rolls her eyes and I try not to let it hurt my feelings. "As entertaining as that does sound, I think I might have a better starting point."

Her tone lifts at the end and hangs in the air, like she's waiting for me to catch it.

"Like what?" I see that familiar mischief in her eyes that I've missed so much and I find myself smiling. Whatever she wants, I'm not going to be hard to convince.

"While my mom's busy tomorrow at one of her fancy-shmancy parties . . ." Gretchen's lip curls a bit in disgust as she brings her laptop over to me. "We'll be doing something *so* much better."

Chapter 2

Evite recovered from Gretchen Dubois's computer, sent from Liv Greenway on June 10 at 9:12 a.m. –

The time has come.

We've talked about it for months.

Now it's happening and I have four words for you.

CATACOMBS

OFF LIMITS

TOUR

Everyone meet at Sacrée Fleur in Montmartre tomorrow at 8 and we'll get sustenance before we meet up with the guide.

■ ■ ■

The Evite is all in black and white—and, thank God, English—with a Halloween theme. Skulls and bones decorate the margins.

The first comment beneath the Evite is from the same person who sent it, Liv Greenway. It reads, *P.S. Gretchen, I know you said your cousin should be in town, bring her.*

It isn't that I don't want to go to the Catacombs; the Ossuary is at the top of my Must-See list. The maze of caves and tunnels beneath Paris sounds incredible. I've wanted to learn more about it ever since I saw a documentary last year. The documentary focused on the off-limits areas and all the people that sneak in and explore them. And I've done my share of urban exploration and geocaching. The Ossuary is one thing. It's the official tour—totally safe and legit. This Evite is talking about an off-limits tour—which is kind of the opposite and illegal.

I'm a little shocked this is even something Gretchen wants to do. She was always more rebellious than me, but it was more in her attitude than her actions. She still mainly followed the rules when we were younger. We both did . . . and I haven't exactly grown out of that.

Gretchen, on the other hand, I'm starting to have serious questions about.

She bounces in anticipation. "Well?"

"It sounds incredible, Gretchen"—I see her excitement falter at my clear reluctance—"but it's against the law, right? Don't get me wrong, I'm sure it would be amazing, but getting arrested isn't exactly part of my Paris plan."

"Arrested?" Her brow furrows and for a moment she looks just like her mom. "Oh! No, they don't arrest people who do that. Tons of people have done it. It's a very small fine if we get caught, not even worth worrying about."

"Just a fine?" I'm a little relieved that Gretchen hasn't turned into some kind of hardened criminal. And I find myself calculating how much money I brought with me. *Mom, Dad, I know I haven't spoken to you lately, but could you send me some cash to pay for a fine I got from this nice French police officer I met?*

Not happening.

"Relax, Harley." Even after all the time apart, Gretchen still manages to somehow read my mind. "If we get caught, I'll pay your fine. It's so worth it. I've been dying to go. Please don't say no."

She throws her entire being into pleading with me and my reservations shrink a little in the face of it. A fine isn't so bad, *if* my parents never have to find out and I don't have to come up with the money. Besides, it seems like this summer is about learning to throw all my plans out the window. More than anything, though, I want to get to know my cousin again. Isn't going with Gretchen on this adventure an opportunity to do that? She has never gotten me into any serious trouble in the past. I mean, we may have been eleven the last time she had a chance, but still.

"Come on! It will be a great way to meet some new friends I made this year. I promise they don't bite. The guys coming are hot, too. Plus, they're from all over so we mostly speak English when we get together. You'll love Liv, she's so cool." Before I can even tell her yes, she barrels forward. "And how can you even consider a summer in Paris without a little bit of rebellion thrown in the mix?"

And I cave. Truthfully, a little rebellion might do me good.

"How can I say no to non-biters who speak English?" I lean back against the lounge and give her the wickedest grin I can muster. "Besides, you had me at hot guys."

■ ■ ■

After a full night's sleep, a scalding hot shower, and a day filled with caffeine and laughing, I'm feeling much better physically by the time Gretchen and I leave to meet up with the others. Mentally, I'm still a little nervous. We walk past the Place de la Bastille and I stare up at it in awe and wonder if that feeling will ever pass.

Gretchen's phone rings and she stares at it for a few seconds before sending the call to voicemail. Then her pace slows as she starts tapping the screen. When I glance over, I see that she's sending a text to Liv, telling her we are on our way.

I focus on peoples' conversations as we walk past, reminding myself that after a full year at the top of Monsieur Amiel's French class I should be able to understand *something*. It still takes about twenty French words before I hear one that sounds at all familiar. "Bonjour!" is an easy one. I knew that before I ever signed up for French. "*It fait chaud*" is one I definitely agree with. It *is* hot. The sun feels like it's trying to bake me, especially since I'm dressed for the cool air in the Catacombs with a long sleeve shirt and jeans. "*Je cherche*" means "I'm looking for," but I can't make out the last word to figure out what the woman wants to find.

And then I hear one that expresses everything I'm feeling right now.

"*Je suis perdu.*"

I'm lost.

And I really am. The knot of guilt in my chest tightens as I think back for the hundredth time on my conversation with Mom. I've never told her I hate her before, and of course I don't. But I honestly and truly *hate* everything they're doing to me. Swallowing a lump of emotion in my throat, I decide I'll call her tomorrow.

Until then, I won't worry about it. I can't let it ruin one more minute of my time here. I have nearly six weeks in Paris in front of me, my favorite cousin by my side, and an adventure on the agenda for tonight that should be epic.

My summer trip might have been planned because of the disaster back home, but I'm still very happy to be here now.

Gretchen sends off the text and drops her phone in her pocket, but it beeps again immediately. With a groan, she rolls her eyes and digs it out. "Sorry."

"Don't worry about it." I shrug as she checks the screen and I see her expression harden.

"What's wrong?" I ask, fairly certain already that my aunt is somehow part of the answer. Gretchen simply hands me the phone.

Voicemail to text from Model Mom to Gretchen

sent on June 11 at 7:39 p.m. —

Hi Gretchen, I'm wondering if maybe I should ask the Blanchards to check in on you and Harley tonight. I feel terrible for not spending any time with her yet. Will you need anything? Should I have Sofia order you some dinner? Let me know what you think. Miss you.

—transmission successful

I feel my nerves biting at me with the idea of someone checking in when we aren't there. The last thing I want to do is have Chantal mad at me before I even really get to spend any time with her. Gretchen swore that my aunt's party would go very late and we could beat her back home, but if she sends people to check on us . . .

"Don't worry. I'll get her to back off." Gretchen gives me a confident smile, takes her phone back, and starts tapping away on the screen. I start to guide her around people, but she seems to have some kind of sixth sense about texting and walking.

"You have her in your phone as *Model Mom*?"

Gretchen frowns without looking up. "It helps me remember her priorities."

I cast a quick glance at my cousin, hearing the tinge of pain in her voice. I know moving to Paris was hard on her, and things are obviously tense between them, but she and my aunt were so close when they lived in Chicago. Seeing how bad things are now makes me wish I knew how to help them.

"Who is Sofia?" I ask. Chantal is obviously a touchy subject, and I don't want to start off the evening on a bad note.

"Her assistant." Gretchen sends off the text as we head down into the Metro. She stuffs the phone back in her pocket and straightens her spine. It's like she's trying to literally shrug off thinking about my aunt. "There. We should be covered."

"Good." I adjust the weight of the backpack I'm carrying. We both have one, and even though they're a little heavy, the weight reassures me. At least we'll be prepared. Each pack is stocked with a couple of water bottles, several granola bars, a light jacket, and a flashlight. I shift the straps again and decide to try another subject change. "Do you think we brought enough?"

"I told you." She adjusts her pack a bit, looking slightly annoyed. "I don't know how long the tour is or who else might have thought to bring supplies. Better to have enough for everyone."

"Maybe we can convince them to take turns carrying the bags then," I mutter, slipping the metro pass she hands me into the slot at the turnstile. Even when I try to avoid touchy subjects, it seems like she could snap at anyone over anything.

She shrugs. "If they want to share, they will."

When we get to the platform, I'm so glad to have Gretchen with me. The subway map is intimidating. I'm fairly certain I would miss three trains while trying to figure out which one I'm supposed to take. "I was surprised your mom was already gone when I woke up from my nap. I didn't expect the party to start this early."

"Oh, no." Gretchen laughs. "It doesn't start until later. She was meeting up with her stylist to spend the next three hours getting ready for it. God forbid anyone notice a wrinkle or gray hair. Aging gracefully isn't a thing my mother understands."

"Ah, that makes more sense."

She squints at me. "You know naps aren't good for getting your jet lag adjusted."

"How can a power nap be bad for anything?" I ask as we make our way onto the train and find a seat. "It actually has the word *power* in it."

"Yeah, I guess maybe this time is the exception." Gretchen tosses her head and shrugs. "Screw the jetlag. Whatever it takes so you aren't falling asleep tonight. Nobody is going to be carrying you out of the Catacombs, I'll tell you that right now."

I scowl in mock disappointment. "I thought that was why we were bringing along the hot guys you mentioned."

She winks at me. "They have other uses."

Chapter 3

Text from Gretchen to Model Mom sent

on June 11 at 7:42 p.m. –

> Lay off. We're probably going to watch a movie at home. We'll get our own food. We don't need a babysitter. You do your thing and we'll do ours. You don't even have to think about us, exactly the way you like it.

—transmission successful

■ ■ ■

Gretchen and I arrive at Sacrée Fleur promptly at eight. A girl with straight blond hair floating around her shoulders stands out front, bouncing up and down on her heels. A very sparkly camcorder hangs on a strap over her left shoulder. Gretchen smiles wide and waves when she looks our way.

Her eyes light up and she kisses Gretchen on both cheeks when we get to her. She's taller than me, but shorter than my cousin.

"This is my cousin, Harley." Gretchen indicates me. "Harley, this is Liv."

"I've heard so much about you!" Her Midwestern accent surprises me.

"Good, I hope." I smile.

My cousin shakes her head, giving me a thoughtful look. "Nothing good."

"All good," Liv corrects, and her nose crinkles up as she smiles. "I've been wondering, though . . . Harley, huh? Like the motorcycles?"

"Yeah," I respond, even though my parents would cringe to hear her say that. With an accountant for a mom and a librarian for a dad, the idea of either of them being hard-core bikers naming their kid after a motorcycle is laughable. The truth is much nerdier. Dad loves comics and Harley Quinn was always a favorite of his. So he convinced Mom to name me Harley Bryn Martin.

My parents can't agree on what type of milk to buy, but somehow were in total sync on the choice to name me after a villain.

"You just got here, right?" Liv shifts her weight back and forth on her orange sneakers.

"Last night." I cross my arms, a sudden rush of nerves making me feel cold even in the heat. I'm not sure if it is coming from meeting Gretchen's friends or from our slightly illegal after-dinner plans. "How long have you been here?"

"Almost four months." Liv adjusts the barrette holding back her hair on one side. "I was here for the last semester abroad program and I'm staying on for the summer."

"I'm jealous. I'd love to stay that long."

"Our guest room is always available." Gretchen gives me a look that tells me she's serious, and I wonder if there is any way I could take her up on that. If I could stay with them, I might be able to afford a school here. It would mean getting away from my parents. It could be exotic and amazing—if I could get accepted and somehow learn French in one summer.

"Maybe after I finish my senior year." I gesture toward Liv's camcorder, which has an intricate design on the side in purple rhinestones. "Are you here as a film student?"

"An aspiring filmmaker," Liv corrects me with a grin, holding her camcorder out and brushing her fingers along its side. "I'm going to be a senior, but I'll be applying for AFI soon."

I try to place the initials, but come up empty.

"American Film Institute," Gretchen says, reading my mind again. She opens the restaurant door for us. "Liv is an overachiever, making the rest of us look bad on a daily basis."

"I might not if you didn't make it so easy." She beams over her shoulder at Gretchen as we walk in. "AFI is a small school, but is has the best program out there."

Her description reminds me of the School of the Art Institute of Chicago. My mind floods with memories of the countless open lectures I attended there, always dreaming of enrolling. I scold myself for not moving past this already. But dreams are hard to let go of, especially when you work so hard to achieve them. A sinking sadness threatens, but I force it away. Not tonight. Tonight is for fun, excitement, and new friends.

Liv leads the way over to a table in the corner where four guys and a girl are laughing and talking, and I feel nervous all over again.

I'm fairly outgoing and like meeting new people, but I also like spending time alone. Sometimes I think I'd be totally happy living on one of those little ships in a bottle as long as I had my Doritos and a lifetime supply of Dr. Pepper. This is *a lot* of new people at once, but I'm going to be here for half the summer. Making new friends to spend it with is a good idea. Who knows? Maybe I can even have one of those Paris summer romances that seem inevitable in the movies.

Liv and Gretchen greet everyone at the table with a hug and a kiss on the cheek as I try not to fidget awkwardly behind them. Then Gretchen beckons me forward and introduces me to her friends. "This is my cousin, Harley."

"Hi," I say, trying hard not to feel like a lost puppy being offered scraps of food.

Liv gestures to the tallest guy at the table. "This is Anders Koskela. He's from Finland and was in a few classes with me last semester." He nods at me, and I can't help but notice he's the only one not smiling.

"This is Maud from Amsterdam," Gretchen jumps in, indicating a black girl with big, beautiful light brown eyes. She might be my height, possibly a little shorter. Her black hair falls like a dark curtain around her shoulders. "Maud's got some kind of built-in radar for finding great parties."

"The parties find me." Maud gives me a relaxed grin.

Liv points to a guy with a strong jawline and olive skin who looks a couple of years older than me. "Paolo is Maud's Latin lover."

Paolo chuckles and Maud shrugs with a laugh.

"He's an artist staying at a commune near here," Gretchen adds.

She indicates the guy next to him with shaggy auburn hair and intense bright green eyes. "That's James, Paolo's roommate. He's from London."

James waves, but looks a little bored.

I turn to face the last remaining member of the group. His blond hair hangs long and straight to his collar, a smattering of tiny freckles bridges his nose, and his brown eyes meet my gaze. He's really cute already, and it only gets better when he smiles.

"And last but not least, this is Henri Pelletier." When Liv says his name she pronounces it with a French flourish.

"Are you a local?" I ask before Liv gets the chance to give any further details.

"No, we all met through students-abroad social events mostly. I'm here for a summer music program," he says, but I'm confused because I definitely hear a French accent. He goes on to clarify, "I'm from Quebec. I'm French-Canadian."

"Ah." I nod, and then turn my eyes on the rest of the group. "Thanks for letting me crash your plans for the night."

"Lovely ladies are always welcome," Paolo answers.

Gretchen and I drop our backpacks next to the chairs and the three of us slide into the empty seats. I catch the scent of something amazing and groan as the waiter passes by with a tray of food. I didn't realize I was so hungry.

Henri chuckles. "Finally, someone who understands."

"Because all *you* think about is food—" Liv begins.

"Hey, we all have jobs to do." He rubs one hand across his stomach. "*I* ensure that we all eat delicious food in a timely manner. *You* make sure everything we do is caught on video for your future blackmailing pleasure."

Liv lifts up her camcorder and points it at him, pressing the record button. "Have any other insights you'd like to share?"

Henri leans in and looks directly into the camera. "Liv Greenway is a spectacular human being."

"You're forgiven." Liv closes her camera and pats him on the head as I try my hardest to decipher my menu.

■ ■ ■

Liv trains her camera on the table and pans across all the empty plates.

"This is all that remains after the destruction." She mimics a deep movie trailer narrator voice. She points the camera at me and asks, "How was your first real Parisian meal, Harley?"

I pat my stomach and stretch my arms. "So good I think I may enter a food coma."

We had the most delicious cheese and bread platter, croissants, *souppe de poisson*, and about a million other things that I don't remember the names of. Anders gives me a slight smile from the end of the table and takes another drink of his after-dinner coffee. James whispers something in Paolo's ear and I hope it isn't about me, but when he looks my way I get the distinct impression it is.

Liv stops recording and places her camera back on the table. "Good. I love this place."

"I'd give it an eight." Henri holds up his hands, displaying his vote on his fingers as though the rest of us might not understand otherwise.

I pretend to be offended. "That's pretty picky. What would've made it a ten for you?"

"Entertainment."

"That has nothing to do with the food." I fold my arms over my chest.

"It has to do with the ambiance," Maud chimes in. Paolo nods and James yawns, checking his watch.

Gretchen taps on her phone screen and frowns. "I wish they had wi-fi."

"What kind of entertainment would you prefer?" I ask Henri, already feeling more comfortable with the group. Something about Henri sets me at ease. Gretchen being by my side doesn't hurt either.

"I'd never turn down a good dinner theater." He winks at me. "What about you? What do you find entertaining?"

I tap my fingers on the table, one at a time, thinking. "I really like good live music. For this place, I'd say an acoustic guitar and a singer . . . or maybe a bluesy sax and a small band with no singing."

Liv jumps in. "Interesting choice. I think saxophones are kind of overdone, though. Maybe something else, like a flute?"

"No. Not a flute. The reason saxes are overused is because they have such a sexy sound." I shrug, gesturing to the candles on the table and the low lighting. "It seems like it would fit the tone of this place."

"Good point." Liv laughs and puts her elbows on the table, leaning toward Henri with a smirk. "Did you know that flutes aren't sexy, Henri?"

James sputters a laugh from the other side of the table, and I wonder what I walked into.

"Maybe she hasn't heard the right person play one. Besides, I don't need an instrument to enhance my sexiness." Henri smiles back at Liv, though there's a slight edge to his voice. "I like the flute because it's sophisticated . . . just like me."

Everyone laughs and Gretchen shoots me a look like she's not sure if she should join in or jump to my aid. It all seems to be in good fun, though, so I give the briefest shake of my head.

"You play the flute?" I ask, taking a sip of my French Dr. Pepper and trying not to make a face. The taste was a bit of a shock when I had one last night with our pizza, and I'm still not used to it. It tastes only slightly like American Dr. Pepper, but it's better than nothing.

"Yes." Henri's expression softens when he turns to me. "And a lot of other even less sexy instruments."

James lifts his dark brows and leans back, crossing his arms over his chest. "Those exist?"

I lean slightly closer to Henri, intrigued. "What else do you play?"

"The accordion, the flugelhorn, and the piccolo."

I blink twice. "Seriously?"

"No." He grins. "I play the drums, guitar, piano, and harp, but I'm best with the flute."

I don't even try to hide how impressed I am. "That's a lot. I have zero musical talent."

"That's okay. You make up for it by being a world-renowned instrument critic." His eyes sparkle at me in the candlelight. I feel a slight heat in my cheeks. It's nice to know that flirting, at least, is a universal language. I'm starting to wonder if this summer may actually have the potential to be amazing despite everything else I have going on.

"Harley has skills." Gretchen finally gives up on her phone and puts it on the table. "She can look at any building and tell you what period of style influenced it. Tell me when that wouldn't come in handy."

I shoot her a mock glare. "I can also tell which beam I should knock down to collapse a building on top of you."

"Ooh, à la Wicked Witch of the West?" Henri laughs at the dismay on Gretchen's face.

"East, dummy," Liv says. "West is her sister that goes after Dorothy."

I check my watch and realize it's already past nine o'clock. It takes me almost thirty seconds to do the same math as yesterday to figure out what time it is back home. Jet lag might not have hit me as hard as I expected, but my brain is definitely dragging a bit today.

Gretchen interrupts my thoughts. "You hear that, Harley?"

I turn to look at her, realizing I missed a significant chunk of conversation in that thirty seconds.

"Sorry." I shake my head.

"Paolo set us up with Roland Lambert, one of the most prominent local cataphiles, to give us our tour tonight."

"What's a cataphile?" I ask.

Anders is the one who answers me. His Finnish accent is strong and I have to listen close to understand. "It's what they call the people who are obsessed with the Catacombs. They like to go down and explore them."

"Oh, cool. He sounds like he'll be perfect." A thrill of fear and excitement shoots through me. Now that I think about it, I remember cataphiles being mentioned a few times in that Catacombs documentary.

"I heard this creepy story once." Paolo leans across the table like he's telling us the most important thing ever. "The guy who was in charge of finding a way to get all the bones into the Catacombs, they say his spirit is still down there, that the owners of the bones he moved won't let him leave."

James groans. "Of course he is."

Maud releases an uncomfortable giggle and swats Paolo on the shoulder. "Come on, ghosts?"

"There are a million stories like that." Henri leans back, putting his hands behind his head. "I saw this video online from a university student who was recording down there. It's super creepy. It doesn't show what he saw, but he looks terrified and drops the camera. The last thing it recorded was his feet running away from whatever he saw. I guess someone found his camera later, but *he* never came out."

An involuntary shiver slides down my spine, but when Gretchen starts laughing it fades away.

She holds her fork in front of her, pretending it's a microphone, and does her best announcer voice. "No idiots were harmed in the making of this film."

"Whatever." Liv waves the stories away and drinks the last of her water. "Monsieur Lambert has been doing this longer than anyone else. I'm glad he agreed to take us. I asked a friend who is a cataphile, and she said she heard he was retired."

"What can I say, I'm very persuasive—and so is money." Paolo shrugs then checks his watch and climbs to his feet. "And actually, we're supposed to meet him in twenty minutes, so if you're all finished . . . *Allons-y!*"

Chapter 4

DÉFENSE D'ENTRER!
LES INTRUS SERONT POURSUIVIS
AVEC TOUTE LA RIGUEUR DE LA LOI!

The sign is posted at the top of the stairs leading down into the edge of the open-air quarry. I can tell even in the dark that it's gypsum, and can barely contain myself. Whether it makes me a dork or not, I love it. The mines and quarries of Paris were all created to mine gypsum and Lutetian limestone. Gypsum is used to make plaster of Paris and the limestone is the foundation of Paris architecture. Steps have been carved carefully into the stone leading down until they disappear into the darkness of the pit below. *That*, I don't love so much.

Gretchen grins at the sign and then at me. "I love being a bad influence on you."

"I know the first part is basically 'keep out.'" I stare hard at the rest of the words, but I don't recognize enough to make sense of them. "What does the rest say?"

"'Trespassers will be prosecuted to the fullest extent of the law,'" Anders says, and I feel cold at the words. I know I can't back out now, but I've never willfully broken the law like this. I rub my hands over my arms until the goosebumps beneath my sleeves disappear.

"Catacops shouldn't scare you, the architect that still haunts the tunnels should," Paolo whispers in my ear, and I jump.

"Architects are about as scary as Mickey Mouse," I scoff to hide my embarrassment, "but what are catacops?"

Henri is the one to answer, his voice taking on a reassuring tone. "They put together a specific group of police for trying to keep people out of the Catacombs back in the '90s or something. Don't worry, they won't find us. Everything I read online says the mines are too big for them to actually watch over all of it."

"It's only a fiiiii-ine," Gretchen drags out the last word. She grabs my hand and pulls me down the stairs behind her with a bright smile. I hold tight to her shoulder, forcing her to slow down. She might not have a backpack to carry anymore—Anders offered to carry hers before we made it a block outside of the restaurant—but I do. Gretchen said she'd take turns carrying mine so my shoulders get a break every now and then.

The others all brought packs of their own except Maud. Paolo brought stuff for her in his pack. It's definitely fair to say that Gretchen and I aren't the only ones who wanted to be prepared.

We climb down carefully because some of the stairs are crumbling and we each lose our footing at least once. Heights are not my friend, so I keep both hands on Gretchen's shoulders and step where she does. When we finally get close to the bottom of the quarry, a figure steps out of the shadows ahead of us. I stop abruptly, holding Gretchen back until the man comes fully into view. Once I can see him, I relax. He looks more like a grandpa on his way to go hunting and fishing at his cabin in the woods than one of the catacops, which happens to be the main type of person I'm afraid of running into at the moment. His hair curls in short white poofs around his balding head, and he has a neatly trimmed grey beard. A pair of high-tech goggles hangs around his neck. He looks about fifty and very fit.

"Paolo?" he asks, squinting up at us.

"Yes, it's us." Paolo makes his way to the base of the stairs and shakes the man's hand. "Thank you for doing this."

"You're welcome." He gives Paolo a tight smile before turning to address the group. His accent is heavy, but he's fluent in English and I don't have to work too hard to understand him. "I'm Monsieur Lambert. First, I'm going to take you to see some bones, then we'll go deep into the tunnels where very few ever go. Some guides will bring people to the Left Bank where locals gather to throw parties."

Maud grins at the rest of us, which makes me wonder if she's been to one of these parties.

Monsieur Lambert gives her a disapproving glare before continuing. "If you want to go there, you should find those guides. The Catacombs and these quarries are not for parties. They are for exploring our history."

I don't let my surprise show on my face, which is more than I can say for Gretchen, who is frowning deeply. She's in this for the adventure, and the guide is making it sound like a school field trip. Which, to be honest, makes me even more excited.

"Once we're inside, don't touch anything without my permission. No cameras." Liv's hand immediately shoots up, but Monsieur Lambert ignores her. "No loud noises.

And don't touch the bones. These are people. Before you do anything, consider whether you would want someone to dig up your grave and do it to you."

Liv drops her hand slowly back to her side with frustration clearly written across her face.

"I will be checking your backpacks before we leave. No one will be taking any *souvenirs* home from this expedition."

It takes me a second to realize he's talking about bones. What kind of weirdo would want to take the bones of long-dead strangers home? What would they even do with them? Use someone's skull as a dining table centerpiece or a supremely creepy paperweight?

"If anyone needs to use the bathroom, I suggest you go back up out of the quarry and find a bush to squat behind. It will be a while before you get another chance."

We all thought ahead and took advantage of the bathroom at the restaurant. Still, I'm suddenly very glad that Sacrée Fleur doesn't offer free soda refills. Hopefully we'll be out before I need to go again.

After no one moves, Monsieur Lambert turns toward the shadows he emerged from. "Then down we go."

As we line up behind him, I catch Gretchen's gaze. She rolls her eyes. I give her two thumbs up. Then we follow our guide into the massive tomb beneath Paris.

■ ■ ■

The entrance to the Catacombs is tiny and there is no way I would've seen it without a guide here to show us the way. M. Lambert calls it a "cat flap," which I guess means *scary narrow tunnel into complete darkness*. After removing our backpacks and pushing them through in front of us, we have to crawl, single file, through several feet of passage before it opens up into a bigger cave. Good thing I'm not claustrophobic. The air inside is at least ten degrees colder than it was outside, and it's musty. M. Lambert pulls out a flashlight once we're all through the cat flap. The cave we're in is smaller around than I thought it would be, maybe only ten feet wide, but it's so tall I can't see the ceiling in such low light.

I'm disappointed to see graffiti scrawled on the walls, and it's obvious from the way our guide turns up his nose at it that he feels the same way. When I see the famous "Je suis Charlie" that I've seen spray painted all over Paris, I decide not to judge. Unity is rarely a bad thing.

At the opposite side of the cave from our entrance, I see an off-shoot tunnel that looks like it goes nearly straight down. I hope to God it doesn't.

"If you have a torch, now is the time to use it." M. Lambert's voice echoes even though he speaks quietly.

"Torch?" I whisper to Henri, who has taken a spot by my side.

"It's what the Brits call a flashlight." He reaches into his bag and pulls out one that looks industrial size.

James pops up next to him and shakes his head, imitating a perfect American accent. "Those wacky Brits."

We laugh.

"Oh, right. I knew that." I tug my yellow flashlight out of my pack and turn it on. It's not as bright as Henri's, but at least I'm certain it has new batteries. Gretchen and I put them in before we packed our backpacks—and I might've thrown in an extra set of batteries when she wasn't looking. Just in case.

It's immediately obvious that M. Lambert's flashlight is about twice as bright as everyone else's. An expression of disgust crosses his face as he looks at all of ours. "If you ever do anything like this again, bring LED torches. They're brighter and last much longer."

I look at my yellow flashlight and find myself feeling oddly defensive about it. "I didn't know there was a *wrong* kind of *torch*," I mutter to myself. Liv starts laughing beside me.

James shines his light up above us and chuckles. "Blimey."

With all the extra light, we can see that the ceiling is covered with bats. On instinct, I tuck my head in and hunch my shoulders.

"Don't bother them and they won't bother you." M. Lambert's tone is a warning. "You should enjoy this now. There won't be many other living things besides us down where we're going."

"That's cheery." Maud regards the bats warily, giving an involuntary shudder.

As our guide leads us over to the tunnel on the opposite side, it's a relief to see that it has more carved stairs and isn't simply a drop that we're supposed to rappel down or something. Paolo whispers something behind me and Maud giggles, but as the stairs go on and on and on, we all fall into silence and focus on taking careful steps. Tripping and taking our entire group out in the process is absolutely something I can see myself doing.

"How far down are we going?" Gretchen whispers, but the sound carries.

"The sections vary in depth, but we'll be starting out at almost a third of a kilometer, nearly a hundred feet down," M. Lambert replies, and Gretchen grunts in response.

The stairs seem to go down farther than that somehow. I walk until strange muscles in my legs get sore and I'm hot despite the fact that the stone walls grow a bit colder with each step. The air feels moister the farther down we go. It gets so humid that the walls start to feel damp, and I'm even more worried about slipping. The steps started out decently wide, but they're beginning to feel narrower. The stairway seems to be closing in on us, becoming less like a tunnel and more like a tomb.

And I can't tell if it's real or a cruel trick my mind is playing on me.

Once we finally reach the bottom, we come out into a long tunnel and I breathe a sigh of relief. Those stairs were starting to make me feel sick. The echoes of our footsteps bounce around us for long enough that I wonder for a second if more people are coming down behind us. Then the sound fades to nothing.

Henri stares at the walls around us in awe. "The acoustics are great here."

"It depends on the section," M. Lambert says. "Here they are very good. In other areas, you can talk and someone nearby won't be able to hear you. Some tunnels hide their secrets better. They absorb the sound rather than amplify it."

"Hey, what's this say?"

He walks over to help Maud read something on the far side of the room.

"Maybe that's why people like to use the Catacombs for P-A-R-T-I-E-S." Gretchen spells it out like M. Lambert is a toddler.

I give a choked laugh. "I'm pretty sure he can spell."

Gretchen shrugs with an impish grin.

I point to the roughly carved walls, which are all slick with moisture. The whitish-gray of the stone reflects a bit of the light from our flashlight beams beneath the sporadic spots of spray paint. "This is the limestone they use all over Paris. I hate that people covered it up to paint their stupid names."

Gretchen puts her arm around my shoulders and squints at me. "I know my fun-loving cousin is in there somewhere." She taps my forehead with her finger. "Let her come out to play?"

I grin and push her arm off with a playful shove. "Nope. No fun for me."

"Pity." She folds her arms and gives me a mock disappointed look as I wave her off and go back to checking if all the walls in this area are limestone.

This tunnel feels almost spacious compared to the stairs, even though the ceiling is only a few inches above Anders's head. A dark line runs down the center of the ceiling. It doesn't look like more graffiti, but I don't know what else it could be. Liv looks up to see what I'm staring at and I see the hand gripping her camcorder strap twitch.

"That black line is from the torches of Catacombs workers," our guide tells us when he sees where we're looking.

I frown at my flashlight. Gretchen laughs and nudges my elbow as she walks past. "This time he's talking about regular torches, like with fire, you dork."

I roll my eyes and whisper, "Maybe this is why Americans call them flashlights, because it's less confusing."

"Yeah, nothing about American English is confusing." James's sarcastic tone has taken on a biting quality. I give him an uncomfortable smile and turn away.

"You can find similar marks in many of the smaller tunnels." M. Lambert turns to watch us, and Liv releases the camcorder strap. She shoots our guide a dejected and surly look, so I give her shoulder a sympathetic squeeze before hurrying to catch up with Gretchen.

"The Catacombs are the remains of very old limestone and gypsum quarries beneath Paris." M. Lambert leads us through the tunnel as he speaks. "At the entrance to the public section, the Ossuary, there is a sign that reads, '*Arrête, c'est ici l'empire de la mort!*' Does anyone know what that means?"

Liv speaks up immediately, her eyes glued to our guide. "Stop! This is the Empire of Death!"

"*Oui. Très bien.*" He nods and she lights up like he gave her an A+ on a paper. Paolo nudges Henri, and they both laugh.

I'm grateful for all of our flashlights. With them, it's fairly bright ahead of us, but when I look behind us it's nearly pitch black. No matter how hard I try, it's still difficult to imagine that nearly three hundred miles of darkness and death stretches out beneath Paris, the City of Light.

"About those Catacombs parties?" Gretchen whispers once I'm back by her side.

I lift one eyebrow. "You seem awfully focused on that piece of information."

"I like learning things." Her tone is playful as she goes on. "I'm pretty sure I read somewhere that the Catacombs were originally constructed to hold Napoleon's numerous disco parties when they inevitably raged out of control."

I recognize what she's doing and a warm feeling spreads through my chest. We spent so many nights as kids lying awake and making up crazy stories about people—sometimes historical figures, sometimes our parents or neighbors or teachers. Gretchen was always the best at it. It's one of my favorite memories.

I whisper back, "That makes perfect sense. Napoleon was famous for his dancing style. I think he was the original inventor of the mirrored disco ball."

She grins so wide and bright that for an instant she looks eleven years old again. Then she taps one finger against her temple like she's in deep thought. "You're right. I'm pretty sure I read that somewhere, too. The disco ball and the hot pants."

"The perfect combination."

We both burst out laughing. M. Lambert turns around to give us an unamused look until we tone it down to giggling behind our hands. He leads the way out of the first tunnel and into a much bigger cave. I gasp when I see what's in it.

Bones. So many bones. More bones than I would've believed could fit in one room. I shiver and instinctively wrap my arms around myself. They're piled neatly against the walls to form patterns and designs from floor to ceiling.

I'm relieved to see that there is almost no graffiti in this section. At least they showed some respect for the dead here.

Gretchen points out a diamond shape made entirely of human skulls, and there are femurs lined up to make the outline of a face. It's incredible and intricate and beautiful . . .

And oh so creepy.

I start counting the skulls, and I get over a hundred without making a dent. M. Lambert notices what I'm doing.

"There are over six million skeletons resting in the Catacombs." He turns to address the whole group. "That's three times more than the current living population of Paris."

"Wow . . ." Gretchen breathes, and it feels like a surprisingly inadequate word.

"It's hard to even imagine that many people in one place." I shine my flashlight over an intricate pattern made out of what I think are rib bones.

"They're not people anymore." I turn to see Henri standing a few feet back from me. His face is blank as he stares at the bones.

"What do you mean?" I try to keep my voice light, even though this setting puts me on edge.

"Didn't you hear Paolo?" His face cracks in a wicked grin. "They're *spirits* now." He emphasizes the word, drawing it out. I half expect him to pull a Ouija board out of his backpack.

I smile and shake my finger at him. "*Shh*! They'll hear you."

I back away from the diamond design, trying to take it all in. Henri moves up next to me and nudges me with his elbow. "It's kind of tragic."

I'm confused until I follow his gaze and see Liv. She's staring around, her eyes huge, both hands wrapped around her camcorder. She has it tucked under her chin and almost looks like she's saying some kind of prayer to the gods of film.

Moving over beside her, I speak quietly. "It seems like a dumb rule to me."

She looks confused before I tap one finger on the top of her camera. Liv's face breaks into a sneaky smile. She pushes the power button on the camcorder, throwing a glance over her shoulder at M. Lambert.

I move my body until I'm in between Liv and our guide. "Stay at the back of the group and put it down if he looks your way."

Liv whispers, "Thanks!" before slipping away from the group and closer to the shadows.

I'm inspecting an archway made entirely of bones when I get the feeling that someone is behind me. My skin prickles and I spin around, finding myself staring into the empty eye sockets of an entire row of skulls. They form the top of a pile against the opposite wall. I try to shake off the eerie feeling as I head back toward the center of the room.

"The quarries have been here since the thirteenth century, but the bones were only moved down starting in 1780 because overcrowding in the city's cemeteries became a health issue. It took twelve years to relocate them all." M. Lambert gazes around, and it's easy to see in his face how much he loves it down here. I wonder if I look the same when I stare at Frank Lloyd Wright's Robie House or the Art Deco tower of the Chicago Board of Trade Building.

"This is so crazy," Gretchen says as we follow our guide into another tunnel. This one is wider, very long, and has bones stacked along the walls on either side.

"It's incredible." I'm mesmerized. I can't seem to take my eyes from the bones. I wonder how they died and who they were. I wonder where they were originally buried and if they'd be happy knowing they ended up like this. An archaeologist might be able to find out, but to me they are genderless and nameless. No matter what color their eyes, hair, or skin were, they're all the same now. It's like someone was trying to make a point: death is the great equalizer, no one escapes it.

The Catacombs stretch on and on and on. We walk past alcoves and giant piles and pillars, all made from human bones. It's quiet and peaceful and chilling. The farther we go, the more still the air is. That motionlessness combines with the moisture and makes the air feel even heavier, like it is weighed down with the millions of lives the massive tomb holds.

I draw in a deep breath and end up coughing on dust.

M. Lambert meets my eyes, and for the briefest moment I see dark humor in his. "The air down here has actual human bone dust in it."

My eyes go wide and I cough harder as some of the others laugh. Maud looks like she's going to throw up, and Liv turns up her nose, so at least I'm not the only one who thinks the idea of breathing in other people is freaky.

I shine my flashlight behind us. I know there is no one else here, but the inky darkness that shrouds everything creeps me out. I roll my shoulders, trying to shake the feeling off, but it clings to me like the water clinging to the walls.

The next alcove we pass has a white stone cross in between two tall obelisks. The skulls seem to stare at the religious symbol, at me, at each other. They simply stare, forever.

I feel like one of them is watching me, then the one next to it, and the next one. All these eye sockets that seem to see me when I know they can't.

I need to squash that idea before it takes root. I wrap my hand around Gretchen's arm and move faster. We slip past Henri, Maud, and Paolo until we're at the front of the group.

Only then can I resist the urge to look back over my shoulder and shine my flashlight at those skulls again.

Each cavern and tunnel we pass through seems smaller than the one before, and I'm hyper-aware of exactly how far underground we've come. I'm glad we took this tour, but I'm ready to be done and get out of here. I desperately want some outside air. Clean air. Non-bone-dusted air.

And a deep anxiety settles in when I realize that nearly a hundred feet of stone, dirt, and bones currently separates me from fresh air in my lungs and the starry sky above.

Chapter 5

■ ■ ■

We pass into a rougher section of tunnels where there are much fewer bones. The ones here lie in big piles instead of organized patterns. My momentary panic eases, mostly because I'm so focused on not hurting myself or anyone else. We're in narrower passages with more cat flaps that we have to push our backpacks through and then crawl in after them. Needless to say, we're all much dirtier now. I duck to avoid a rough piece of stone jutting out at an angle and narrowly avoid hitting my head on a different one. I keep moving, spotting one of many areas that looks caved in. The farther in we go, the less graffiti there is, until it disappears altogether.

Short tunnels with abrupt turns connect to larger caves with multiple tunnels leading out. It's confusing, but M. Lambert doesn't hesitate. He seems to know the Catacombs unbelievably well, and that reassures me. It truly is a maze down here. We take the left tunnel, then the right, then a crevice on one side of a huge room before a tunnel down and another one back up.

It's mind-bogglingly complex, and we've gone so deep now that I'm starting to hope he's leading us to a different exit. We've walked for what I'm sure must be miles. I pull out my phone. It has no signal, of course, but it shows the time. It's well after midnight. We've been down here for three hours. Surely he'll lead us out soon.

Paolo seems to be having the same thoughts I am. "Are we heading toward an exit on the Left Bank? We aren't going all the way back to where we started, right?"

Gretchen perks up. "Isn't that where you said the parties are?"

Monsieur Lambert stiffens. "You paid me to give you a guided tour." He shoots Paolo an indignant glare. "Perhaps you should just enjoy the Catacombs and let me do that."

Paolo shrugs and turns away, and I'm glad that he asked instead of me. Behind me, I hear Liv whispering into her camcorder and smile to myself. At least she's making the most of this experience.

I'm close enough to her that I'm surprised I can't hear what she's saying. Actually, everything is kind of eerily quiet. We must be in one of those tunnels that absorbs sound. We pass another half-wall of bones before turning the corner and following M. Lambert into a large room. Massive pillars line the room on each side, and each one is constructed entirely of bones.

All fear falls away as I move closer to study them. The aspiring architect part of my brain shoves the creeped out part aside and I stare in amazement. Bones are strong and hard, but they're nothing like stone. When stone and bone meet, stone wins every time. I rub my forearm where I have a healed fracture to prove it. But someone has used mud and some kind of plaster to make this pillar stronger than the bones are by themselves.

"Liv?" Henri says behind me, and I turn to see him leaning out of the room into the tunnel we just came through. "You have to come check this out."

"Wow!" Liv whispers as she enters, and the sound echoes.

I step back from the pillar to join them, shaking my head in awe. "This place is such a strange balance of scary and incredible."

Liv's camcorder is up to her eye again and she moves closer to the nearest pillar, zooming in on some of the bones. She no longer seems to care about our tour guide catching her. As I stand by Henri and Gretchen, the three of us tense, watching Liv and M. Lambert like we're waiting for two storm fronts to collide and hoping we don't get caught in a tornado.

It doesn't take long before M. Lambert notices. "I made it clear that I didn't want you recording."

I flinch. After several hours of mostly quiet, his shouting feels deafening. Apparently his rule about no loud noises doesn't apply to him.

Liv's spine shoots up straight and I see fire in her eyes when she spins to face him. I notice she doesn't turn her camera off when she puts it on the ground pointed at M. Lambert. Odd, but I guess catching drama on film is sort of a career goal for her.

"Seriously? This place *needs* to be captured." Liv walks up to him, holding her flashlight down by her side. "Besides, I thought you meant you didn't want me recording *you*."

"No! *No cameras.* That's what I said." He rolls onto the balls of his feet, like he's trying to appear taller than he actually is. "I don't even know why I agreed to do this. I don't give tours anymore, and it's because of kids like you."

Henri, Gretchen, and I hurry closer to them. I'm not sure what to do here, but I'm certain that these two arguing isn't good for anyone.

"Come on, Liv." Gretchen reaches for her arm, but Liv jerks away without even looking at her.

"I'm not doing anything wrong! Why can't I record it? I need the footage. I'm going to use it for one of my projects to apply for film school this fall." Liv crosses her arms, and when the flashlight beam shines straight into M. Lambert's face, she smirks slightly instead of angling it away.

He growls and swats the flashlight out of her hand. "Then go on the regular tour and get it. This place isn't for people who can't appreciate it. It's sacred and should be protected."

Liv doesn't back down. "It's not like I'm destroying it. I don't understand why you're being such an ass about this."

"Come on, Liv. Back off." Henri picks up Liv's flashlight and puts one arm around her shoulders, leading her away from M. Lambert.

As I watch them, I wonder if there has ever been anything romantic between Henri and Liv. Not that it's really my business. But Henri is cute, and if there is no hope there, then I'd rather know from the beginning. When Henri catches my eye, I turn away, but I keep listening.

"You know how important this application is to me. I told you how hard I've been working. Going to AFI is the only thing I've ever wanted." Liv's voice is soft now, pleading. I feel an instant kinship with her. The way she talks about AFI matches exactly the way I feel about SAIC.

I strain to hear Henri's reply as I keep my eyes on Maud, Paolo, James, and Anders walking around one of the pillars at the other end of the room.

Henri responds in quiet soothing tones. "I know, but we'll get you some great footage another way. This doesn't need to be a big deal."

Liv moves back into my peripheral vision with a sigh and scoops up her camera. Her lips form a full-on pout as she hovers her finger above the power button. "Fine, but I'm not sure what we'll find that could possibly be better than this."

M. Lambert stands nearby, glaring at Liv, waiting for her to turn off her camera. Across the room, I see a slight rain of dust fall from the top of the pillar the others are looking at. Paolo is bent over behind it like he's examining something. I squint, focusing my flashlight on the falling dust, and I see the dirt around the bottom of that particular pillar is thicker than around the others. It looks different too, like powder . . .

Anders takes a step back from the pillar, shaking his head. "This doesn't look very stable."

James shoots Anders a look before saying, "You're one to talk." Anders stiffens.

Everything seems to slow down as Paolo pulls a skull from the pillar, holding it out teasingly toward Maud. My heart stops and my limbs go numb as I realize that the thick powder around the pillar is crumbled plaster. "No," I say softly, but our guide must hear me because he spins around.

M. Lambert reacts much faster than I do. He runs, arms stretched out and body rigid with panic. Maud recoils from Paolo in disgust as he puts down his flashlight and pulls another skull free from the pillar.

"Stop!" M. Lambert shouts. "Don't touch that!"

"Run!" I scream.

Anders steps back, pressing himself against the wall. Maud and Paolo simply freeze, whipping their heads around to look our way. I hear the rumbling before I feel it. Paolo must too, because he grabs Maud and James and jerks them back hard toward the far wall. Grabbing Gretchen, I drag her over behind the pillar I examined earlier. It's strong, sturdy, and it might be our only chance of not being buried alive. As we rush past, I shout Henri's name.

"What in—" Liv says.

"Move!" Henri pulls her toward me so fast she drops her camera and stumbles into Gretchen and me.

Our world vibrates and then a roar of noise fills my ears. Rocks crashing, bones and stone cracking, people screaming. I'm screaming too. I've never heard so many people sound so desperately afraid. Flashlight beams spin wildly about before all the light is dimmed by falling dust and debris. Gretchen and I hold tight to each other and I close my eyes against the dust that burns them like fire.

The shaking seems to go on forever until suddenly it stops. Seconds pass in eerie silence. My lungs burn and Gretchen coughs against my shoulder.

Somebody moans. I think it's Henri. I reach for him, finding his jacket and gripping it.

"Are you okay?" I try to say, but the words aren't clear. My voice sounds raspy and broken.

I open my eyes a little. The dust is settling, and if I squint I can see a bit without my eyes burning. Not that there is much to see. There are spots of light shining through the dust cloud in a few places, but most of the flashlights have been buried. I'm afraid to sit up straight, terrified that the shaking will begin again and the ceiling will fall in and crush us all. My breathing comes in tight gasps as I fight to push away the panic. The air burns my throat and lungs until I'm coughing again.

Henri digs out his big flashlight and shines it around the room. "Oh no," he whispers.

Gretchen and I shift our position until we can see where he's looking. My stomach rolls and I feel like I might be sick. Where the farthest pillar stood, now there is a massive pile of dirt, rocks, and bones. Nearly half of the room is caved in. The pile reaches up to the ceiling. Two of the five tunnels out of the room are blocked.

Henri reaches for my hand on his sleeve and grips it tight. "Is everyone okay?"

"I am," I answer at the same time Gretchen says, "I think so."

"Yes, are you?" Liv says with a trembling voice.

"Yeah." He turns on his knees to face me and I see a small gash on his forehead oozing blood. "Can you come and look over there with me, Harley? You said you know structure and I don't want to cause another cave in."

"I'm no expert, but it's probably pretty unstable," I say, hesitating a moment before climbing to my feet. Yes, I'm terrified, but so is everyone else. If I can help, I want to try.

And although I'm not an expert, I might be the only one here with a clue. I *have* spent a lot of time reading architecture books and magazines and checking out buildings. That combined with my limited experience in urban exploration could really help here. Once you know what to look for, it isn't that hard to recognize the signs that something is structurally unstable. I join Henri and we carefully make our way across the cavern.

We both know what we're looking for in the debris, so neither of us says it out loud. The last thing the Catacombs needs is more bodies.

That morbid thought sends an uncontrollable shudder through me and Henri shoots me a concerned glance.

"Be careful!" Gretchen whisper-shouts from behind me, and I nod without turning around. I wrap my arm through Henri's and we take one cautious step at a time. On our side of the room, it's mostly random loose rocks that have fallen, but before we go far, the rocks become bigger. I stoop to pick up my yellow flashlight as we pass and my hand is shaking so hard that the beam jumps around.

I point the beam up at the ceiling and stop to study it. The cracks aren't too scary here, which indicates good structural integrity. It's much worse the closer we get to the pile. Where the pile reaches the ceiling the rocks and dirt look like they're compressed. That's good. Everything that has fallen is currently supporting the ceiling now. It's replacing the pillar for the moment, and that's mildly reassuring.

We freeze when we hear movement near the right side of the pile.

"Maud? Paolo? Are you okay?" I call softly. The echo from before is gone. All the rubble buries the sound now, just like it tried to bury us.

Glancing back toward Gretchen, I notice she's found her red flashlight. Liv sits beside her. She doesn't have her flashlight, but she has found her camera and has it trained on us. It irritates me this time. People could be hurt here and recording our search for them isn't helping anyone.

"Anders? Can you hear me, man?" Henri's voice is no louder than mine, and I'm glad. You never know what could set off another collapse in a situation like this.

"Help me!" James croaks, and then immediately starts coughing. Henri and I move slowly toward his voice, and he curses at us for taking so long.

"Calm down." I keep my voice low and soft, but don't even attempt to hide my frustration. "If we hurry, we might cause another collapse and bury you completely. So shut up and wait."

Once James is in view, I can tell he's fine and not trapped in rubble. I'm angry until I spot Paolo and Maud behind him. She looks okay and is free, but Paolo's arm is stuck. James bends over and starts pulling rocks away near Paolo and I feel a rumble. "Stop!" I hiss.

James stands up and stares at the ceiling wide-eyed until the rumbling stops. Henri and I make it to his side and I bend down to get a better look. Paolo grunts in pain and Maud looks up at me with terrified eyes. "How can we get him out?"

I swallow as my stomach rolls. I want to help, but we're talking about life and death here. That's a lot of pressure to put on what I remember from books, a little geocaching, and some guest lectures. Pushing my fear aside, I study Paolo's arm. It's buried up to the elbow beneath a huge rock. "Can you feel your fingers?"

Paolo nods.

Carefully, I get down on the floor and look under the big rock. Smaller stones support it and pin his arm in place. If I move the smaller stones, the rock will crush his arm. I need leverage.

"Maud and James, when I say so, push down on that side of the rock as hard as you can."

Maud glares at me. "Won't that hurt him more?"

I give a firm shake of my head and pretend that I know for certain what I'm really just guessing. "It will help me get him out if you push on the very edge—but only when I say, okay?"

They nod and move into position.

Henri is at my elbow. "What can I do?"

I point to the smaller rocks. "They are the only things keeping the rock from crushing him, but they're also pinning him in place. When Maud and James push down on that side, I need you to lift up as much as you can on this one. Try to tilt it enough that I can move the rocks so Paolo can pull out his arm."

Paolo blinks at me. "You sure this won't just crush my arm?"

"Honestly, no. But if anyone has any better ideas to get you out, go ahead and tell me."

They all stare at each other doubtfully, but no one responds.

"Harley? Is everything okay?" Gretchen asks from across the room.

"Yes. Now, *shh*." I say just loud enough for her to hear me before turning back to the others. "You guys have to keep the rock shifted long enough for Paolo to take his arm out *and for me to put the rocks back*. Dropping it could destabilize this whole pile and cause another cave in."

Henri looks at Paolo. "You ready?"

Paolo nods. His olive complexion has gone sickly pale.

I take a deep breath through my teeth to keep the dust out and then grab hold of the rocks I have to pull free. "Go!"

James and Maud push down on their side as hard as they can and Henri lifts with all his strength on the opposite side. At first nothing happens, then the rock moves just a bit and Paolo screams.

James and Maud start to ease up, but Henri growls, "Don't you dare!" through gritted teeth.

I pull the first rock free, but have to wiggle the second one and roll it on its side. Paolo jerks his arm out and the whole room starts to shake as I shove the rocks back in.

"Get back!" Henri says. Releasing the rock, he grabs my arm and drags me a few feet away before I even have a chance to react. We both duck, huddling together and covering our heads until the trembling subsides.

After a few seconds of silence, James crawls out from behind the pile, dragging Maud and Paolo with him. Maud clutches three flashlights to her chest. Paolo holds his arm gingerly against his body and blood stains his shirt near his wrist, but he gives me a weak smile. "Thank you."

"Of course." I start doing a silent head count, and my chest tightens. Anders is still missing.

Maud stumbles toward Liv and Gretchen. All three embrace without speaking. Henri pats James on the back and receives a one-armed hug from Paolo as he passes. Then Henri and I move around toward the other side of the pile, the last place we saw Anders.

"Anders? Are you okay?" Henri's voice is more frantic now. I watch the ceiling for signs of trouble, trusting him to guide me. I step on something that rolls under my foot and I grab on to Henri's shoulder to stop from falling. Once I'm steady again, I look down and see the base of a mangled flashlight. Henri stops walking and I feel his shoulders slump.

"Oh God."

Henri's face is pale and he looks stricken. The triumph of freeing Paolo is gone in a heartbeat, and I don't want to look where he's looking. I don't want to see what he's seeing. For an instant, I wonder if I can just grab Gretchen and run. Get out of here, get out of Paris, and never look back.

But I know I can't. Tightening my grip on his arm, I follow Henri's gaze to the ground a few feet ahead of us. Blood—new blood—and old bones. A bloody skull rests on top. It stares at me, red drops glistening in the beam of my flashlight. I look under it and to the side. There's more blood. And then I see him.

Monsieur Lambert is lying on his back in the rubble. His face, the source of all the red, has been crushed so badly on the right side that it's almost unrecognizable. I turn and push my face against Henri's shoulder, closing my eyes and trying to keep breathing. I feel sick. While I was looking for the others, I had completely forgotten about our guide.

Gretchen is on her feet behind us. "Is it Anders? Is he . . ." Several seconds pass before she finishes, her voice choked with emotion. "Is he dead?"

The sound of someone moving over rocks comes from nearby, and Henri jumps back like he expects M. Lambert's body to come crawling out of the pile to grab him.

"No, I'm here." Anders's faint words come from somewhere near the left side of the pile.

He limps into view. He has bloody scratches on his arms and a gash on his forehead to match Henri's, but other than that he looks okay.

Anders approaches us a bit unsteadily, and I let go of Henri's arm as they embrace. When they pull apart, Anders carefully approaches M. Lambert. He tries to get close enough to check for a pulse, but every time he's nearly there, the rocks shift and he has to back off.

"Be careful. It's really unstable," I say.

"I think we all know that by now," James sneers as he examines the cuts on his arms. I gape at him for a moment before closing my mouth and looking away.

"You don't need to be a jerk about it." Gretchen jumps to my defense, and Henri is right behind her.

"Knock it off, James."

Anders moves around the pile to where he can reach one of M. Lambert's feet. He takes off the shoe and sock and puts his hand on the top of his foot.

"Can you get a pulse there?" I whisper to Henri.

"Yes. It's harder to find, but we don't seem to have many options."

After a few seconds of silence, Anders stands back up, expression grim.

Gretchen moves a few steps closer. "Is he—?"

"I can't find a pulse. It looks like his head and chest were crushed." Anders looks nearly emotionless, but his voice cracks a bit on the last word.

"He's dead?" Maud asks with wide eyes.

"Yes." Anders's tone is even now.

"How can you be so calm?" Maud's hands flutter at her sides like she doesn't know what to do with them. "He's dead. There is a dead body ten feet away from us. Why aren't you guys freaking out? Why—"

"We are," Gretchen responds, cutting her off. "We're just doing it quieter than you are."

I walk carefully back toward Gretchen, feeling numb. I'm so cold I can't stop shivering. No one speaks, but when another rumble shakes the room, we all jump. Maud wraps her arms around Paolo and sobs quietly against his chest. He pats her back with his one good arm and clenches his teeth against the pain when he tries to move the other one. He has pulled back the sleeve and I see deep scrapes around his wrist that are seeping blood, but that isn't the worst of it. His skin is covered with angry red and purple splotches all the way from wrist to elbow. It must be broken, and I'll be surprised if there isn't more than one fracture.

Now that I'm not actively doing something, the horror of our situation blankets me just like the dust settling around us. It falls onto every surface, into every crevice, until it has thoroughly coated everything. I find myself scanning the ceiling again and again. Is that crack new or am I being paranoid? I've never been this scared in my life. The fear won't let me breathe, or even think. I tell myself to take a breath in when I'm scanning the ceiling to the right and then let it out when I'm scanning to the left. That's what I focus on. When I forget to do that, my breath starts coming faster and faster until I feel like I might black out.

Finally, Liv says the words we're all afraid to say. "How the hell are we going to get out of the Catacombs without our guide?"

No one answers. Gretchen slumps until her head is on my shoulder. Maud cries harder.

And I just keep breathing.

Chapter 6

Voicemail to text from Model Mom to Gretchen

sent on June 12 at 12:15 a.m. –

Hi Gretchen, it's me. I called the home phone to check in and you didn't answer. I'm not sure if you're punishing me now or what. I'm hoping you're at home and sleeping already. You know you don't want to be grounded while Harley is visiting. Anyway, I thought maybe we could go to Angelina for breakfast. You can introduce Harley to the best hot chocolate in the world? We can talk about it in the morning. I love you, honey. Please be safe.

—transmission failed

■ ■ ■

I don't want to hold still anymore. If I do, I'm terrified these caves will swallow me whole. I'll sink into them and become just another body, just another skull staring at nothing.

The others argue about what to do while I recover all the backpacks and gather them together. I start organizing their contents and Gretchen squats down to help me with shaking hands.

"We've come so far. I'm sure he had to be leading us toward an exit." Liv's tone sounds raw with emotion bubbling just below the surface. "There is no way he was going to take us back the way he brought us in. We're probably three hours from that entrance, and I don't know about any of you, but there's no way I could remember all those twists and turns we took."

The rest of us shake our heads.

"But we have no idea where he was going." Anders grips the front of his jacket with both hands. "At least if we head back, we can try to remember together."

"That's crazy," Paolo says, and when I glance his way I'm happy that I can't see his mangled arm anymore. Maud and Henri helped him take of his jacket and tie it into a sling to keep his arm from moving too much. "If we head back and can't find the entrance we came in, then what? What do we do at that point?"

The muscles in Anders's jaw flex taut. "It's no crazier than wandering forward into unknown areas and hoping we magically find an exit. At least we know the areas we've gone through are safe."

I stare up at them, stunned that even after crossing an ocean and going one hundred feet underground I still can't escape people fighting around me. Maybe it's me. Maybe I put off some kind of vibe that makes everyone angry.

Maybe I can't avoid it.

"Yeah . . . this room was safe at one point, too." James tosses a pebble hard at the wall and glares at Anders. "Until you started walking around in places where the guide didn't say we could go."

"Don't act like I did this," Anders growls. He points an accusing finger at Paolo. "Walking through that side of the room didn't cause the cave-in. Pulling skulls from the pillar almost got us killed."

"Knock it off," Gretchen groans, tucking her knees up underneath her as she stares down at our supplies. "You two arguing about everything is bad enough even when we aren't trapped in a stupid maze of tunnels."

"Maybe you shouldn't have given them anything to fight about, then," Liv mutters, and Gretchen shoots her a look that can only be described as a death glare.

I lift my eyebrows at my cousin. It's not hard to tell that James and Anders aren't exactly buddies. I never would've suspected it was about Gretchen, though. She gives me a small and unnecessary shake of her head. I know this isn't the time to ask her about it, even though I'm desperate for a distraction.

"Please." James crosses his arms over his chest and lifts his chin disdainfully at Liv. "She didn't mean that much to me."

Gretchen jerks her head up. She couldn't look more shocked if he slapped her. I'm not even certain exactly what they're talking about and I want to punch him. I didn't like James much before, but now I'm starting to hate him.

"Then she deserves better." Anders takes a step forward, obviously feeling the same way I am.

"This isn't helping," Henri says, pushing his fingers through his hair and stepping in between them.

"Someone is dead, you guys." Liv looks around at us all with a dark expression.

"Yeah, whose fault is that?" Maud's voice is so quiet I'm not sure I heard her.

It's silent for a few seconds and Liv frowns. "Are you blaming *me* for this?"

"No one should follow Anders, ever," James mutters, and I see Anders's hand clench into a fist by his side. I wrap both arms around myself. Wishing I could hide from all of them. Take Gretchen, and maybe Henri, and go off on my own.

Maud ignores him, answering Liv with a slightly apologetic tone now. "I'm not blaming you. I'm only saying . . . if you hadn't been distracting M. Lambert by using your camcorder, he might've warned us in time."

"Warned you not to be idiots?" Liv looks dumbfounded and furious. "He told us not to touch the bones already. This wasn't new information."

Paolo shifts his body like he's trying to block Maud from Liv's retaliation. "He warned you not to record anything too."

"Me turning on my camcorder didn't bring down half the ceiling!" Liv's voice shoots up in volume and the cave around us rumbles. We all duck again, panicked eyes searching the ceiling, arms up to protect our heads. My pulse pounds so loud in my ears that my head aches. When the slight vibration settles with only a fine shower of dust, I have trouble catching my breath again.

"Enough," Henri says, quiet but firm. "We don't have any good options, but we still need to pick one."

I clear my throat. "We have twelve water bottles, twelve granola or protein bars, seven flashlights, one extra set of batteries, one of Gretchen's workout T-shirts, seven jackets, and one first aid kit that consists of mostly Band-Aids, ibuprofen, and antibiotic ointment."

I wait for them process this information. No one responds, and I try to force my voice not to reveal how absolutely freaked out I am when I continue. "Monsieur Lambert's flashlight was crushed. Did he have his pack on him?"

James nods, eyeing me like he's trying to figure me out. "I don't think he took it off the whole time."

Deliberately looking away from him, I focus on Henri. "I doubt we can get to it if it's under him."

"No." He frowns. "It's too unstable to be trying to shift or move anything over there. It could bury us all."

"Right." I look back at the others. "Whichever way we decide to go, we need to try to conserve the food and water as much as we can."

"But we'll get out before we have to worry about that, though . . . right?" Maud's whisper borders on frantic, and when no one reassures her it seems to make things worse. "I mean, we were outside only four hours ago, guys. *Stront*! We have to be able to get out before we're all—I mean— without water and food we'll—we'll—" She stops, her expression one of absolute despair. Paolo pulls her against his shoulder again, gritting his teeth against the pain.

Gretchen digs her phone out of her pocket and holds it up, squinting at the screen. "Everyone check to see if you have a signal."

"Down here?" Liv looks skeptical.

"It doesn't hurt to check," Gretchen mutters, sticking her phone back into her pocket. I pull out my phone and the others all try theirs as well, except Paolo, who didn't bring one. We all get the same result. No signal. Gretchen sighs. "Let's turn them off for now, then. Save some battery life to check later."

"We should conserve light too," James adds, his expression grim. "We don't want to end up lost down here in the dark."

I shudder at the thought.

"Good idea." Gretchen's icy tone makes her words sound flat. "We should only keep one on at a time. You go first."

"Let me guess, Anders can be next?" He smiles tightly.

Gretchen mimics his expression. "Only if your performance is disappointing."

His smile falls, morphing into a glare, and she stands up with a groan, turning her back on him as she speaks to the rest of us. "Sitting in this half-caved-in room definitely isn't the best plan. Let's take a vote. Everyone who wants to try going the general direction we were already heading and look for an exit there, raise your hand."

I raise my hand along with Liv, James, Paolo, and Maud.

"Then that's the plan," she says.

We use the first aid kit to patch up our worst cuts and scrapes and give Paolo a few ibuprofen to help with the pain. I put everything back into the backpacks and hand them out. Maud grabs Paolo's before he can take it from me. I know he must be hurting pretty badly when he doesn't protest.

As soon as we're all ready, I start leading the way toward the two unblocked tunnels on the other side of the room. Gretchen calls my name, and when I turn around I notice that I'm the only one who still has my flashlight on besides James.

"Oh, right." With fumbling fingers, I switch it off and slip it into my backpack. My skin prickles, cold and clammy. A pool of light cast by a single bulb is now all that stands between us and the shadows. They suddenly feel malicious to me. Closing in, they touch us here and there, but it's only a caress compared to what they have in store.

James steps forward and hands me his flashlight. I'm stunned, wondering if what's going on in my head is really that obvious even to a near stranger. He shrugs. "This way you can lead and look for any sections that might collapse before we go into them."

"Sure." I turn, gripping the blue flashlight tight. Picking my way along carefully, I stick to the outside of the stronger pillars where the ceiling still looks fairly stable. Less cracks, and most of the stone here looks to be chiseled instead of crumbling, so it *should* be safe.

"Wait." Henri's voice echoes. He's the only one who hasn't started following me. When we look back, he gestures helplessly toward the collapsed section. "Do we leave him down here?"

"We can't dig him out or carry him, so . . ." Liv frowns.

Paolo bows his head. "This is the place he loved best. I think he wouldn't mind being left here."

"Shouldn't we bury him the rest of the way, at least?" Henri takes one step toward where M. Lambert lies quiet and still amid the rubble.

I sigh. I hate having to say this, but it's true. "We really shouldn't move any dirt right now. That side of the cave is too unstable."

"Okay." Henri bows his head for a few seconds before moving to join the rest of us. I feel terrible for leaving our guide in here, but I really don't know what else we can do.

"Once we get out, we'll tell someone. Maybe they can send someone to get him," I mutter, trying to make myself feel better. Gretchen squeezes my shoulder, and I see the same worry in her eyes that I know must be in mine.

"I'm not sure I want anyone to know about any of this." Liv sounds like I feel: insecure and scared.

Paolo shoots her a glare. "We're telling someone."

Liv lowers her head and keeps walking.

We separate, momentarily turning on a second flashlight so we can scout the two tunnels for about fifty feet. They look pretty similar. Both are relatively small and have a few offshoot tunnels. The one on the right is farther away from the cave-in, though, and the new-looking cracks in the ceiling of the tunnel on the left make our decision for us.

"I think we should try to head mostly to the right, without going back the way we came, of course, and go up whenever possible," Gretchen says. Anders gives a short nod of agreement, and I'm relieved when no one else argues and this becomes our official plan.

I can't stop thinking about my conversation with my mom. I wish I could take back my awful words. The last thing I said to her was "I hate you." How could I leave things like that? I was so angry, but it's no excuse. Heavy over my every breath, every thought, every step, hangs the fear that those could be the last words she ever hears from me.

I won't let those be my last words to her. I *can't*.

I wish instead that I'd told her—or anyone—about our plans to come to the Catacombs.

"Will anyone know where to look for us?" I ask as I lead the way into a tunnel that angles up.

Gretchen walks beside me, her face twisting into a frown. "Did any of you tell anyone we were coming down here?"

"I said Anders and I were visiting my cousin." Henri glances at Liv. "Didn't you do something similar?"

She nods, looking miserable.

Gretchen looks to Paolo. "What about you?"

"The commune won't care if James and I aren't there. They don't keep track of the residents," Paolo says with a grimace.

"If anyone misses me, they'll assume I'm with him." Maud tilts her head toward Paolo.

"What about you?" I ask Gretchen as I lead the way down another tunnel to the right. "I know you didn't tell your mom where we were going, but won't she check your computer or something? Maybe find that invite?"

Gretchen gives a short and bitter laugh. "I keep my laptop locked up tight. It requires a password and a fingerprint to access it. There's no way she's getting in there unless she gets help from a hacker at least as good as me. And she doesn't know anyone like that."

I groan, thinking that Mom and Dad wouldn't be trying to reach me at all for at least a couple of days. "At least Chantal will get the police involved once she realizes we're not home, right?"

After several seconds pass without an answer from Gretchen, I lift the light until I can see her face. Her lips are pressed into a firm line.

"What?" I'm confused. "Why wouldn't she?"

Gretchen's expression doesn't reveal much. "This wouldn't be the first time that she's come home and I haven't been there."

I'm too surprised to think before I speak. "That doesn't sound like you."

Her eyes harden and I can almost *feel* her glare. "I guess when you stop returning phone calls and emails for months at a time that things might change. You don't know me, Harley."

A tight pain starts in my chest and I whip my face forward again, walking in silence. My shock quickly fades into anger. I might not have been the best pen pal, but it definitely went both ways. But my mind betrays me by bringing up all the times when she emailed or texted or called and I was too busy to respond right away—or at all. Okay, maybe it was more me than her, but she wasn't perfect at keeping in touch either. In the last year, I was the one whose messages went unanswered. But why do *I* feel guilty when we're stuck in this entire situation because of *her* convincing me to go on an off-limits tour of the Catacombs?

I'm quiet as I lead the way down tunnel after tunnel with no sign of an exit. We're moving slower than before. Paolo needs help from James and Henri to get through the smaller sections where we have to crawl, and although I'm pretty sure he's in shock, his pain seems to be getting worse the farther we go. Maud keeps randomly bursting into tears. At first, I felt for her, but now I really want her to get a grip. We're all upset and scared, and this isn't helping. Plus, the way her sniffles echo is starting to give me a pretty serious headache.

We come to a room even bigger than the one with the pillars. I shine James's flashlight around to check it out. There are six different tunnels leading out. Random piles of bones are scattered around. Someone took hundreds of skeletons here and sorted them into different piles. The nearest one is all skulls, probably over two hundred of them. Unlike the arranged stacks, these have been thrown into a pile. Some are upside down or facing backward. One in the center stares straight forward, straight at us—straight through me.

Maud stumbles and falls to her knees. She doesn't try to get back up, and I can't blame her. The adrenaline rush from the cave-in seems to have faded and every step feels harder to take. I'm so tired. My neck aches and I rub it. I'm still afraid to stand up straight. Without thinking about it, I've been walking with hunched shoulders, subconsciously trying to protect my head from potential crushing death.

"Can we take a break?" Even with the ibuprofen, every word Paolo speaks is tinged with pain, and when I shine the flashlight on him, I'm amazed that he's still so pale when the rest of us are flushed with exertion.

I search the ceiling for the telltale signs of cracks and crumbling or rotted wooden beams. But nothing here hints of instability. "Yeah. This looks like a safe place to do that."

He sinks down beside the nearest wall, leans his back against it, and closes his eyes. We're all tired, but the dark circles under his eyes stand out in stark contrast to the new pallor of his skin. It scares me. The others relax, some standing, some sitting, as they have quiet conversations. I prop the flashlight so it's shining on the ceiling above us.

The reflection off the whitish-gray stone makes the pool of light a little bigger.

Dropping my backpack to the ground, I take out my phone and turn it on to check the time. I blink at it, my bleary eyes not focusing on the bright screen right away. I'm startled to see it's almost four in the morning. No wonder everyone is so wiped out.

"Do you have a signal?" Gretchen speaks from right near my elbow, and I jump. "Sorry. I didn't mean to sneak up on you."

"No signal. It's fine. I'm just exhausted." I try not to sound angry and hurt about our earlier conversation, but I fail. "I'm sorry I wasn't better at keeping in touch."

"I'm sorry for saying it. I'm not mad at you. I just missed you. It hasn't been easy." Her eyes are full of sympathy as she looks up at me and shrugs. "But I guess things aren't exactly going smoothly for you either."

"Not exactly, and I missed you too." I give her a hug, resting my head on her shoulder. My arms and legs feel so heavy now, more like logs that I'm dragging along with me than limbs. When I release her, she pulls out her phone and turns it on.

"I'd be shocked if any of us could get any kind of signal down here." I lift my hands over my head and stretch my back.

"Shocked in the very best way possible. Might as well check." Gretchen gives me a wistful half-smile before walking slowly around the room, holding the phone up above her head.

I'm afraid to sit, but my aching legs tell me I should. Once I do, my whole body feels like it's trembling even though I'm sitting still. My throat and eyes still burn from all the dust and I desperately want some water. But I can't be the first one to take some after being the one to suggest that we ration it.

I distract myself by watching Gretchen. She's far enough away that the light from her phone screen shining on her face makes her look like a bobbing disembodied head. It's bizarre. Her lips twist into a frown that deepens the longer she moves around. Finally, she comes back and sits down beside me.

"No luck, huh?" I ask, examining the scratches on my arm to make sure none of them are still bleeding.

"No." She squints and turns her head toward me. "Did you see anything metal in the bags when you went through them?"

I think for a second. "There was a pocket with some paper clips and pens in one of them. Why?"

She taps her fingers against her lips. "I wonder if I could make something to enhance the antenna on one of our phones."

I doubt that any antenna would allow us to get a signal this far underground, but I shrug. "Worth a try."

Gretchen pushes a strand of purple hair behind her ear and starts looking at the case on her phone. "We'd have to be closer to the surface, I think. Plus, it might take me some time to figure it out . . ."

My fingers clench as I respond. "Anything that could help at this point is good to try."

Gretchen bites her lip. "Right. I'll see what I can do."

Henri eases himself onto the ground next to us. "I wonder if maybe we should try and sleep for a bit here."

My instinct is to argue. I don't want to sleep in the Catacombs with a pile of skulls watching us. I'm not sure if I can . . . but my body yells out in protest and my headache throbs to match.

"Yeah, we probably should. It's late." Gretchen points back to where it looks like Paolo is already asleep. "He really looks like he could use it."

Glancing at the structure of the room again, I shrug. "This is a safer place than most down here."

Henri gets back to his feet. He moves like an old man as he turns slowly toward the others. "We're going to sleep here for a bit. I'm going to check out one of the tunnels to use the bathroom and take my phone for a light. Don't follow me unless you want a show."

Liv and Maud don't look happy at the idea of sleeping here either. I hear them muttering, but neither of them make an argument out of it.

Gretchen and I look at each other. I've had to go for quite a while now, and it's to the point where I'm sure I won't get any sleep without doing that first.

"Let's go together?" I say, and am relieved when she gives a fervent nod of agreement. Leaving the flashlight where it is, we pull out our phones. We wander back to the tunnel we came out of since we're already familiar with that one. We find an offshoot with no bones. Both of us decide that's a requirement, to show respect for the dead and because we don't want any skulls watching us. We take turns, one of us standing guard in case of . . . I don't know what.

By the time we come back, most of the others are sprawled out and trying to sleep. The flashlight is off—

good for conserving light, bad because now only our phone screens are lighting the darkness. Only Liv is still sitting up, whispering into the lens of her camcorder, a tiny spotlight on the front casting her features in harsh angles and shadows. Paolo hasn't moved. When Gretchen shines the light from her phone around, I can see his chest is rising and falling in a slow, even rhythm. Maud is curled up with her head on his leg. Her sporadic crying has died down to a whimper. James rests a few feet away, curled up with his back toward the group.

Gretchen and I turn off our phones and try to find the softest parts of our backpacks to use as pillows. We curl up, facing each other. I close my eyes and wonder how I can possibly sleep when I'm still shivering.

"Harley?"

I open my eyes, and in the faint light from Liv's camera I see Gretchen looking at me, half her face covered by her jacket collar. "Yeah?"

"I'm sorry." I'm surprised when a quiet half-gasp/half-sob comes from her. "We shouldn't have come here. I'm sorry I got you into this."

"Shh . . ." I pull my backpack closer to her and give her a hug. Stretching out on my back, I lie by her side and whisper, "This isn't your fault. And we're going to find a way out of here. I promise."

I speak the words as much for me as for her. We both relax, side by side, and fall asleep.

Chapter 7

Voicemail to text from Model Mom to Gretchen sent on

June 12 at 3:07 a.m. —

Gretchen. You better call me back immediately, young lady. I'm home and you're not. You haven't pulled a stunt like this in months. I thought we'd moved past it. I know you're still angry at me for moving us away from New York, but this is immature. I'm very disappointed in you. You are responsible for your cousin. She's in a strange city where she barely speaks the language. You both better come back home safe. We'll discuss your punishment when you get here.

—transmission failed

■ ■ ■

Monsieur Lambert finds me in my dreams. His crushed head drips blood as he reaches for me. The skin melts away from his hand, leaving only exposed bone. The ground beneath me shakes and I fall—down and down and down. He falls with me, trying to grab me with his bony fingers. My heart pounds against the walls of my chest so hard and fast it aches. My screams echo through the darkness, but I can't run. There is nothing to hold on to as we fall forever. Down here, there is no escape. His broken and bloody mouth is barely able to form the words as the bones of his hand finally close around my throat.

"If I'm not leaving, neither are you."

■ ■ ■

I jolt awake with a start and the first thing I hear is Maud crying again. With a moan, I roll over. Every part of my body aches and I wonder how on Earth I managed to sleep at all. Gretchen is already sitting up and glaring with blood-shot eyes at Maud. She holds James's flashlight, which is on again, in her lap.

The others are all awake and I wonder if any of them slept better than me. I'm much colder than I was before. It could be because I burned through all the calories from dinner and now I don't have anything left for fuel. Or it could be because moving generates heat and I've been lying still. Either way, the cold seems like it's seeped through my clothes and into my skin. I zip my jacket up all the way and push my hands into the pockets. It doesn't help much.

Maud leans against Paolo's chest, whimpering. His eyes are closed and his skin doesn't have any more color than before we went to sleep, and now he's shivering. I feel bad for him and wish I could help. He's still using his jacket as a sling, so he must be even colder than me.

Henri sits a few feet away, going through his backpack. I shift into a sitting position and cross my legs, rubbing my eyes and then stretching my shoulders. I turn to look at my cousin. "What time is it?"

"Almost eight." Gretchen's already low voice sounds gravelly. So, maybe four hours of interrupted and night-mare-filled sleep? Not great, but better than nothing. James's flashlight dims a bit before coming back. It's already running low on batteries.

James looks up from where he is sprawled out on the ground to my right. "Looks like it's almost Anders's turn."

A low growl escapes Gretchen and Anders's back stiffens.

Liv gasps, pointing at something behind us, her eyes huge.

"Did you see that?" Her whole body seems to vibrate with pent-up tension. We all look where she's pointing and Gretchen shines the light in that direction. It's only empty space and more limestone. "I . . . sorry. I thought I saw something moving over there."

"With all the shadows, it's probably just your tired brain playing tricks on you," Henri says, patting her shoulder.

Maud's sobs get louder and I groan under my breath.

"God, would you please *shut up*?" Anders snaps.

Paolo's eyes fly open. "What did you say to her?"

"I asked her to shut up."

Paolo climbs carefully to his feet and faces off with Anders. Maud sits in shocked silence, her eyes huge as she watches the confrontation.

"Leave her alone. She's afraid." Paolo wobbles a little, but that doesn't keep him from standing his ground.

"We're all afraid!" Anders yells in his face. "She's making an awful situation even worse, and you started all of this by messing with that pillar in the first place."

I look on in surprise. Anders did his fair share of arguing last night, but he kept his cool better than the others. Not this morning. He's flat-out shouting, even though we've established that isn't a good idea down here. There's obviously an angry streak buried under that calm exterior. James jumps up to his feet and I let out another groan. We're going to start last night all over again. But before it goes any further, Paolo swings his uninjured arm and slams his fist into Anders's face.

James freezes, a half-dazed smile on his face.

"Whoa, everybody calm down." Henri is up and between them before Anders gets a chance to retaliate. Blood trickles from Anders's nose and it's clear from the fury on his face that he wouldn't hesitate to hit back if Henri wasn't in the way.

"I'm taking a piss." Paolo picks up James's flashlight and stomps off through the second tunnel on the right.

Anders stalks away through a different tunnel, pushing away Henri's attempt to make sure his nose is okay.

"Bathroom break before we start walking again, then," Gretchen says. "Everyone meet back here when you're done and you've cooled off." She gets up and helps me to my feet. The others head off through different tunnels.

Gretchen and I duck back into the same tunnel we used last night. We only use her phone this time and there is so much darkness. My skin prickles. I remember what Liv said about seeing something moving and shiver. That nightmare really freaked me out. It's given me an absurd paranoia that we aren't alone, like someone is watching us—and waiting. I swallow, my eyes searching as I shine the small light into every dark corner. Even though I know it was only a nightmare and that all the stories about bad supernatural juju in the Catacombs are simply stories, it still creeps me out. I can't wait to get back to the rest of the group.

After we both take care of our business, we hurry back to the cavern. Henri is already there and holding an unopened water bottle on his lap.

He holds it up. "You think we could each have a sip?"

Gretchen and I both nod.

"Ladies first." He twists off the lid and hands it to Gretchen.

She takes a swallow before passing it to me with a wink and saying, "If anyone in this situation is afraid of germs then they need to re-evaluate their priorities."

I grin back, and it feels good to let a bit of the tension seep out of me for a minute. "Agreed. There are too many other things to worry about down here." I take my swallow before passing it back to Henri.

I get my flashlight out so we can turn off our phones. The others straggle back, and I'm relieved that Maud has stopped crying. My persistent headache thanks her.

Henri passes the water bottle to Maud, Liv, James, and Anders as they come in and we wait for Paolo. None of us speak and I notice both Maud and Liv are shivering now too. I pull my jacket tighter around me. It really is cold down here. We need to get walking again. I hold my flashlight in one hand and press the other hand against my jeans to warm it up.

Gretchen scoots closer to Anders. I wince when I see that his cheekbone is an ugly red and starting to swell.

My cousin reaches out and touches the swollen part gently. He meets her eyes and everything hard and stiff about him seems to soften. It's surprising to see him melt like that. I smile to myself. Falling for the last guy I would expect seems so much like this new Gretchen that I'm getting to know. She catches me watching and gives me a small smile. When I turn away, I catch James watching them, too, pain in his expression. For the first time, I feel a little bad for him.

I shiver again, and Henri scoots closer to me until his left side is against my right. It's surprising how much it helps, and when I whisper "Thank you" to him, he pats my hand in response. The warmth of his hand on mine is so reassuring that I grip it without thinking before he can pull it away. I'm as surprised as he looks, but I only have an instant to wonder if it was a mistake before he smiles and weaves his fingers through mine.

It's probably good that it's so dark in here, because now I'm blushing.

I look around the cavern, mostly to avoid Henri's gaze. With only one flashlight casting back the darkness, we can't see much beyond our small circle.

"Is Paolo the stalk-off-and-pout type?" I finally ask. "Do we need to go find him?"

"N–not usually." Maud looks over at me with worry in her eyes. "You don't think he was caught in another cave-in, do you?"

I shake my head. "No. We would have felt the shaking if that happened. I'm sure he's fine."

"He could be lost, though." Liv frowns and stares off toward the tunnels.

"That's true," Anders agrees. "The tunnels seem to weave in this section, and a few of them interconnect."

"Let's go look for him." Henri climbs to his feet and pulls me up beside him, still holding my hand. "Turn on two more flashlights. Split up into groups, and if you start feeling lost at all, head straight back to this room and wait for the rest of us."

Anders and Gretchen walk into Paolo's tunnel with her light. James joins Liv and Maud as they head into the one on the right. Henri turns his big flashlight on and we walk into the one on the left. It's completely silent for the first minute and I feel the awkward need to lighten the mood.

"Too bad you didn't bring any of your instruments down here." I heave an exaggerated sigh as he shines his light into an empty alcove on the left. "I could really use some music to criticize right about now. It's an excellent distraction."

Henri chuckles. "I tried, but the drums wouldn't fit in my backpack."

I throw him my best deadpan expression. "I think that's how you know that it's time to invest in a bigger backpack."

He matches my serious tone, but even in the dim light I can see the laughter in his eyes. "Oh, it's the first thing I'm doing once we're out of here. Heading straight for the giant backpack store."

I laugh, and he squeezes my hand, rubbing the side of it with his thumb. It sends tingles shooting up my arm.

We talk about what things are like back home in Chicago and Quebec as we check two more offshoot tunnels. One is a dead end, but the other seems to intersect the tunnel Paolo took.

"Your mom is a doctor?" I ask after he tells me she works in a hospital.

"Yeah, my dad, too." He kicks a small pebble in front of him as we continue to the left.

"Wow, is there any pressure from them? Do they want you to be one too?"

"There used to be, but once I told her there was no way, my mom backed off." He sounds relaxed, which I hope means he doesn't feel like I'm prying.

"Does your dad still pressure you?"

"Oh, no." He shakes his head. "I actually don't see him much. He moved to Toronto after the divorce."

I wish I could kick myself. I know from personal experience what a painful topic this can be, and I still manage to walk right into it. Welcome to the Catacombs Confessional; now tell me all the worst things about your life. Time to extract my foot from my mouth. "I'm sorry. I didn't mean to—"

An ear-shattering scream bounces off the walls from a tunnel ahead of us and to the left. I grab Henri tighter and he pushes me behind him.

"Everyone! Come here!" Liv's voice is frantic.

Henri and I run toward her voice. It sounded like it was nearly on top of us, so I'm surprised when we have to search quite a ways down the tunnel to find them. Sound travels bizarrely down here. By the time we find them, my body has gone from cold to hot. I'm panting and my heart is racing. All my senses are on high alert.

James is closest to us. He's leaning forward with his head against the wall. His eyes are closed, his hands clenched at his sides. Maud crouches on the floor with her back to us, her body racked with sobs. Liv stands over her, one hand across her face and the other holding James's flashlight.

"What the—?" Henri cuts off as we get close enough to see what Maud is crouched over. Paolo lies sprawled across the tunnel floor. I gasp, dropping Henri's hand to cover my mouth. Paolo's eyes are open, but they look vacant, staring up at nothing. It isn't until Henri's flashlight beam hits the ground next to him that I see the pool of blood extending from his head. It's too much blood.

"Paolo?" Henri moves quickly, dropping to Paolo's side and checking for a pulse. Gretchen and Anders rush in behind us.

"What happened?" Gretchen grabs Liv's shoulder. "We heard a scream. Are you okay?"

"Paolo." It's the only word Liv can get out.

My thoughts are stuck on an endless loop: *Please don't let someone else die. Please don't let someone else die. Please don't let someone else die.* I have to get a grip, to focus on something useful. If Paolo hit his head on something, there has to be a reason, and I have to make sure no one else will get hurt while we're trying to help him.

Moving around James, I search the ceiling and walls for signs of instability, but the tunnel looks sturdy. By the time I'm confident that we aren't at risk of another collapse here, I'm on the opposite side of Paolo. From here I can see a gaping wound on the side of his head. It's a weird color, and it takes me a moment to realize I'm looking at part of his brain. I suddenly can't draw in a full breath. I lean against the wall of the tunnel. Lifting my eyes back up to the ceiling, I put all my energy into not throwing up.

"I–I can't—I can't find his heartbeat," Henri stutters.

"Let me help." Anders moves down beside him and lifts Paolo's hand off the ground.

A low growl comes from Maud. "Don't you *touch* him!"

She launches herself across Paolo, shoving Anders's hand away and grabbing Paolo's fingers. She presses them gently against her face, kissing the tips of each one. Anders falls back, pure shock in his eyes.

Henri stands up. He keeps shaking his head over and over. "How did this happen? How?"

Liv shines the shaking beam of the flashlight on a rock near Paolo's body. The top of it is smeared red with blood. "I–I saw this. Maybe it fell on him or something."

"You s–sent him here," Maud chokes out through her sobs as she glares at Anders. "This i–is your fault."

Anders stares back in wide-eyed disbelief.

"Shh . . ." Gretchen kneels behind Maud, whispering soothing words to her that I can't quite make out. Maud starts to breathe a little slower. I'm both numb and on fire. This is—was—a person. I might have only just met him, but Paolo was funny and charming and alive, and now he's dead. My eyes drift back to the rock covered with Paolo's blood. A feeling sinks deep down into my bones: the Catacombs doesn't want us here.

This is a place for the dead and we don't belong.

I turn my head to look into the pitch-black tunnel. The darkness is so thick that it feels alive. I know my eyes are playing tricks on me, but it seems to be moving. It's waiting for us. Waiting for all of our lights to go out, one by one.

Suddenly Gretchen is there, wrapping both arms around me in a tight hug. When I feel her hot tears against my neck, it jolts me back into focus. This is my cousin. It's Gretchen. She's one of my favorite people in the world and I refuse to let her die. We *have* to get out of here somehow—*all of us.*

If one rock can fall and hit Paolo, then more could fall and we need to get the hell out of here.

I gently pull myself free from Gretchen's arms, squinting up at the ceiling again, searching for the crack that killed him, trying to find the spot where that rock fell from. I pick up Henri's big flashlight from where he dropped it and shine it all around the ceiling. I should be able to find where the rock fell from, but I don't see anything. This tunnel is kind of narrow. The soot from workers' torches has blackened most of the ceiling and upper walls here. I definitely don't see any white or gray from freshly exposed limestone.

Swallowing, I move around Paolo's body, careful not to look at the wound again, and crouch beside the bloody stone. I take a deep breath, draw up my nerve, and roll it over.

Grayish-white limestone on all sides.

I fall on my butt and scramble backward. There isn't any soot tarnish anywhere on that stone. What does that mean?

It means the rock didn't fall from the ceiling or high up on the wall, at least not in this particular tunnel.

It means it could have fallen out of a lower section of wall, but it had to be far too low to hit Paolo on the head.

It means the only way this was an accident was if Paolo tripped and fell backward, landing hard enough to kill himself when his head hit that rock. And from the position he's in, that seems impossible.

It means that one of the people around me is a murderer.

My whole body starts to tremble. I wrap my arms around my legs and stare up at the others. James stands with his back to the wall. Henri still holds one of Paolo's hands, his whole body curving in on itself. Gretchen has moved back by Liv and they're trying to comfort Maud. Anders is the only one watching me. When I look up at him, he seems to know what I'm thinking. He curses and kicks the wall. The question is whether Anders figured it out at the same time as me . . .

Or if he knew already because he's the one who killed him.

Gretchen looks over at me. "Are you okay?"

I clear my throat twice before I can get my voice to work. It comes out small and quiet. "I don't think this was an accident."

Chapter 8

Transcript of 112 Emergency Call placed by Chantal Dubois

on June 12 at 9:09 a.m.

(For use in criminal case #41773)

112 Operator:

Please state the exact nature of your emergency.

Chantal Dubois:

My daughter and niece are missing.

112 Operator:

When and where did you last see them?

Chantal Dubois:

Yesterday afternoon, they were here at my flat.

112 Operator:

Can you give me your name and address please?

Chantal Dubois:

Yes, I'm Chantal Dubois and my flat is at 9 Boulevard Richard-Lenoir. My daughter is Gretchen Dubois and my niece is Harley Martin.

112 Operator:

Do you believe they went missing from that location or did they leave after you last saw them?

[silence]

112 Operator:

Ms. Dubois?

Chantal Dubois:

[muffled]

I don't know.

112 Operator:

Have either of them ever run away before?

Chantal Dubois:

[quiet sobbing]

Not like this. God, it's been months. She always comes back by morning. She always answers her phone or at least sends a text. This is different. Please help me.

112 Operator:

We're sending an officer to your location. Please stay on the line until they arrive.

■ ■ ■

"What do you mean it wasn't an accident?" Henri looks at me, his skin gray beneath the light reflecting off the stone walls. I feel dizzy, like my brain is spinning and my heart is beating too fast and too wildly for my blood to get where it needs to go.

Blood. For a place famous for bones, we've seen way too much blood in the Catacombs.

My eyes drift back down to the puddle beneath Paolo's head, and I cringe. I regret speaking up. I should've thought this through more. Letting a killer know you're on to them in a confined space like this is a terrible idea, but I can't take it back.

"What do you think happened to him?" Liv asks, looking from Paolo to me in confusion.

"That rock didn't fall from up high," I finally answer. "There's no soot on it like on the ceiling here. And if it fell out, it would expose white rock behind it. Where could it have fallen from?"

96

The others glance around the tunnel, doubt and fear stamped plainly on their faces. As we're talking, I'm scrambling to piece together who could have done it. When Paolo walked off, who went next?

Anders.

I think he went into a different tunnel, but what if it connected to Paolo's?

"I know what you're thinking, and I don't want to believe it either," I mutter, tightening my arms around my legs. I know it hasn't gotten colder in here, but it feels like the temperature has dropped at least ten degrees since we found Paolo. I'm surprised I can't see my breath. "So please, give me another explanation . . . give me *any* other explanation for what happened."

Anders is still watching me. His posture is rigid. "Who could've done it?" he asks.

And even though Anders makes the most sense, I have to admit that it could've been any of them. Everyone separated after Paolo left. Gretchen is the only one I know didn't do it because she was with me. "I'm not sure."

Gretchen sits next to me, switching off her flashlight. Between Henri's and James's, we have plenty of light without it. "You think one of *them* killed him? These are my friends, Harley."

"*Perkele*," Anders mutters under his breath. He leans back against the wall and crosses his arms over his chest. His eyes are full of panic and something else. Is it fear or guilt?

I could be making a mistake assuming that Paolo was killed while we went off for our bathroom break. He could've been killed during the search just as easily. Maud,

James, and Liv found him. What if one of them killed him and the others are lying to help their friend cover it up? Looking at Maud, though, I doubt that she's acting. Her grief is too pure, too terrible.

Without even thinking about it, my eyes drift to Gretchen. I don't want to even consider it. But can I be certain that she isn't involved?

"I really don't know." I don't want Gretchen to look to me to answer this question. Like she said before, I barely even know her now, let alone her friends. My pulse pounds louder in my ears as I watch the way they react.

"Maybe some of those creepy ghost stories are actually true? Maybe none of us did this?" Liv's voice is so soft it borders on wispy.

"That's crazy." Henri squints into the darkness and rubs one hand across his forehead, leaving a smear of dirt. I glance up at James, who has been unusually quiet, but then I catch the death glare he's giving Anders. He's actually saying plenty.

"What are our other options?" Gretchen's voice has a slight edge of hysteria to it. "I would rather believe something supernatural is going on than that one of you did this."

A long silence stretches out and I can feel the tension increasing with each second. It hangs over our heads like the city far above, threatening to crush us, to suffocate us in darkness and bury us for the crime of living in a place intended for the dead.

"Maybe there is someone else down here with us?" Henri stares into the shadows beyond our flashlight beams.

"Have any of you seen anyone else?" I whisper back, my eyes following his gaze. The darkness is so thick and heavy it seems to have substance. Each particle of dust we kick up swirls in it. It's more like tar than air. It's suddenly hard to breathe. I'm trembling again, and I don't fight it this time.

When I look back up at the group, they're all staring out into the darkness as well. The same fear I feel crawling through my nerves is stamped on every face.

Henri lowers his head to his chest. "I haven't seen anyone. If I had, I would've asked them to help us get out of here."

"It's still possible, though." My eyes are drawn out to the blackness again. I keep expecting it to change or move. "If they knew the Catacombs well, another cataphile maybe, they could be down here with us and we might not know."

"What if it's friends of Monsieur Lambert?" Gretchen's voice cracks. "What if they're angry that we got him killed?"

"The collapse was an accident." Henri frowns. "Anyone with any sense would know that."

"Does this look s–sensible to you?" Maud lifts her head from Paolo's chest. Her eyes are wild and unfocused until they land on Anders. Then they fill with the purest rage I've ever seen. "*You* did this. You killed him."

Anders shakes his head and steps back until he's pressed against the wall. "I didn't."

"You were fighting with him," Liv says softly. "He punched you."

"People have punched me before and I didn't kill them." Anders inclines his head pointedly toward James then stares at Liv and Maud like they've lost their minds. "Why would I do it now?"

"You went into the c–caves right after him." Maud's angry statement is broken by a half-sob in the middle as she climbs to her feet.

"I didn't kill him." Anders looks both terrified and furious. I might even feel bad for him if I didn't agree with most of Maud's and Liv's points. Anders flings his arm wide, pointing at all of us. "Didn't you all go into the caves right after we did?"

"He's right. We did." Henri climbs to his feet as well, standing between Anders and the rest of us. "It could've been any one of us."

Anders's posture relaxes a bit, but it doesn't last long.

"You need to stop defending his actions," James says. "We all know who did this."

Anders wipes his hands across his face, releasing a growl of frustration. "You're crazy."

"It could have been any of us," Henri repeats, trying again to diffuse the situation.

"Yes. Anyone but me or Harley." Gretchen shifts closer to me. "We were together the whole time."

I hesitate to agree and she turns on me in surprise. "What? We were."

"I know." I want desperately to agree with everything she's saying, but it isn't *all* the truth. "But that's if we assume that he was killed before we started looking for him."

She recoils like I slapped her across the face. "Are you saying you think I could've done this?"

"No!" I rush to reassure her, but from her hurt expression I can tell she knows that I have doubts. I feel guilty for even thinking it, but it's been years since I knew her really well. I *know* she wouldn't have done it back then . . . I *hope* she wouldn't do it now. That's the most positive I can be at the moment.

Maud doesn't give me a chance to explain myself. Instead, she fires back at Henri and Gretchen. "Of the rest of us, who else would've killed him? Who else had a reason besides Anders? No one. He and Paolo never got along. You both know that. They've never liked each other."

"That's not true." Gretchen scoots away from me and climbs to her feet, and the temperature seems to drop another ten degrees in an instant. "They were friends until—"

"Paolo took my side. Surprising how rare that kind of loyalty actually is." James shoots an angry glare at Henri, who waves it away with a disgusted shrug.

"You can't honestly believe that Anders killed Paolo because I broke up with you." Gretchen is getting angrier by the second. "I knew you were self-centered and egotistical, but I never thought you believed you were *that* important."

"This is crazy. What did I ever do to make you think I could kill someone?" Anders looks like he wants to disappear into the wall behind him. "We didn't always agree, but I'm not a murderer."

"We aren't going to figure this out right now, guys." Henri puts his hands up like somehow that will make everyone stop. "We have to keep going or we'll never get out of here."

"You want us to leave Paolo?" Maud pins an accusing glare on me as I stand up, even though I'm the only one not involved in this argument.

"I—I don't—" I step away from her.

"We'll send someone back for him, Maud," Liv says softly, dropping an arm across her shoulders.

"We can't bring him. I–it's really not possible." Gretchen's voice catches with emotion.

Maud crouches down over Paolo, a fresh wave of sobs racking her frame. It's heartbreaking to watch her. She obviously really cared about him. She reaches out to his right wrist and undoes the woven leather band around it. She has to wrap it twice around her own wrist to keep it from falling off. Liv helps her secure it in place.

By the time she gets back to her feet and settles Paolo's backpack on her slim shoulders, the crying has stopped. Her eyes are icy and filled with hatred when she glares at Anders.

"Fine. We can keep going and send someone back for Paolo." We all turn toward the tunnel entrance in somber silence, but freeze when Maud continues. "But Anders can't come with us."

"What?" Gretchen gasps, her eyes wide with shock. Anders doesn't look surprised. I'm not sure why, but this makes me suspect him even more.

Liv's hands shake by her sides. "She has a point. If we think he killed Paolo, why would we let him stay with us? What if he decides to kill someone else?"

"*Voi helvetti*! I'm not a murderer!" Anders moves away from the wall and growls out the last word low and fierce. I'm the closest to him and I jerk back on instinct. His mouth hangs open for an instant in genuine surprise at my reaction. "Do you believe them?"

I close my mouth and look away. I don't know what to think. I agree that he has the best motive. Even before the arguing started, I thought so. But I'm tired and scared and I can't even believe this is happening. Twenty minutes ago, I didn't think any of them were capable of murder. Now I *know* that someone is. My hands tremble as I press my cold fingers against my mouth, letting my breath warm them. The cold feels like it's sinking deeper into my skin with each second.

"Of course she doesn't," Gretchen says beside me.

"Yes, she does," James says over her, his tone triumphant. "Admit it, Harley. You'll feel safer if he's not here."

My exhaustion and fear build to suffocating levels. I can't think straight and my vision seems to go red. I see Paolo punching Anders again and again, and then Paolo's brain and all the blood, and I shudder before finally giving in.

"Well, I might feel safer. I think—" I clear my throat and ignore the shocked glare from my cousin. "I don't know most of you, but if you all think . . ."

"That's the majority then," Maud whispers vehemently. "Anders isn't coming with us."

My stomach plummets to my feet. There are seven of us left, and I just cast the deciding vote. I wobble on my feet, feeling light-headed, and Liv throws an arm around my shoulders to support me. I don't know how I ended up taking the opposite side against Gretchen and Henri, but I immediately regret it.

"You should be glad that I *don't* kill people," Anders snarls, and I'm not sure if it's directed at Maud or me.

"Stop. You can't be serious." Henri stares at Maud in shock. "If we send Anders off by himself, he won't survive. I don't think he did this, and even if I did, we'll become murderers ourselves if we send him off alone. Don't let this place turn us into monsters."

"We won't be safe with him around," Liv insists.

"The majority should decide." James's tone is ice cold.

The angry stares from Henri and Gretchen are getting to me. I regret my decision even more now, but for some reason I can't back down. "None of us are safe down here, no matter what."

"We need to stick together," Gretchen pleads. "We're safer together."

"Does this look safe?" Liv gestures at Paolo's body.

"We can't *make* him leave us," Henri challenges.

"What if we won't go anywhere unless he leaves first?" Maud's question sounds more like a threat.

I feel sick to my stomach. This situation has spiraled out of control so fast.

Gretchen rolls her eyes. "Then maybe we should leave *you*."

"Maybe no one should leave anyone." Henri shifts to stand between Gretchen and Maud. "Our best chance to get out of here is together."

"Not with one of us killing the others." Maud glares at Anders.

"For God's sake, we don't *know* it was him!" Gretchen shouts in frustration. When dust falls from the ceiling, we all flinch.

"We need to get out of here," Liv murmurs softly into the following silence.

The pain and anger is fresh in Gretchen's eyes when she pivots to face me. "You don't *really* think it was him?"

I want to lie and take it all back. I wish I could tell her I don't suspect Anders, but he is so hard for me to read. There's something about him that I don't get, and I'm terrified of everything and everyone around me right now. So I whisper the two words that I can't seem to get past: "Who else?"

Her face fills with pain. She likes him way more than I suspected. Instead of reassuring me, this makes me press my lips tighter together. If she likes Anders that much, she might not be able to see him clearly.

And there is no way I'm risking Gretchen's life simply because she may have a crush on a psychopath.

Henri sighs, sounding resigned and disgusted. He hasn't looked my way in a while, and after this I'm not expecting him to. "Can we at least make sure he has enough supplies?" he asks.

"Just make sure he doesn't take too much," Maud growls.

Without a word, Anders unzips his backpack and dumps the contents on the ground for our inspection. I take his extra water bottle from the pile and add a granola bar from my own backpack. Even as I move, I can't believe what I'm doing. Guilt and regret sink down into my bones.

"A full bottle of water, two granola bars, his phone, and his flashlight. He'll have as much of a chance to get out of here as the rest of us. If we get out first, we'll send someone for him. If he gets out first, hopefully he can do the same.

Splitting up might actually increase our chances." And I fully believe that could be true, even though being generous to him now can never undo the damage I've already done by siding against him.

I try not to think about how I would feel being sent off on my own down here. The heavy and cold air, the darkness, the sounds that disappear or echo on endlessly, the twisting maze of tunnels—it all freaks me the hell out. Why I ever thought this would be a fun adventure, I don't know. Getting lost in the darkness, all alone . . . Can I really send someone else to that fate? Everything in me tells me it's wrong to send him away, no matter how scared I am, but my eyes fall on Paolo's body and I know I can't take it back.

Henri takes Anders's backpack and places the little pile of supplies into it. With every movement, he seems angrier. When he finishes, he hands the bag to his friend, unable to look him in the eye. Anders has lost the fire and anger from before. Now he looks like he's trying really hard not to panic.

"I'm really sorry, man," Henri sighs. "Do you want me to come—?"

"No. They have the supplies . . ." Anders trails off and his eyes go from Gretchen to Henri. "Keep each other safe, and send someone for me when you find your way out."

"You know I will." Henri's entire body is tense with worry.

"I do. And I'll do the same." Anders squeezes his shoulder, and when Gretchen reaches out for his hand, he holds it for a moment before walking past us. He turns his flashlight on and I see the beam shaking as it cuts through the darkness.

"*Perkeleen hullut*." He turns down a side tunnel, out of sight. He's heading back the way we came, and I wish I could back up time to match.

Chapter 9

12:47 p.m. [Beginning of recording]

[Liv Greenwall has the camera propped up on something and is looking into it.]

> **LIV:** (whispering) I haven't recorded for a while, but I'm not sure who to trust anymore so talking to myself seems like a good idea.

[Liv frequently glances over her shoulder. She picks up her camera and pans it across the tunnel walls around her. She appears to be alone in a small tunnel. She turns the camera back to her.]

> **LIV:** I think he's after us. I mean, I don't think Anders really left. I don't want to scare Maud more, so I haven't told the others, but I think he's still following us. I keep seeing movement behind us. He's not—

[Henri Pelletier's voice comes from off-camera.]

> **HENRI:** Liv? Where are you?

[The camera jerks as Liv grabs it.]

12:49 p.m. [End of recording]

■ ■ ■

By afternoon, my stomach rumbles with every step and I'm starting to feel weak from hunger. Maud isn't crying anymore, but she moves along beside us like a ghost. She's a living, breathing reminder of the people we've already lost in here and I can't make myself look at her. Henri and Gretchen aren't talking to me, and I feel so guilty that I don't blame them. I know I made the wrong choice. I'm still not sure Anders didn't do it, but I know that sending him away was a mistake.

James hasn't spoken except when asked a direct question, and Liv isn't much better off than Maud. She's rambling about Catacombs ghost stories she's read online, about people who have gotten lost in here and then escaped only to be sent to an asylum.

Finally, Henri says the three words we're all thinking: "Shut up, Liv."

When we started off, we went the opposite direction of Anders. James's flashlight died about five minutes later. We're using Liv's now and she insists on holding it. Our path looks like it's going mostly straight and I feel like we've been walking for hours, so I don't understand how we end up back in the same room that we slept in last night. Gretchen crumples to a sitting position on the floor. I stand awkwardly beside her, not sure whether I'm welcome to sit by her.

"Maybe we should take a break to eat something and share one of our bottles of water," I say, dropping my backpack to the floor and stretching my shoulders.

"Yeah. Then let's try a different passageway." Henri sits on the other side of Gretchen. I sink down to the floor as well, feeling so relieved that he's talking to me even though he has every right to be angry.

Fear made my decision for me. I won't let that happen again.

But even while I'm feeling guilty for voting against Anders, I can't stop watching the shadows and wondering if we made a possible murderer angry and then set him free to stalk us from the darkness. Brilliant, Harley. Apparently, my motto is: *Keep your friends close and give your enemies every possible opportunity to take you out.*

"Do any of you have lipstick or any makeup with you?" Liv asks. She stays standing while Maud and James take a seat nearby. Gretchen squints up at her.

"Seriously, Liv?" She sounds disproportionately angry, and when I touch her arm she shakes me away. "You sound like my mo—"

She cuts off the last word and her eyes fill up with tears. I know how she feels. I've been trying to keep my mind off my parents, but I can't help wondering if they even know yet that I'm missing. Has Chantal told them? Have they called to check on me?

Is anyone looking for us?

I go through our bags and find two lipsticks and a tube of mascara. When I hold them out, Liv takes them with a mumbled, "Thanks."

"What are they for?" I ask, holding the water bottle out for her to take the first drink.

She sits down cross-legged in front of me and grabs the bottle. "I thought we might want to mark the walls as we go. Make sure we don't go in any more circles."

"That's a good idea." Henri scratches his head like he's wondering why he didn't think of it.

"Sorry, Liv." Gretchen pats Liv's leg. "Good plan."

"Thanks. I figured it was possible we had a few things between us that would work." Liv is careful not to drink too much before passing on the bottle to Gretchen. "I asked Maud first. She had a gloss, two eye shadow compacts, two lipsticks, a liquid liner, and two mascaras."

I laugh, and Gretchen has to cover her mouth to keep from spitting water out.

"Careful, that stuff is like liquid gold at the moment." I nudge her with a half-smile.

She manages to swallow. "I know, believe me."

"I know we need to be careful, but I'm starving. Can we split two?" Henri pulls two granola bars out of his pack and holds them up. When the rest of us nod, he opens one and breaks it apart, handing us each a piece. We all pop our pieces in our mouths, and from the moans you would think we were back in the bistro eating gourmet French cuisine. Henri tosses a piece to James and then stops before opening the next bar. "Did Maud go to the bathroom?"

I glance around, and she's not here. "I didn't see her leave."

"She's been so quiet since . . ." Gretchen trails off.

"Where did she go?" Liv asks James.

He frowns. "She didn't say anything."

"Why didn't you stop her?" Gretchen demands.

Before James can answer, there's a muffled noise from the darkness behind me. Liv shines her flashlight back there. Maud is curled up into a ball next to the tunnel Paolo died in. Her head is on her knees. She must've heard us talking;

she isn't even ten feet away. When she lifts her head, her eyes look flat and emotionless. It scares me how empty she seems when she was so full of life and fun yesterday. She's like a different person now. The Catacombs are sucking the life out of her.

It makes me wonder what I might look like right now.

"I can still hear him." Her voice breaks and she closes her eyes. "I hear Paolo."

Henri walks over to her, takes her hand gently, and pulls her to her feet. "Come have some food and water."

"I don't want any." Her voice is weak, her legs shaking as he leads her to a spot beside Gretchen.

Henri opens the next granola bar and pulls off a piece slightly larger than the ones the rest of us already had. He hands it to Maud.

"You need to have some." Liv scoots closer to her and nudges the hand with the granola up toward Maud's mouth. Maud sighs and takes a bite, but I don't see any of the pleasure or relief in her face that I saw in the others.

The water bottle has made its way back to me. Only Maud and I haven't had our drinks yet. I sip it slowly, savoring the cold water on my lips and tongue. I don't realize how dry my throat is until I take my first swallow.

It is hard—surprisingly hard—to stop myself. I want to drink it all. It tastes so good and I know my body needs more. The others made it look so easy to take their share and pass it on. Somehow, I force myself to stop and pass the bottle to Maud.

When she looks at it and turns her nose up, it's all I can do not to pull it back and drink every last drop. Instead, I put it in her hand and she drinks what's left.

"Any luck on the phone situation?" I ask Gretchen. There was anger in her eyes when she looked at me before. Now I only see betrayal. I don't know which is worse.

"I don't have anything that will boost the antenna enough. Not from this far underground, anyway." Her whole face seems to curl downward in disappointment. "But I'll keep trying."

I shrug with a sigh. "What else can we do?"

"Exactly."

We take a tunnel to the right this time, being careful to mark our way with one of the lipsticks. The few offshoots we check lead to dead ends or downward-sloping tunnels that are completely flooded—and swimming an unknown distance through murky water that reeks is something none of us are willing to do. The middle tunnel keeps going on and on, and eventually the offshoots disappear. I start feeling hopeful that it could lead out . . . until it dead-ends. We're about to turn around when Maud stops us.

"Wait, what's that?"

A piece of rock juts out from the wall in front of us. There's a cat flap beneath it. It's narrow, pitch black, and long enough that I can't see out the other side.

"You want to go in there?" Liv asks Maud. Liv's fingers twitch around her flashlight.

"Better that than walk all the way back and end up in that stupid room again." Maud shakes her head fiercely. "I don't want to be that close to Paolo. I don't want to accidentally go down the tunnel and see him . . . like that."

We all feel the same. None of us want to wander back into the tunnel with Paolo's body. At the same time, this cat flap is barely wide enough to fit Henri's or James's shoulders through. It's going to be cramped and I have no idea what is waiting on the other side.

And just as I'm thinking there's nothing in the world that can make me crawl into that cat flap, Gretchen steps forward. "I'll do it."

I grip her arm. "We don't even know what's in there, Gretchen. It may not lead anywhere."

"It may lead out," Liv responds, but I can tell from the way she won't look directly at the tunnel that she won't be volunteering to take the lead.

Henri drops his backpack to the floor. "I'll go."

I can't let either of them go. *This* is something I can do to help them. Something I can do to make up for what I did before. It's an opportunity to face my fear and be stronger than I was with Anders. I have to do it.

"No." I drop my pack down beside his. "I'll do it. You come through last, bring my bag, and make sure we don't leave anything or anyone back here."

He begins to argue, but when my eyes flit to Maud, he stops and gives me a quick nod. "Sure. I can do that."

"Are you sure?" Worry is etched across Gretchen's every feature. "We can always turn back."

"No, they're right. Going back to the same place over and over will never get us out. I'm the best choice. I can make sure wherever this leads is safe and stable." I drop down onto my hands and knees and put on a brave smile. I hope they don't notice my whole body is shaking. "You know I'm not claustrophobic. I'll be fine."

"I'm holding you to that." She pats my head with her cold fingers. I dig my flashlight out of my bag and turn it on. Gripping it tight, I move toward the opening of the cat flap. Once my head is inside, the air feels thicker. I'm stirring up dust with every movement, and I'm immensely relieved when after the first five feet the passage widens a bit. The others call out to me, asking if I'm okay and what I'm seeing.

"I'm fine. It's really tight at first, but then it opens out a bit." I start coughing and cover my mouth. With each cough, the jagged walls of the cat flap stab into my sides. I focus on taking slow, deep breaths through my nose until the coughing subsides. I decide not to speak again unless something dire happens. The others might worry, but I don't want another mouthful of dust.

"Harley?" Henri calls out.

When I don't answer, they all start talking.

"What's wrong? Should we try to pull her out?" Gretchen asks.

"She passed a curve in the tunnel and I can't see her anymore, but I can hear her. It sounds like she's crawling," James says.

With a stroke of genius, I tuck the barrel of my flashlight down my cleavage. I secure it with my bra and revel in how much easier it is to crawl with both hands free. I haven't always embraced my curves, but right now I'm thanking God for my breasts.

The cat flap seems to go on and on. It gets narrower and I feel like it's pressing in on me, taking my air away. My foot catches on something and I'm stuck. My heart pounds so hard my vision starts to darken, and I rest my head on my hands until everything steadies. With one hard kick, I free my foot and keep moving.

I'm not sure if it's a cruel trick of my brain, but every section in front of me looks too small and I'm certain I won't fit through it, yet somehow I do. I just keep moving. Not crumbling into a weeping mess is the hardest thing I've ever done. The only thing that keeps me going is knowing the others are counting on me. If I can't do this, Gretchen probably won't get out of the Catacombs alive. The next section of the cat flap is wider, but the bottom is covered with small, jagged rocks that cut into my hands and knees. My arms cramp, my shoulders and knees throb in pain, and the only thing I can hear over my heartbeat is Gretchen as she starts to cry.

I hear some sort of scuffle behind me and then James says, "Going in there right now won't help her, Gretch. If she stops moving, then we'll talk about it." His tone is soft and kind.

"Please. Let me go get her. *Please.*" She sounds so desperate and scared. I have to say something.

Thinking fast, I move my flashlight out of the way and pull my shirt up to cover my mouth so I won't choke again. "I'm fine, Gretchen," I call softly. "Just wait. It's hard to talk in here."

"Okay, she's okay." Henri sounds extremely relieved. "Be careful, Harley."

Once I readjust my shirt and have my bra-light ready to go again, I get moving. When I round the next curve, I see what seems to be an opening ahead. I gasp in excitement, start coughing immediately, and my flashlight falls out of its oh-so-secure holding place.

That's when I see the floor clearly. Against the wall ahead of me is a half-crushed human skull. It blends in so well with the jagged stones on the bottom of the cat flap that it takes me a second to realize what I'm seeing. Then my breath comes too fast and my stomach churns. The skull looks exactly like the rocks I've been crawling on. I've been scratching myself up on crushed bone fragments.

I freak and try to get off them and end up slamming my head against the ceiling. I can't get enough oxygen. My lungs burn. I'm hot and cold and my vision spins. Tears spring to my eyes. I wrap my arms around my head and think of Gretchen and my parents. I have to talk to my mom again to tell her that I love her. I think of the others that are all depending on me to get to the end of this cat flap.

So I do what any other resourceful girl pretending to be brave would do: I tuck my flashlight between my boobs, angle it up toward the ceiling, and try not to look down at the dead people I'm crawling over. When I get to the partial skull, I shove it out through the exit ahead of me. Maybe if the others don't see it, they won't realize what they're crawling over and freak out like I did. We don't all have to end up with burning lungs and a monstrous headache.

At the other end of the cat flap, I wonder for a moment if I've found an exit to the outside, but it's far too dark in here. Whatever this cavern is, it's massive compared to the other places we've seen so far. The cat flap comes out two feet above the ground, so I unceremoniously flop into the dirt when I pull myself out. For a minute I just breathe, stretching my arms and legs and working out the kinks. My flashlight shines up at the smooth stone ceiling of the cavern. It looks far sturdier than anywhere we've been. In this huge room, my single beam of light barely pushes back the shadows and I feel suddenly alone and vulnerable.

I roll over, backing up against the wall beside the cat flap. The shadows around me seem to be crowding in, reaching out, coming after me. I shake my head and blink several times. Then, as suddenly as it started, it stops. The darkness is only darkness.

"I'm through," I call as loudly as I dare into the cat flap. I hear muffled words of relief from the other side. When I get on my knees and shine my light into the cat flap, I see red blood smeared across the walls in places and on the crushed bones at the bottom. I almost freak out again before I realize it must be mine. Shining the light across myself, I see that my elbows and knees have fresh cuts that are welling up with blood. I also have a nick on my right forearm and two long scratches along my stomach. One is deeper and flowing freely. I'm definitely going to need Gretchen's first aid kit.

Gingerly, I touch the spot on my head where I hit it against the ceiling of the cat flap. There's a big goose egg there, but no blood. Sighing, I settle in for a long wait and shine my light back into the cat flap. "Gretchen, you come through next and push your pack in front of you. Be careful. The bottom's covered in sharp rocks."

I leave it there, deciding that more details won't help them right now.

They don't need to know how long or tight the tunnel is.

They don't need to know this end doesn't look any more like an exit than where we've been.

They don't need to know that they'll have to crawl over the crushed remains of the dead in order to get to me.

Chapter 10

Missing Persons Reports Filed June 12th at 13:29 at

Paris Central Police Dept.

(For use in criminal case #41773)

NAME:	Gretchen Eleanor Dubois	Harley Bryn Martin
CASE CLASSIFICATION:	MISSING	MISSING
MISSING SINCE:	6/11/2020	6/11/2020
LOCATION LAST SEEN:	11th Arrondisement, Paris	11th Arrondisement, Paris
PHYSICAL DESCRIPTION		
DATE OF BIRTH:	May 24, 2003	August 8, 2002
AGE AT TIME OF DISAPPEARANCE:	17 years old	17 years old
RACE:	White	White
GENDER:	Female	Female
HEIGHT:	5'10"	5'8"
WEIGHT:	52 kg	55 kg
HAIR COLOR:	Purple (Natural, blond)	Auburn
EYE COLOR:	Hazel	Blue
ALIAS/NICKNAME:	N/A	N/A
DISTINGUISHING MARKS:	Pierced ears and naval	Pierced ears. Broke arm two years prior to disappearance.
DENTALS:	Available	Not available
FINGERPRINTS:	Available	Available
DNA:	Available	Available
CLOTHING & PERSONAL ITEMS		
CLOTHING:	Jeans, black long-sleeve shirt and jacket, black boots.	Jeans, green long-sleeve shirt, red jacket, gray Nike sneakers.

JEWELRY:	Three silver rings on her right hand.	Unknown
ADDITIONAL PERSONAL ITEMS:	Backpack with unknown contents.	Backpack with unknown contents.

CIRCUMSTANCES OF DISAPPEARANCE		

Gretchen Dubois and Harley Martin were last seen leaving the Dubois flat at 9 Boulevard Richard-Lenoir on the evening of June 11th. Mme. Martin is visiting from the United States and it is unknown where the girls were heading. They both wore backpacks and had phones with them, but authorities have been unable to connect with either device since the reported disappearance.

Mme. Dubois has a history of missing her curfew, but never for this length of time. Mme. Martin has no history of running away. Neither of them have had any contact with family or friends since leaving that evening.

INVESTIGATION AGENCY(S)—If you have any information, please contact:	
AGENCY NAME:	Paris Central Police Department
AGENCY CONTACT:	Inspecteur Bernard
AGENCY PHONE NUMBER:	23.1.55.36.25.08
---	---
AGENCY NAME:	American Embassy
AGENCY CONTACT:	Consular Official: Maurice Williams
AGENCY PHONE NUMBER:	08.49.10.22.07.13

■ ■ ■

Henri tumbles out of the cat flap and onto the floor. The rest of us are still applying ointment and Band-Aids to our scratches. He huffs and tilts his head in my direction.

"I can't decide if I wish you would've told me exactly what to expect in there."

"I wondered if I should. Good thing you don't have your giant backpack of instruments." I give him a slight smile. "It definitely wouldn't have fit through."

He closes his eyes and lets out an enormously disappointed sigh. "And I would have been so crushed to leave it behind."

Maud sits on the floor, staring back at the cat flap. "Can we block it off?" Her voice surprises me when it comes out rough and low.

James looks up, lifting his eyebrows. When he looks at her there's something wary in his expression, and I wonder if he sees what I see. "The cat flap?"

"Yes." She turns to look at him, and I can't put my finger on what it is about her that sets all my nerves on edge. There is a tinge of madness to her, a total loss of hope—maybe that's the best way to describe it. I can see it in her eyes. "We have to stop him."

"Stop who?" Henri asks, but I can see from his frown that he knows exactly who she's talking about.

"Anders." When no one responds right away, she goes on, seeming desperate to convince us. "I saw him. He's following us. He's furious I made him leave and he—I think he—"

"Maybe we shouldn't have made him leave, then," Henri mutters.

"She's right," Liv says. "I thought I saw something too."

I scowl at her. I know that I'm as much at fault for sending Anders away as either of them, and I'm still not convinced that he didn't kill Paolo, but the last thing Maud needs is someone encouraging her paranoia.

"What?" She looks at me in wide-eyed surprise. "I'm not sure it was him, but I know I saw something moving in the darkness."

Suppressing a shiver, I look at Henri. It's obvious that he thinks they're being paranoid, and that reassures me.

"He isn't following us. And we can't block off the cat flap." He speaks slowly, like he's explaining to toddlers. "At least not until we're sure we have another way out of here."

"Look at this!" Gretchen's tone is pure hope and excitement. I spin my head around so fast my throbbing headache gets worse. I have to close my eyes against the pain for a moment.

"What the . . ." Henri is on his feet and frantically pulling me up before I get a good look at what is freaking everyone out.

Is that . . . a headlight?

Gretchen is waving her flashlight so excitedly that it takes me a second to make out what looks like a subway train. Whenever her light hits the headlight, it bounces back at us, almost blinding me. It's about 100 yards away from where the cat flap dumped us out.

I scan my flashlight across the ground, almost afraid to hope. Then I find them. Tracks. Subway tracks. They're covered in dirt and dust and some pieces are so rusted through that they've broken, but they're still subway tracks. Excitement bubbles in me and I grip my flashlight tighter as I shine it all around, trying to take in everything at once.

Gretchen's excitement dims a little as apprehension creeps in. "This has to be a way out . . . right?"

"It would be a pretty useless subway if it didn't lead anywhere." Henri turns off his flashlight, sticking it in his bag. He jogs ahead to share Gretchen's light and I stay back, scrutinizing the tunnel we're in. It's wide and arched, big enough for two trains to pass each other. I'm surprised by how old everything looks. This track obviously hasn't been used in a very long time.

Maud doesn't move. I recognize the flashlight she's holding as Liv's. The one we've been using since James's died. It's still pointed at the cat flap, and it flickers. My chest tightens as I think about how long we might have light left. I've avoided bringing that up because it's the scariest prospect to me, but I assume the others are thinking about it as well. Turning my flashlight off, I slip it into my backpack. Liv stands up next to me and we walk slowly toward where Gretchen and Henri are shining her light on, in, and under the train car.

"*Station fantôme,*" Liv whispers.

I squint at her, wondering if I heard her right. "What did you say?"

She looks surprised, like she didn't notice me walking beside her. It scares me. Maybe we're all in even worse shape than I thought. "Oh. I said it's a ghost station. There are a few of them beneath Paris. I heard about them from one of my teachers. Most of them have been shut down since the beginning of World War II. It's probably one of those."

We're close to the train now and it definitely looks old. I frown and kick the track with the toe of one shoe. The rusted metal disintegrates on impact. "That sounds about right. What else do you know about them?"

She shrugs, and some of the color returns to her cheeks. "Not much. I know some of them have been used as restaurants and one was opened up for an art exhibition. Obviously not this one, though."

"Guys!" James shouts from the opposite direction, and we rush back to see what he has found.

"This end." He shines the beam of Maud's flashlight across the tunnel, well back from the cat flap and the train. The entire arch is closed off by a sturdy brick wall. James's shoulders curve in like everyone's exhaustion has fallen on him to carry. I feel it too; it's the weight of hope. "They sealed this part off."

Without a word, Gretchen pivots and runs the opposite direction, past Maud, who still sits on the ground staring into the cat flap, and past the train.

"Gretchen!" I yell after her. "Don't go off on your own."

I reach into my backpack, frantically searching for my flashlight. Henri grabs my hand and stops me, reaching in to retrieve it for me. He easily finds it and turns it on.

By the time we're moving, her light is rounding a corner ahead and she's out of sight.

"Gretchen!" My heart seems to clench so tight that it feels like every beat might be its last. Henri and I run at full speed. As we're approaching the curve, my toe catches on what has to be the only spot of rail that isn't completely rusted through and I tumble to the dirt.

Pain explodes in my wrists and knees and I cry out. Henri is crouching beside me in an instant.

"I'm sorry." He takes my flashlight, trying to examine my injuries and blinding me in the process. "I tried to catch you, but I missed."

"Yes. It's totally your fault." I wince as I sit up. "You are the reason I'm an enormous klutz."

He laughs with relief. "Are you hurt?"

My knee throbs, I've skinned my palms, and my left wrist might be sprained, but that's the worst of it. I didn't break anything. "I'll be okay. Go catch Gretchen." I push him gently away.

"Okay, I'll be right back."

It's only when he runs off with my flashlight that I realize my mistake.

The dark closes in on me immediately. It's silent and oppressive and I hate it. The air doesn't move. It hangs heavy with dust and water, and now that I'm alone in the darkness, it feels like one more thing that could crush me.

I keep thinking my eyes will adjust and I'll be able to see better, but there is no adjusting to this. I can still see a hint of light around the corner where Henri and Gretchen disappeared, but that's it.

The sound of my breathing fills my ears and the darkness around me swirls. I swear I can feel it churning. Something moves in it. What is it? What's coming? Even though I know logically that there's nothing there, I feel like something stalks us in the darkness, watching and waiting. Could Maud and Liv be right? Is Anders following us? I shake off the idea. I *do not* want to follow them down that path.

The air seems to grow heavier moment to moment, like it's thickening into a soup that my lungs weren't meant to breathe. Then I stop breathing. I hold perfectly still, but something still moves. I can hear it now. The darkness is alive with it. Is someone else breathing? Did someone whisper my name? My pulse pounds in my head and I twist to look behind me, but all around there is only inky black nothing. Someone could be next to me, almost on top of me, and I wouldn't see a thing.

I can't hold my breath anymore without passing out, and now my ears fill with my breathing again. I'm panting and I can't stop. Screw it. I'd rather fall again than stay here in the darkness for another second. I get to my feet and head toward the curve and the very dim light coming around the corner. I force my body to move slowly. I will not let panic rule me. I'm stronger than this.

I have to be.

I stumble twice, but manage to avoid falling. In the silent darkness I have nothing to distract me from the way my body screams at me. It wants food. It wants water. It wants sleep.

But more than any of that right now, *I want light*.

Rounding the corner, I see Gretchen curled in a ball on the ground. Henri crouches over her, gripping her shoulder and shaking her. "Gretchen!"

She turns to face me as I get closer. Tear streaks cut through the dirt on her cheeks.

"Are you okay? What happened?" I'm still breathing too fast when I reach them. The edges of my vision start to dim and I shake my head violently in an attempt to stop it.

"She's okay. Breathe slower, Harley." Henri cups my face in his hands and makes me look at him. "Calm down."

His steady eyes and soothing words get through and I do as he says. One deep breath, then another. Everything settles back into place. Henri lets me go and I look down into Gretchen's devastated hazel eyes.

"It's closed off too." Her voice cracks. "They walled off both ends."

Henri hands me my flashlight and I have a look around. She's right. This section of track is sealed off completely from the rest of the subway. We won't find an exit here.

I reach down with my right hand to help Gretchen to her feet. "Let's go back to the others, rest for a bit, and have a snack." I look at Henri and he nods in agreement. We both turn to walk back.

"Then what, Harley?" Gretchen doesn't move to follow us. Despair seems to have seeped into her bones and I don't know how to get it back out.

"Then we'll keep looking until we find the way out," I answer. She needs me to be strong now and I'm going to do it. For her. I reach out and squeeze her fingers.

Gretchen starts walking, and Henri stops me before I can follow her.

"Are you hurt?" he asks, bending down to examine my beat-up jeans and the fresh blood seeping through on my right knee.

"My left wrist got the worst of it."

He stands straight and takes my hand gently. "Can you move it?"

I try and pain shoots up my arm. I wince. "Yes, but it isn't fun."

He nods. "I think I can brace and wrap it with something back at the train. You should take one of the ibuprofen. It should help with the pain."

"You sure you don't want to be a doctor? I think you might have missed your calling here."

He grins wide enough to drive away some of my fear and I'm suddenly so glad he's here. "That's only because you haven't heard me play . . . yet."

"That sounds tempting enough to make a girl keep fighting to get out of here alive," I answer playfully.

"It's a promise." He wraps one arm around my shoulders and rubs my arm with his palm, lending me some of his warmth. "Once we're all out of here, I'll give you a private concert."

"The full majesty of the flugelhorn on display?" I snuggle closer to his side and smile up at him as he chuckles in response. "Finally, I have a reason to go on."

Chapter 11

Voicemail to text from Model Mom to Gretchen

sent on June 12 at 8:56 p.m. –

I know you probably aren't getting these messages. I wanted to hear your voice, honey. I went to the police today. Wherever you are, we'll find you. I know you're scared. I know you wouldn't do this willingly. If someone has you, please do whatever they say. I wish I knew where you and Harley went when you left here yesterday. Hold on to each other. Protect each other. Keep each other safe. I love you more than you know. I hope I get the chance to tell you that.

—transmission failed

■ ■ ■

James holds the flashlight for Gretchen and Henri as they work to pry open the door of the train. It takes a few minutes, but the wood strains and finally cracks open. Gretchen and Henri lead the way inside using Gretchen's flashlight. I move to follow them, but James grabs my elbow.

When I turn to face him, I'm surprised by how uncomfortable he looks. He keeps his voice low enough that I have to strain to hear him. "Did she . . . has she ever said anything to you about me?"

I briefly considering lying, but it won't help him. "No." He looks so disappointed that I hurry to add, "But she hasn't talked to me about any of you."

Now he looks genuinely surprised. "Really? Why not?"

I peer at my cousin through the grimy windows of the train. "I guess we aren't that close." It actually hurts to admit it out loud.

When I get on the train, Gretchen turns to face me. "There's obviously no power in here, but some of the compartments have old cushions."

Gretchen picks one up and squeezes it. Dust flies out, but it doesn't disintegrate like I expect.

"They're filled with some kind of down or something. It's held up pretty well. Maybe we could stop for a bit and sleep in here? The thought of having a pillow is turning me into a wimp." Her eyes droop with exhaustion and I know mine must be doing the same.

"Sounds good to me." I shrug, glancing back toward the doors of the train. I'm nervous about going to sleep and making ourselves that vulnerable after what happened to Paolo. But in here might work. An enclosed space where we can at least block the doors should make me feel safer . . . assuming the killer isn't still part of our group.

I shudder, pushing aside the thought as I inspect the train interior. Everything is covered with a thick layer of dust and dirt, but other than that it's been preserved pretty well. Most of the windows are still intact and the benches have ornately carved backs. Although I don't know much about train design, I recognize the Art Nouveau elements that were popular in early 1900s Paris.

When I turn around I almost run into James. He's been standing so quietly behind me that I didn't know he followed me inside.

"Did you hear Gretchen's idea?" I ask as I slide awkwardly past him.

He nods. His eyes linger on my cousin as she tries out different train seats. "Anything that doesn't involve sleeping on the ground again is a genius idea."

"My thoughts exactly," I murmur, but he doesn't act like he hears me.

■ ■ ■

My dreams are full of living darkness and bones again, but with a couple of pieces of rusted track propped against the inside of the train doors, at least I sleep. I dream of Anders wandering through this maze of tunnels as his flashlight sputters and dies. In the darkness, he screams my name and says his death will be my fault. I bolt upright, panting. It's pitch black. As much as I want to conserve the light, I hate sleeping down here in the dark.

I lie back down on the big pile of cushions we made inside the train, closing my eyes again. It doesn't take long before I have another nightmare. This time I'm trapped inside a wall, my head one more of so many skulls. I'm still as stone as I watch and wait. Wait for my friends to die, like me. Wait for them to add their spirits to all of those in the Catacombs. I watch Anders kill Paolo. But instead of staying down, Paolo gets up. His head is bloody, his skull smashed. He hits Anders again and again with his flashlight. Over and over until Anders is just as bloody, just as broken.

Then they both turn on me.

When I wake up the second time, the others are already up and moving. Gretchen sits beside me, not fully awake yet. My stomach growls loud enough that she hears it. She blinks and her lips curl into a small smile before it fades away.

I know I need to help her. If she gets lost in despair the way Maud has already, this is going to be much harder. Then I get an idea.

"You should try to get a signal here."

She looks around the train car doubtfully.

"Sometimes I can get a signal in the subway. Maybe we're closer to the surface here than we have been."

Gretchen doesn't look hopeful, but she pulls out her phone and leaves the train.

Once I get up and stretch, I pull out my own phone and turn it on. It reads 5:58 a.m. on June 13th. I have no idea what time we went to sleep, but it feels like we didn't rest for more than a few hours. This place is really messing with my head. Time loses all meaning when you have no day and night.

I power my phone off to conserve the battery and get off the train. Gretchen kicks through the dirt by the railing a few feet away, searching the ground with her phone light. I wonder what she's looking for. Before I can ask I get distracted by Maud. She's just standing there hitting Liv's flashlight against her leg again and again. She stops and flips the switch on and off—nothing.

James stands nearby holding Maud's flashlight. It's the one providing light now. We've lost another one.

"Liv's is dead?" I ask with a sinking feeling.

Nothing down here scares me as much as the idea of losing all of our light and being stuck in the darkness. Nothing.

Maud nods, but doesn't speak. Her face is wet from crying, and I can't help thinking what a waste of water it is. Even with the bottle of water we shared before going to sleep, my lips feel so dry. I wonder if it's possible to get so dehydrated that you can't cry.

Then I hear the most miraculous sound in the world: Gretchen's phone dings with an incoming message. I gasp and run to her, James and Henri close behind. "Was that what I think it was?"

Gretchen stands on top of a mound of stones next to the brick wall that blocks off the station. Her phone dings again, and then a third time. She's removed the phone's back panel and stuck a piece of semi-rusted metal into it. I assume it's boosting her antenna. Bless my cousin and her geeky tech genius.

"It doesn't look like I have a signal, but I must be connecting somehow. I'm getting messages!" She jumps up and down and the stones beneath her wobble. I reach up to steady her. All the others have gathered around now and I see excitement on every face.

"From who?" James tries to get in a position to see, but can't get high enough.

Gretchen looks at the screen and her voice shakes with emotion when she answers, "My mom."

I sympathize. I know all too well the regrets she probably has. "She sent you texts?"

"No, it's a voicemail to text thing." Gretchen is crying now. Her voice is raw as she scrolls through the messages. "She went to the police. They're looking for us."

"Oh, thank God," Henri whispers beside me.

"Do they know where to look?" I ask.

"No. I need to send her something to let her know where we are." Gretchen hits reply on the last message and types in the word *Catacombs* with shaking fingers.

"If this goes through, I'll send her more information. If I make the message too long, it might not go through." She holds her phone up as high as she can before pressing send. It tries for a while before I see a message pop up on the screen.

—Message failed to send

"Damn it!" Gretchen pushes the resend button. Again, and again, and again. We check all of our phones, but Gretchen's is the only with a connection. I give her a break and try to send the text so she can go eat her share of granola bar and water. Then Henri takes a turn walking around with the phone held high, trying to find a spot with a better signal, but he has no luck either.

The sudden hope brought by the messages coming through has been crushed by our inability to respond. It weighs us down like a cinder block in a lake and we can't seem to get free. The despair in everyone's faces is as scary as the darkness around us. I have to look away.

After trying again and again for over an hour, Liv is the one to finally say what we're all thinking. "We need to move."

Gretchen shakes her head. "Getting a signal here is our best chance."

"Either the message went through or it didn't. I don't think staying here longer is going to help." Henri looks sad to admit it, but we all know it's true.

"Sitting here isn't doing us any good." I wrap my left arm around Gretchen's shoulder, careful not to bump my braced and bandaged wrist. "When I was looking for a signal, I found a bigger cat flap leading up at the other end of the tunnel. We should try that one and see where it goes."

"Fine. Let me keep trying until the battery dies, then we can go." Gretchen sighs. "I'm never going to take my phone signal for granted again."

"You're probably the only one of us who never has." James gives her a wry smile, and it surprises me when Gretchen returns it.

Maud and Liv split up for bathroom breaks. James is still trying to help Gretchen with the phone, so I decide to be helpful in a different way.

"I'm going to check the train one more time for anything we can use." I use my phone to light my way as I climb back into the train car. I'm there for about twenty minutes before I hear someone else climb in behind me.

"This seems like more fun than what's going on out there." Henri gives me a half-smile and I roll my eyes.

"I hope she can get it to send."

"Me too." He moves toward the opposite end of the car, pulls out his own phone, and starts looking around too.

"Well, thanks for coming to help."

He has a coughing fit as a cloud of dust from a cushion puffs up around his face. Still, he gives me a thumbs-up before moving his search to the opposite end of the car.

I continue looking under rotted seat cushions, under the seats themselves, and digging through the luggage racks. I rummage through everything and come up empty. When I get to my feet after checking under the last seat, Henri is holding perfectly still and staring at something in his hands.

I power off my phone and walk up to see what has him so absorbed.

He clutches a ratty old piece of paper so tightly his fingers shake. When I look over his shoulder, he meets my gaze with eyes full of anticipation. I swallow hard and he holds the paper so I can see it better. It is weathered and worn, but more from use than from age. There's no way it's been in this train since they shut down the station. I'd be surprised if it's been here for more than a couple of years. It's hard to make out the lines and faint scribbles at first, but then I see the words *Station Fantôme* and a sketch of a train below it. I gasp.

I adjust Henri's phone light to see better. There are paths and tunnels sketched all around, and several drawings and words that are too faded to make out. One path is darker, though, like someone went over it a couple of times. At one end, it plainly reads *Sortie.*

Exit.

My hope flares to match what I see in Henri's face and I throw my arms around him in a spontaneous embrace. He gives a choked-off laugh of surprise before picking me up and spinning me around.

"It's a way out," he whispers against my hair, and my heart speeds up even more.

I pull back enough to see his face, feeling a desperate need to see someone else sharing my excitement. As if seeing it in him will prove to me that it's real, that what I'm feeling is justified. I need to see that I'm not deluding myself. After all the despair that has been weighing everyone down over the last couple of days, it's even better than I could've imagined to see real hope in Henri's eyes.

He seems to feel the same, because he gives out a hoot before pressing his lips to mine. The kiss is so sudden and unexpected that I freeze up completely. Then I melt into him. His lips are dry to match mine, but warm and surprisingly soft. They send tingling sensations through every cell. I press my body against him and we fall against the wall of the train. He moans as my fingers twist into his hair, and he lifts me off my feet and tighter against him. My head spins in such a haze of happy intoxication that the sound doesn't even register until Gretchen clears her throat a second time.

I pull back with a surprised gasp and blush hotly under my cousin's knowing smirk. "I was coming to tell you my phone died, and I thought I heard Henri shout, but I'm guessing it was for a different reason than I thought."

I say the one thing I know will completely take her mind off what she walked in on. "We found a map."

"Wh–what?" she stutters, rushing forward to see the paper Henri holds out in front of him.

"What do you say we get out of here?" I grin at my cousin's astonishment and reach out to squeeze Henri's hand. For the first time since the cave-in, I let hope run hot and free through me and enjoy every moment of it.

Chapter 12

Text from Gretchen to Model Mom sent on June 13 at 6:13 a.m. −

Catacombs

−transmission successful

■ ■ ■

We come out to tell the others the good news, but we don't even get a chance to speak before Maud's flashlight beam dims and then dies. My heart sinks again as Gretchen uses the light from my phone to find her own flashlight and turn it on.

Even with the map, I don't know if we can make it to the exit. Our supplies are dwindling. I hear someone's stomach growl, but I'm not sure whose. Mine aches like an empty pit and I'm sure the others feel the same. To our credit, no one is complaining about it yet.

"You can probably just toss that, Maud." I say as I notice she is still clutching her dead flashlight tight in both hands. I move toward where I left my backpack when I was walking around trying to find a signal on Gretchen's phone. Before I make it more than a few feet, Maud's voice stops me.

"Wait. Didn't you say we had extra batteries?"

I was hoping she'd forgotten about them. Even knowing that we're trying to conserve our lights, Maud has been using her flashlight for even the slightest excuse. That's probably why her batteries died so quickly. As cruel as it may sound, I don't want to waste our backups on her.

"I'm not sure they even fit yours, plus I think we should save them," I reply, quiet but firm. Maud looks shocked for a second, and when she opens her mouth to argue, Gretchen jumps in and cuts her off.

"My flashlight is plenty for now. We should use the others before taking out the backup batteries."

Maud still tries to argue, and their voices fade away as I turn and jog back toward the other end of the tunnel.

I round the final curve before the wall and pan my little phone light back and forth before me, looking for my pack. When my light lands on the bright blue of James's jacket, I stop in surprise. He's kneeling between the tracks with his back to me. I wonder what he's doing alone here in the dark. I pick up the pace, jogging toward him. "James?"

He doesn't turn around or even flinch. I slow, my insides filling with ice. I suddenly don't want to walk any closer, afraid of what I'll see. But my feet keep moving, drawn to him like a magnet.

"James?" I move around to his side, crouching down.

James is dead on his knees, and it's immediately obvious why he never fell over. A three-foot-long piece of rusted metal has been stuck through his chest. The other end is wedged against the ground, pinned in place by his bodyweight, propping him up like some sick puppet. Blood drips from his slack mouth into a massive pool below him. His eyes stare endlessly into the darkness.

I scramble away, sucking in a ragged breath, but it doesn't come back out. My mouth is stuck open in a horrible, soundless scream.

A rat crawls across my hand, heading toward James, and now I'm screaming. I can't move or run. I can't even drag my gaze away from James and his dead eyes.

Henri is suddenly in front of me, blocking my view of James. He pulls me toward him, pushing my face against his shoulder. My screams stop, but my body keeps shaking. Even with my eyes closed, clinging to Henri, I still see James in my mind. I still hear the blood dripping from his open mouth.

"James? Oh my God." The pain in Gretchen's voice snaps me out of it a bit. I pull myself away from Henri's shoulder and search for my cousin. James might be her ex, but she must care for him a lot. She needs me now. I have to focus on that.

Gretchen is standing in front of James's body in total shock. Her hand keeps lifting like she wants to touch or help him and then falling back to her side again. Liv and Maud hang back when they see Gretchen's reaction, and I think that's probably the wiser choice.

"Who did this?" Henri releases me and gets back on his feet. His tone is defeated. "How could this happen again? Who killed him?"

He turns accusing eyes on Liv and Maud.

"We didn't do it." Liv's eyes are wide with shock. When he doesn't look convinced, she says, "*We didn't!*"

"It's Anders. I told you he was following us." Maud raises her fist like this is some sort of twisted victory. Then she points at Henri. "I *told you!*"

140

"Where would he be hiding?" Henri asks, shining the flashlight into the empty darkness.

Maud is too busy staring into the shadows with open paranoia to respond.

"What if it's not any of us?" Liv wraps both arms around herself, rocking back and forth. "What if it's just fate? Maybe we were all supposed to die in that cave-in and now the Catacombs are making sure it happens. Maybe the bones hate us for coming and their spirits are still—"

"Stop it, Liv," I bark, and I'm on my feet and in her face before I realize what I'm doing. Her mouth snaps shut so hard I hear her teeth click together.

I put an arm around Gretchen and guide her away from James. Henri is right. Someone did this. I can't think of a situation in which James could accidentally impale himself like that. There's no doubt this was another murder.

And it could have been anyone. Maud and Liv each took a bathroom break, so they were both alone for long enough to do this. Only Henri couldn't have done it because he was in the train with me.

Except he wasn't. Not the whole time. He could've done it before he came into the train.

"Did James say where he was going when he left you?" I ask Gretchen.

"No." Gretchen pushes her hands up and pulls hard on her hair. Her eyes are wild and unfocused. She keeps turning like she wants to go back to James, but I don't let her.

"Gretchen." I gently lift her chin until she looks me in the eye. "What happened?"

"We got in a fight. He didn't tell me where he was going. He told me where *I* should go . . ." She bursts into tears and I pull her into a hug.

I steer Gretchen toward the train. She's sobbing against my shoulder, muttering something I can't quite make out. It kind of sounds like, "I didn't mean to. I didn't mean to."

I pull back, staring hard at my cousin's face as my body flashes ice cold again. "What are you saying?"

Her eyes are closed and she's pressing her fingers against them. "I shouldn't have said the things I said. It's my fault."

Relief floods through me and I feel terrible for believing even for a moment that Gretchen is capable of murdering her ex-boyfriend. The Catacombs are changing me. They're messing with my head.

"This isn't your fault, Gretchen." I pull her into another hug, careful to angle her away from James. Unfortunately, this means I have a clear view of him.

"He left—he left right after Henri did. When he left me, he was running to catch up with Henri . . ." Gretchen sniffles, leaving the sentence hanging heavy with implication. I shake my head.

"Henri wouldn't do this." I'm shocked that Gretchen would even suggest it.

"I don't want to think he would either. I don't want to think any of them would." Gretchen lowers her head onto my shoulder. Her words come out in shuddering whimpers. "All I'm saying is he could have. It would have taken someone strong to do . . . *that*."

Henri is trying to lower James gently onto his side. Liv is holding the flashlight for him, and even from here I can see Henri's whole body trembling. My heart aches for him;

this was his friend too. Gretchen isn't thinking straight, that's all there is to it.

"I'm just saying, please be careful," she whispers.

"I will, but you don't have to worry about me. I'm fine." I pat her back in a futile attempt to give her peace in a place of nightmares. "We're going to find a way out of here. I promise."

"I'm a mess, I'm sorry. I know. I just keep thinking that if I hadn't fought with him, maybe he wouldn't ha–have ended up—" Her words cut off, strangled by her grief.

"No. Shh ... you didn't do anything wrong. I don't understand what's happening down here, but we *have* to stop letting people go off alone." I smooth her hair and speak softly and firmly. Doing a perfect job of looking like the calm rational one, while on the inside I'm still absolutely freaking out. I scan the darkness, seeing menacing movement where there is none, seeing threats that may or may not be real. How could someone be after us in the darkness? Wouldn't they need light? How would they get around in the pitch black without running into things? We would hear that, right? Is someone really there? Someone out of sight? Or is the murderer one of the people in the light? The ones standing right in front of me? How do I know who to trust when the world is this upside down?

After a couple of minutes, the others join us without a word. It's time to go. There's no food or water left in James's backpack, but his phone still has a little battery life left, so we take it and leave the rest behind.

Henri's shoulders hunch as he leads us to the cat flap I found. Gretchen stops crying and falls into some kind of mute anguish. Liv has her camera clasped under her chin like it's a talisman to ward off evil. Maud's darting eyes search every shadow, every patch of darkness. She's growing more and more paranoid, and I'm not sure that's a bad thing anymore. Maybe she's the sane one. Someone *is* hunting us down here, picking us off one by one, and we don't know whom to trust.

We have every right to be terrified—and I am, down to my very core.

■ ■ ■

Once we get past the narrow entrance of the cat flap, it's big enough that we can walk through at a crouch. I follow close behind Henri, watching the ceiling and walls for signs of instability. I'm glad I'm not leading the way alone this time. After what happened to James, I'm not sure I'd make it through another experience like the last cat flap.

The floor slopes in an upward angle now. Maud keeps lagging behind, so Liv agrees to bring up the rear and herd her along. We've gone through three lipsticks already and we're only marking the intersections. Hopefully the map will make this an unnecessary precaution, but after wasting part of yesterday going in circles, it's better to be safe.

I cast a worried glance back at Gretchen. Henri at least mutters something about the caves every now and then. Gretchen hasn't spoken since she stopped crying, and it's scaring me. I totally understand, though. James is—was—someone she cared about. And we don't even know if Anders is still alive, which is something I really don't want to think about right now. I just wish I could do something to help her.

The silence is eerie and it continues long after the air lightens and the temperature starts to drop. I try to think why getting closer to the surface would make the air colder, but I can't come up with anything. The part of the map marking the area ahead of us is smudged and it's hard to tell what we're walking into, so we take each turn and new section slowly. Still, we've made it nearly halfway to the exit, and knowing we may be heading in the right direction brings a bit of relief.

We take a sharp turn and walk out into the biggest cavern we've seen so far. It's big enough that I can't see the ceiling, and the lack of stars is the only thing that makes me certain we haven't found the exit.

"What *is* that?" Gretchen says, clutching my arm, and I would be incredibly relieved to hear her voice again if she didn't sound so disturbed. She's staring hard at the ground twenty feet in front of us. I follow her gaze, and I can't make sense of it either. The floor of the cavern is a huge expanse of shining blackness. It looks like the ground abruptly falls away, becoming a slick pit to hell.

Henri picks up a small rock and throws it as hard as he can. There's a splash, and then the floor ripples out in widening circles beneath Gretchen's flashlight beam.

"It's a small lake." Henri frowns, consulting the map again. "What the hell is an underground lake doing here?"

Liv looks from the water to Henri in confusion. "Is that on the map?"

His mouth tightens at the corners, but he doesn't respond. Everyone but Maud gathers around the map, trying to make sense of the smudged lines and drawings. I keep staring at the scribbles on the paper after Liv and

Gretchen give up, hoping to see something to make this fit, but I come up empty. The lines that continue sporadically through this smudged section look too much like the tunnels we already came through to think they are meant to be anything but more tunnels.

"Could the lake be new?" I whisper.

Henri gives me a dejected shrug. "Or the map could be older than we thought."

"Maybe we can make our way around and figure out which tunnels start off on the other side?"

"Won't that take too much time?" Liv uses the hem of her dirty shirt to polish the lens of her camera.

Henri squints at the water ahead. "If this water is drinkable, we could drink as much as we want and refill all the bottles. That should buy us some time."

"Catacombs water?" Gretchen's tone is completely flat.

Even from this far away, just looking at it makes my mouth feel dry as the bones down here. I need it in a way I've never experienced before. I want to stick my face in and drink until I burst, but Gretchen isn't wrong. "It could be from a sewer leak, for all we know. How will we be able to tell if the water is drinkable?"

Henri steps forward until the toes of his sneakers are at the edge of the water. He shines the light down into it. "It looks pretty clear. I guess we'll have to try it and see."

Before the rest of us can respond, Henri dips one hand into the water and takes a sip. Gretchen and I exchange shocked looks. I'm not a particularly religious person, but I pray that he didn't just make a huge mistake.

"Seems okay." When he goes for another drink I rush forward and grab his arm to stop him.

"How about we take a break and wait a few minutes to see if you suddenly start throwing up or something before you drink any more of it?"

The hint of a smile that crosses his face makes me wonder if he isn't a little too pleased about how worried I sound. I don't care. He and Gretchen are the reasons I'm staying sane in this pit of bones. I can't handle the idea of losing either one of them, and that seems like more and more of a possibility. I swallow hard, shoving that thought away along with all the other paralyzing fears that I'm struggling to keep locked in a dark corner of my mind.

"What's the point?" Maud mutters, watching the many shadows around us.

Gretchen glares at her. "You aren't the only one who lost someone they care about. Maybe some of us still want to get out of here alive."

Maud looks up at her with a strangely wary expression. "Hope what you want. He won't let us."

"No more, please." Henri's tone holds a warning that comes through loud and clear.

It seems to make Maud at least think twice before answering. "But I saw . . ."

"Anders *isn't* following us." Gretchen sounds like she's on the brink of an explosion. "And if he was, I would run to him and ask to join him so I could get away from *you*."

Maud's haunted expression hardens into a cold glare. "Careful or you might get what you want."

"Stop." I pull Gretchen away from Maud. "I'm sure you're right and he isn't following us."

Gretchen's eyes fill immediately with tears. "Why couldn't you have taken his side earlier?"

My guilt hits me like a punch to the gut. "You're right. I was afraid and I made the wrong decision. I should've listened to you. I'm so, so sorry." I try to sound as certain as she is of Anders's innocence, but the chill of fear deep in my bones still makes it fall a little flat.

Gretchen's expression holds a hint of the betrayal she still feels. And I can't blame her. I hope that she's right about him, and Maud and Liv are wrong—that he's not the one who killed Paolo and James, that he's not following us in the shadows, waiting for an opportunity to get his revenge.

And I really hope Anders doesn't die down here because I wasn't stronger than my fear.

If Gretchen is right, then maybe Anders already found his way out. Maybe he's alive and well and hopefully not too angry at us to send help.

"I really am sorry," I whisper to her again in the silence.

"Thank you," Gretchen says, hugging me tight. We stay like this for a moment, holding each other up in this place that wants to tear us down.

Liv speaks up, changing the subject. "So if we try to head in the general direction of where the exit is supposed to be, which way around the lake would we go?"

Henri shines the flashlight back and forth across the shore on either side of us. Random boulders and stacks of bones line the shore in both directions. Neither option looks better or faster than the other.

"Let's take a break here and eat something." Henri drops his backpack to the ground. "And wait to . . ." He doesn't finish his sentence, but we all know what we'll be waiting for.

Wait to make sure the water doesn't make Henri sick.

Wait to see whether the massive lake blocking our path represents life or is another symbol of death, like everything else down here.

Chapter 13

From: Eric Martin (EMartin@zmail.com)

To: Chantal Dubois (ModelLife@zmail.com)

Subject: Flight

The first available flight is the red-eye tonight. We'll be arriving at 7:25 tomorrow morning and Amanda and I plan to head straight to the police station and then to the Embassy to see what they can do. Please meet us at the station so we can get an update. Amanda is still furious with you for waiting until this morning to tell us about Harley and Gretchen, but we all need to put our differences aside. All that matters right now is that we work together and focus on getting our girls back.

In all honesty, going into the catacombs sounds like something that Harley would jump at the chance to do. She does a lot of urban exploration, so I don't doubt that they both had their part in this. I'll try to remind Amanda of that on the flight over. Things have been tough over here with the divorce, but this is bigger than all of that. Finding them is our only focus.

Harley and Gretchen are what matter now. Please send any updates to both of us as soon as you hear anything. I'm still hoping that you'll have wonderful news for us when we land.

Eric

■ ■ ■

Food only seems to make my body angry. I've moved past hunger into a strange weakness I've never experienced. My stomach seems to have gone to sleep, and when I eat, the food only wakes it up long enough to remind it how much more it needs. I nibble on my portion of granola bar, trying to make it last as long as possible. Next to me, Liv's belly growls loudly and she wraps her arms around it. I watch as her eyes flit over to Maud's untouched portion.

It sits on the rock in front of Maud as she stares fearfully into the shadows behind us. Her occasional whimpers annoy me more than I would like to admit. I'm afraid too. Shouldn't that make me more patient with her? Still, the anger bubbles up inside me. If Maud wants to die down here so badly, then why are we giving her our precious food? I have to clasp my hands together to stop myself from grabbing Maud's breakfast. I climb quickly to my feet.

"I'm going to walk along the water for a bit." When Gretchen looks up with a worried expression, I reassure her. "I won't go far, but I need a break for a minute."

Henri starts to get up and I put a hand on his shoulder. "You should stay here and keep an eye on things."

He looks disappointed, but when I glance behind him at Maud and Liv, he nods like he understands. Fifteen minutes have passed and he still seems fine, but the water he drank makes me nervous. I know tainted water could take days to make us sick, but we'll probably have to take the chance. If our choices are dying of dehydration or getting sick in a day or two, dying of dehydration seems worse.

Not wanting to risk draining another flashlight, I pull my phone out of my pocket and turn it on. After checking for a signal, I put it on airplane mode so it doesn't waste power trying to connect. Then I turn the screen's brightness down to the lowest setting. It shouldn't drain much battery, and it will drive back the darkness enough to prevent me from tripping over something.

After a few minutes of walking, I can't hear the others anymore—not Maud's whining or Liv's strange chatter. I glance back to reassure myself that they're still there and I'm not alone.

I need to stop being so annoyed at Maud, and even sometimes at Liv. Some of the things James did bothered me too, and now I feel horrible about it. Sure, he was a jerk to Gretchen sometimes, but I'm pretty sure it came from pain over their breakup. And it isn't that I don't like Liv and Maud. I'm sure if we weren't stuck down here and we could spend a couple nights hanging out together in Paris, I would love them. I kick a small piece of limestone in front of me and it skips across the bizarrely still water, causing ripples everywhere.

It's weird how being stuck down here makes me feel so alone, so cut off from the world, and yet also so smothered by this small group of people. I'm torn between wanting them to leave me alone and absolutely not wanting to be down here by myself. Of course, Henri and Gretchen don't bother me, but still, I don't think I'd want it to be only three of us down here.

Especially since that would mean more people dying.

I glance back at the circle of light around the single flashlight. I can't see Gretchen or Maud anywhere. Henri and Liv seem to be deep in discussion and Henri looks angry. As I watch, he turns his back on her and she pulls out her camera and retreats into the shadows to make another recording. Henri squints in my direction and gives a small wave.

I wave back, trying to gauge how far I've come. It looks farther than I thought. The curve of the waterline is pretty gradual, which could mean the lake is huge.

Or it could simply mean it's not a perfect circle. I'd be surprised if it was, actually. Which means I don't know any more about it than I did a few minutes ago.

With a sigh, I shine my faint light around and move away from the lake toward the wall. I should at least use the walk back to look for tunnels that might be on the map.

I come across a narrow tunnel almost immediately, but within a few feet it starts to go down, and as it descends it fills with water. Nothing about it seems like anything I remember from the map, so I turn around. Back in the main cavern, I am forced to move away from the wall at spots by massive boulders or piles of rocks. One tunnel is closed off by what looks like a fairly recent cave-in, and I'm suddenly very nervous about not being able to see the ceiling.

The whole thing could be covered with cracks and on the verge of collapse and we would have no idea.

The thought makes me shiver. I pull my jacket tighter, but it doesn't help. It's like the cold is coming from inside me.

More boulders litter the ground. These ones aren't right up against the wall, so I don't detour around them this time, hoping I might find a tunnel behind them. I keep my eyes on my footing and walk carefully, trying not to stumble on loose rocks.

I keep seeing flashes in my mind of the people who've died. I see Paolo and M. Lambert, their heads broken and bloody. I see James, impaled on a piece of rusted track. I shudder.

My stomach rumbles again and the sound echoes around me like my hunger has created a new monster outside my body. I've only felt this hungry and tired once in my life before. I was attending a series of late night lectures last year called The Hidden Mysteries of Chicago Architecture. They ran the same time as finals week at school. I was so busy I that wasn't sleeping or eating much, and Dad and Mom insisted I slow down. It was the only thing they'd agreed on in a while, but it wasn't until I almost passed out that I decided they might have a point.

Thinking about them makes me sick with longing. I miss them so much it hurts. I've been so busy trying to think of a way to get out and stay alive that I haven't thought about what they might be going through. I assume Chantal told them we are missing by now. They must be so scared. Fresh guilt flows through me for the way I've been treating them lately. All of the problems I blamed them for seem so minis-cule compared to what I'm facing now. So I may have to go to a different college or try to get a grant or student loan. So I have to choose which parent to live with. So what? I'll still get to see them both. Yes, my struggles were real and they weren't easy, but they weren't worth the rift I created between my parents and me. My eyes ache, but no tears come. I want Mom to hug me. I want Dad to tell me that I'll be okay.

I *have* to get out of here alive. Who knows what will happen to them if I don't. They'll both be on their own. It isn't like they know how to rely on each other in difficult times. All they do is fight.

My heart cracks inside my chest. I can't let my death be another thing they can use to tear each other apart.

Goosebumps break out across my skin and I freeze. It feels like someone is watching me . . . or maybe following. I scramble ahead, trying to move faster. My head spins for a moment with the effort, and I stop to catch my breath, leaning against the cavern wall.

When the spinning stops I move on, but I don't know how long I can keep going like this.

Moving back out of a short dead-end tunnel, I rub my dirty hand across my forehead and stretch my back. Shining the light on the floor might help me not trip, but it's far from comfortable. I frown. Something seems different. It's darker somehow. I look at my phone, wondering if it's dying already. It's not. It still has forty percent battery life. When I look back up, my breath catches in my throat.

I can't see the others. That's why it's darker. The light from our flashlight is gone.

My fingers shake as I turn up the brightness on my phone, and it's immediately obvious what the problem is. They aren't gone, I am. While watching my feet, I wandered into a big tunnel without realizing it. The lake, the giant room, and everything else are now out of sight. My body trembles. I fight to keep calm, to be smart. Turning the phone light down again, I backtrack, keeping my steps slow and careful. I hear footsteps behind me inside the tunnel, and my heart pounds louder. I know there is no one there and that the sounds are only echoes, but I keep checking behind me, fighting the urge to run. The last thing I need is to have an anxiety attack and pass out in some tunnel where no one will know to look for me. The air feels heavier even though I know it isn't, and my lungs work harder to breathe.

Finally, I re-enter the cavern with the lake and come back to the short dead-end tunnel. I skirt around a couple of boulders and move closer to the lake. Shining my light back at the wall, I notice a matching dead-end tunnel on the other side of the big tunnel. I'm glad I realized what happened before I got myself hopelessly lost in there.

I'm relieved to see the area lit by our flashlight again. Gretchen has returned, but now she's alone. So much for trying to stop people from wandering off by themselves. I scoff. And immediately realize I'm a hypocrite for doing the exact same thing. Maybe we're all feeling the need to be alone for a minute.

The fear I felt in the tunnel hasn't let up and I don't know why. Something has my nerves on edge. Searching the darkness around me, I pick up my pace and move as quickly as I can manage without getting dizzy. When I look at Gretchen again, my heart leaps into my throat. In the darkness behind her, I see someone crouching. Whoever it is seems to be staying back in the shadows on purpose. The figure stands up to their full height and it's obviously male. It looks too tall to be Henri. It looks more like Anders.

And Gretchen is going through her backpack with no idea someone is sneaking up behind her.

"Gretchen!" I scream, "Behind you!" but the echoes of the lake cavern turn my warning into garbled nonsense.

She looks up, confused, and I growl in frustration. Why does sound carry so far when it's creepy and annoying, but goes nowhere when I actually need it to?

My heart hammers as I start running. Adrenaline pounds through my veins and my dizziness flees in its wake. I start yelling again as soon as I think I'm close enough for her to understand me.

"Turn around!"

Her eyes widen, and the figure behind her retreats into deeper shadow. She spins up into a kneeling position facing the other direction, squinting, but obviously seeing nothing. By the time I'm almost to her, Henri and Liv are back and are looking around in panic.

"What's going on?" Liv asks.

"Harley, what's wrong?" Henri catches my shoulders as I skid to a stop.

"Did any of you see him?" I sputter, my heart refusing to slow down.

"See who?" Gretchen stands and moves closer to me, eyes still searching the shadows around us.

I stop myself short of saying it was Anders. I don't want to encourage Maud and Liv, and I'm really not certain it was him. But I definitely saw someone. "I—I don't know. I thought I saw someone behind you. You didn't see anything?"

Gretchen frowns, but Liv is the one who jumps on my question. "Where did you see them?"

I point to the deep shadows behind Gretchen, and she scans the flashlight over that section. Other than a couple of rocks too small for anyone to hide behind, it's empty.

"That's the area Henri came from." Gretchen gently squeezes my hand as my breathing slows. "Was it him that you saw? In this kind of darkness anyone can look threatening."

I shake my head. She's wrong. I know what I saw. I look at Henri. In the beam of the flashlight, his shadow seems to stretch on forever. Is it possible that the light distorted his figure, playing a trick on my tired mind?

"Maybe you're right," I groan, and my knees wobble. Henri helps lower me to a sitting position.

"Why don't you catch your breath for a minute while I tell you my good news?" He smiles, but it doesn't reach his worried eyes.

"I could definitely use some good news." I take a slow, deep breath and adjust my position to face him.

He leans in like he's telling me a secret, and I feel my lips curving up to match his. "I'm not sick," he whispers.

I laugh in surprise. This is actually very good news. "You're sure you don't feel different at all?"

"Not at all." He shakes his head firmly. "Except that now that I know there is a lake of reasonably safe water, I'm very thirsty."

Gretchen sighs loudly and throws us an exasperated look as she moves toward the water. "You guys keep flirting. I'm going to go have a long drink."

In the light of the flashlight, Henri's cheeks flush a bit. I'm sure from the heat in my face that mine match. He takes one of the empty water bottles from my bag and fills it before bringing it back to me. I hold it in front of the flashlight and am relieved by how clear it looks. I take a long, slow drink and sigh. It's refreshing, and other than a slight metallic hint, it tastes fine.

Liv steps out onto a squat boulder not far from the shoreline and leans over to splash some water on her face. I move to the water and do the same. My skin feels so grimy at first, but improves quickly with a few splashes. Liv drinks a few scoops of water out of her hands as we all fill up, empty, and fill up the other bottles. I drink one full bottle and a half before I have to stop. After days of almost nothing, my stomach feels like it's about to burst with only that much.

Once we've finished, Liv frowns and looks around. "Did anyone see Maud come back from her bathroom break?"

Gretchen looks surprised. "Is that where she went? I thought maybe she followed Harley's idea and went to check the other side."

"She didn't go with you?" I shift position to face Gretchen. "I noticed you were both gone about the same time and thought you went together."

"No. Has she been gone *that* long?" Gretchen's face shifts from confusion to worry in a snap.

My eyes scan the shadows for Maud as I pick up the flashlight. I shine it across the shore and back over the wall. Nothing. "She definitely didn't follow on my side of the shore, but I never saw her come back to the group once I noticed she was gone."

Henri searches through the backpacks, counting the supplies. "She didn't take a flashlight with her—or anything else that I can tell. Even her phone is here. It looks like it's dead, though."

Liv's face has gone pale. "She can't be too far. I mean, she's not crazy. She wouldn't wander off into the darkness without having any light at all . . . would she?"

None of us answer. I'm not sure if Henri and Gretchen have the same concerns I do about Maud, but I get the feeling they do.

And honestly, there are very few things that I don't think Maud is capable of at this point.

Chapter 14

(For use in criminal case #41773)

Investigation Regarding Missing Persons – Gretchen Eleanor Dubois and Harley Bryn Martin

Update current as of June 13th at 20:24. Notable progress and new leads are as follows:

LEAD: Chantal Dubois, mother of missing Gretchen Dubois, reported in this morning after receiving a text from Mme. Dubois with the word "Catacombs" in the message.

> **ACTION TAKEN:** Contacted security for the Catacombs tour of the Ossuary. After circulating pictures of the missing females, it was determined that they have not been seen by any of the staff. It is likely that the girls went into the off-limits section of the Catacombs.

LEAD: Mme. Dubois and Mme. Martin likely went into the off-limits areas of the Catacombs. Assessing their previous behaviors, it seems unlikely that the girls went there alone.

> **ACTION TAKEN:** Reached out to contacts within the cataphile community regarding the missing females. Contacts agreed to circulate photos of the missing girls to those in their community that have been known to give tours to the public.

LEAD: Because it is unlikely that Mme. Dubois and Mme. Martin went into the Catacombs alone, it's possible that they communicated the details of their plans to others by phone or online.

> **ACTION TAKEN:** Notified the cyber division of new developments. They haven't yet been able to access

the information on Mme. Dubois's laptop, but are still working on it. They also set up a trace on both the girls' cellphones so we'll be notified if they connect to the network again.

LEAD: At 18:27 today (June 13) we received a tip from one of our cataphile contacts. They informed us that known cataphile and expert mapper of the Catacombs, Roland Lambert, may also be missing.

ACTION TAKEN: A team was dispatched to his last known address and he wasn't there. We've been unable to decisively confirm this lead. We obtained permission from landlord to perform a search of his apartment and we're still processing that scene for any helpful information. In reaching out to other sources, it seems that no one has heard from M. Lambert since the evening of June 11th, the same night that Mme. Dubois and Mme. Martin disappeared.

LEAD: Contacts within the cataphiles state that M. Lambert vowed he would never take another group into the Catacombs after a difficult experience a few years ago. They also say that no reputable guide would take a group of only two into the Catacombs for safety reasons. It is therefore our theory that whether or not M. Lambert was their guide, there may be more individuals missing that haven't yet been tied to this case.

ACTION TAKEN: Additional staff has been assigned to re-evaluate all recent missing persons cases in Paris and the surrounding area to check for any ties to Mme. Dubois and Mme. Martin that have been missed previously.

ACTION TAKEN: On top of the unsuccessful searches we've completed of the Catacombs located beneath the 15th arrondisement today, there will be a more focused search party of officers led by cataphile volunteers starting tomorrow morning. They will be concentrating on areas of the Catacombs that M. Lambert preferred.

Please direct any additional leads or new information to:
Inspecteur Bernard at the Paris Central Police Department

■ ■ ■

We've barely started the search for Maud when Gretchen's flashlight flickers and dies. Instantly, Gretchen grips my arm and I hear Henri digging in his bag for his flashlight.

"One more down." His voice slams through the silence like a wrecking ball. A note of fear oozes into his normally confident tone. The air around us seems to vibrate with it. I hold tighter to Gretchen and force myself to keep blinking, even though it doesn't matter at all whether my eyes are open or closed. Blinking somehow makes me feel more normal, and the repeated motion soothes me even in this utterly suffocating darkness.

I consider pulling out my phone to help Henri, but it's in my backpack. When I hear Liv moving I assume that she has the same idea, so I wait. Besides Henri, we're the only ones with working phones now—Gretchen used what little battery was left on James's for her bathroom break—and now my flashlight is our last remaining spare. That and a single set of replacement batteries. That's all that stands between us and permanent darkness. I shudder. Liv swears and something hits the stone floor.

"Breaking your phone won't help, Liv," Gretchen scolds her, and it's like I can actually hear Liv stiffening.

"I didn't drop it on purpose," she snarls.

"Almost got it," Henry says, still with that edge of fear. Then I hear what sounds like two people colliding and the unmistakable sound of a flashlight bouncing across the ground.

"Sorry," Liv mutters. There's a rustle as she drops to her knees and starts feeling around on the ground with her hands. There's a splash as she reaches the water and my throat squeezes shut, refusing to let air pass. I pray that we didn't ruin one of our last two flashlights in the lake. My urge to do something is barely suppressed by my fear that I'm more likely to step on or kick the flashlight than I am to find it.

I nudge Gretchen. "Hold my backpack so I can find my phone or flashlight?"

She immediately takes it. Without being able to see, my other senses surge in response. Well, maybe not surge so much as totally freak out. I'm not sure, but I think I hear something that sounds like whispering beneath the other noises we're making. I'm blinking still, over and over, like somehow that will dislodge whatever is blocking my vision. I give up and close my eyes, relying on my sense of touch. I push past all the recently filled water bottles and feel around for my phone or flashlight.

My pulse pounds in my ears. Gretchen shuffles closer and my skin prickles when her warm breath moves over it.

"Where in the hell?" Liv grumbles, and Gretchen shushes her.

"Did you hear that?" My cousin's voice comes out as a whimper.

"What?" I freeze.

"Shh!" She stands stock still like she's waiting, so the rest of us wait too. In the silence, I close my eyes again and listen. Long seconds pass, and the silence is almost as oppressive as the darkness. It's like we're trapped in some version of hell where invisible demons are stealing away our senses.

An overpowering urge to make noise rises inside me— any noise at all. I clench my teeth together. Letting my fears drive me down here will only lead me to bad places. I need to get a grip. I focus on the sound of my breathing to calm my nerves.

Then I hear it. I hold my breath, listening, and I hear it again: the slight shuffle of rocks across stone. But none of us are moving anymore. We're frozen in the darkness. Like if we hold perfectly still, whatever is out there will stop hunting us and go away. The sound came from behind us. Then I hear a soft moan.

"Maud?" I whisper into the void, but only the stifling silence answers me. I refuse to hide in the dark anymore. My fingers finally close over the flashlight and I flip the switch as I pull it out of the bag.

I blink against the brightness and point the beam frantically in the direction the noise came from. I skim the beam over boulders and rocks, trying to shine it into any spot where someone could be hiding. But the light reveals nothing.

I'm not sure whether a random vibration simply knocked some loose rocks free . . . or my mind is starting to break down.

I hope it's the first.

I'm afraid it's the second.

"Aha!" Liv picks up her phone and Henri self-consciously retrieves his flashlight from a spot behind him.

"Sorry," he mutters. "You can turn yours off now."

I nod, but instead of doing as he says, I keep scanning the area where I heard the noise. Even with a light, I can't shake the feeling that something lurks in every shadow. Gretchen nudges me and I flip the off switch, stowing my flashlight safely away again. I can worry about my own sanity if I want, but I don't want the others to know I'm cracking, especially Liv and Maud. The last thing I need is for them to decide that I can't be trusted and send me off on my own like they did to Anders.

Like *I helped them* do to Anders.

The guilt still eats away at me, even after Gretchen forgave me. I shove my hands into my jacket pockets and follow Liv as she takes Henri's flashlight and heads out along the shoreline. We walk the opposite direction of the way I went earlier. A heavy sense of foreboding fills me as I wonder where Maud would go without a light—and why she wouldn't come back.

It's almost impossible that Anders's flashlight would still be working now. I mumble a quick prayer under my breath that he's already out of this hell maze, swallowing back the wave of nausea that ties my insides in knots at the idea of him stumbling around in this darkness alone. My eyes scan the shadows, and in every one, I see places he could hide. My brain is so muddled and tired that I can't seem to decide whether I'm more afraid that I might have killed him or that he's out here waiting to kill me.

Even if Anders isn't the one who killed Paolo and James, wouldn't it be natural for him to want revenge for what we did to him? For what *I* did to him?

I hurry to keep up with Liv, driven by the vain hope that moving forward will let me leave my frightening train of thought behind.

We take turns softly calling Maud's name. We make it around a big curve and follow the shoreline as higher ground forces it to pivot abruptly back toward the other side of the cavern. The ground juts out into the lake here and we climb up until water surrounds us and we're on a kind of rocky outcropping above it.

Liv shines the light around, looking over her shoulder to talk to us. "Should we keep following the water or head back toward the—"

"Stop!" Gretchen shouts, lurching forward with a trembling hand to grab the flashlight and direct it to a spot in the water below us. Exactly where someone might hit the water if they jumped from here. Gretchen's trembling grip is shaking the flashlight so hard that it's difficult to see clearly, so I steady it.

A cloud of black hair floats in the water and I choke on my breath.

"*Merde,*" Henri mutters, and then he's stripping off his jacket and shirt.

"Stop, what are you doing?" Gretchen grabs his arm. "That water is nearly freezing."

He blinks at her. "What else are we supposed to do?"

When she only opens and closes her mouth in response, he moves her gently aside and makes his way to the edge of the outcropping. This time I'm the one to stop him. I grasp his hand and hold it tight. "I understand needing to go in, but we have no idea how deep the water is right here."

"It's only three meters down." He squeezes my shoulder, trying to reassure me.

"Still, if it's only three or four feet deep . . ."

He nods and runs past us back down to a spot that's closer to the waterline.

"Why didn't we hear her?" Liv asks. Her already pale skin is ghostly white. "If she jumped in or fell, why didn't we hear any splashing?"

I have no answer, so I move to follow Henri. He'll need help getting Maud onto the shore.

Gretchen stays put. She's keeping the flashlight carefully trained in front of Henri and me so we can see where to go.

"Why did she go off into the dark in the first place?" Gretchen says softly. "Sh–she isn't moving at all."

When we get to the shore, Henri strips down to his boxer shorts. I get a quick look at lean muscles before I glance away and concentrate on rolling my pants up over my knees. I guess it's silly for me to worry about giving him privacy in this situation. Henri obviously isn't concerned about it.

My gaze goes up to my cousin. Gretchen's hands have steadied and there's a grim determination in her stance. Liv stands beside her, tear-streaked face in her hands. Her wide eyes are glued to where Maud's head bobs in the water. Her lips are moving, but I can't hear any sound coming out.

Sudden violent splashing jerks my attention back to the water. It's not Maud, like I hope. It's just Henri wading out to her. The water is only waist-high when Henri reaches her, and I'm grateful that he listened when I told him not to jump.

I slip off my socks and sneakers, wincing and shivering as I wade into the frigid water to meet him. He's rolled Maud onto her back, and the sight of her beautiful face looking dull and lifeless makes me take an involuntary step away. Her brown eyes are open. They stare up into the shadows above us.

Henri shoves her toward me and I reach out to grab her, helping him lift her out of the water. She's far heavier than I expect and my hand slips as I try to hold on to her wet skin. Liv and Gretchen make their way down to the shore and Liv holds the light while Gretchen helps us lower Maud carefully to the ground.

"She isn't breathing," Henri says. "She isn't breathing."

Gretchen bends over her, fingers pressed to Maud's wrist. Then she looks up at me with tears in her eyes. "I can't feel a pulse."

That's three of our group dead. Four if we include M. Lambert. Five if Anders doesn't make it out. The thought sends a shudder through my whole body. His would be the only death I would feel *personally* responsible for.

I *really* hope he gets out of the Catacombs alive.

"I can do CPR." Henri nudges Gretchen out of the way and kneels over Maud. He starts pressing on her chest, and I notice his skin prickling up and taking on a slightly blue hue. Taking off my jacket, I drape it over his shoulders. At least he didn't get his hair wet. That would make the cold air so much worse.

He offers a quick "thanks" in between compressions.

I rub my hands together, then against my jeans. I stick them in my pockets and then take them out again. They refuse to hold still, so I gather Henri's clothes and bring them over.

"Why isn't she waking up? She has to wake up! It's like I said. The spirits down here won't let us get out alive!" Liv is panicking, and Gretchen tries to calm her down, but I can't make myself help. It's all I can do right now to keep my own terror at bay. I'm not strong enough right now to be responsible for someone else's fear.

Instead, I watch what Henri is doing, trying to memorize his movements. He's counting to thirty compressions each time before blowing two quick breaths into Maud's mouth. I study his hands. Keeping my fear in a vise-like grip, I try to convince myself that this is something I can handle. Still, my voice trembles when I say, "You should get dressed before you get any colder."

"I can't stop."

"Let me try and tell me if I'm doing it wrong." I scoot closer and reach out my hands, placing them over his to make sure I have the right position. My improvised brace makes it awkward and my wrist still hurts, but Henri's fingers feel like icicles beneath mine and I know this is something I *have* to do. The longer he stays in his wet boxers, the harder it's going to be for him to get his body temperature back up.

He frowns. For the first time since we found Maud, I can see how freaked out he is when his wide eyes turn to me. "Have you ever taken a class on CPR?"

"No." I keep my fingers on top of his, learning from touch how hard he is pressing. "But I'm a quick study and I'm watching you. You teach me."

"Okay, compress exactly the w–way I am." Henri shivers hard, and after the next breath he shifts aside and lets me move into position. My heart pounds, embracing the rhythm we're trying to force into Maud.

"Five—six—seven—eight—" We count in unison, and I'm glad because my anxiety makes me want to speed up. If I thought Henri's fingers were cold, I'm floored by the glacial quality of Maud's body. If we get her heart to start again, how can we possibly get her warm enough? The only things we have to burn down here are our supplies, and we need them to get out of here. The questions whirl into a funnel of panic until I clamp down on them, focusing on nothing but the counting. Everything else won't matter if I don't get her heart to start beating first. When I get to thirty, I shift my position the same way Henri did.

"Make sure to keep her head tilted back like that, make a seal with your mouth, and blow two breaths into her mouth." Henri picks up his clothes and edges away from the group.

I do exactly as he says, and I'm surprised by how much Maud feels like a cold plastic doll. It's weird and creepy. I've always wondered if literally sharing your breath with someone would be an incredibly intimate thing, but the life-and-death reality of it is just plain traumatic. Her chest moves up and down with the air I force into her, but otherwise there's no response.

Liv lets out a low cry that is utterly heartbreaking. I don't look up at her. I can't let myself feel the emotion of what's happening yet. If I break down right now, this very important job I volunteered to take on will become much harder.

With a sinking feeling, I start doing compressions again. Henri has backed into the shadows, but I can see enough of his movements in the darkness to know in general where he is.

"I'm still here," he says when he sees me watching him. "I'm not l–leaving you." He's still shivering, and he's obviously trying to stay calm for my benefit. "But I don't want to put dry clothes on over wet boxers . . ." He trails off, and I look away.

I go through five more rounds of compressions and breathing before Henri returns, fully dressed. With each round that passes, my hope ebbs. I'm not seeing even a hint that this is helping. I'm not sure if it's because I'm starving or if CPR is genuinely hard work, but I'm exhausted and my injured wrist is throbbing. Henri slides in, taking over seamlessly. I scoot away, giving him room to work.

Gretchen sits down next to me. Liv sobs silently across from us. Her face is so full of pain. Paolo, James, and now Maud—how does this keep happening? All the questions that the CPR routine was keeping at bay come crowding in. What was Maud thinking? Why would she go wandering off this far without a light? Did she fall off the outcropping in the dark? When she ended up in the water, why didn't she scream for help? Did someone do this to her?

Or did she walk straight into the water, knowing full well what she was doing?

Every inch of my body goes numb and I stare into Maud's vacant eyes. Did this place drive her totally off the edge? Is it only a matter of time before it has the same effect on the rest of us?

"How long do we do this before we know for sure it won't work?" Gretchen whispers. Henri's back stiffens, but he doesn't stop.

I shrug helplessly. "Isn't the fact that she's cold supposed to help? I think I saw that in a movie once."

Henri sighs. "Only if we can warm her back up again." He stops compressions and feels for Maud's pulse again.

"It isn't like there's any wood around here to make a fire." Gretchen frowns, gesturing at the rock walls all around us. "Do bones burn?"

Liv shakes her head, and a sob chokes off part of her answer. "—d–don't think so. Not without s–something like oil or gas."

I look back out at the water and frown. "The water is so shallow here. What happened? Are we even sure that she drowned?"

Henri starts up the compressions again, glancing over his shoulder at the water. "It really isn't that deep, but the rocks at the bottom are really sharp. I sliced up my feet a bit."

"So what, she couldn't stand up?" I ask, incredulous.

"If she fell in from the outcropping, why didn't we hear a splash? Plus, I'd think there would be more cuts and scratches on her, maybe b–broken bones." Liv pulls her knees up under her chin, wrapping her arms around them.

"What *is* that?" Gretchen reaches out to tilt Maud's head up more. She shines the flashlight on Maud's neck and pulls down the collar of her thin turtleneck. We both gasp. The dark skin is marred by an even darker bruise. Henri stops his compressions and rolls the collar down enough to see the whole thing. A ring of bruises encircles Maud's throat. They're about one inch wide in most spots, but thicker in others.

Gretchen and I stare at each other, eyes wide. Then I glance over at Henri. His gaze hasn't lifted from Maud's neck. He touches her bruised skin gently before pulling his fingers back like she burned him.

Liv's sobs cut off abruptly and she scrambles back, turning away from Maud. Her wide, terrified eyes search the shadows, panic seeping from her every pore. "It's Anders.

I knew it. He came back to kill us for making him leave. I told you I saw him. I told you all that I saw him."

Then Henri's flashlight flickers out and plunges us back into darkness.

Chapter 15

VIDEO CLIP #2/Transcript and video footage of Inspecteur Bernard interviewing Anders Koskela. For use in criminal case #41773/Paris Central Police Department/Time stamp: June 14th

6:32 a.m. [Beginning of recording]

[Inspecteur Bernard looks into camera in interview room of Paris Central Police Department.]

INSPECTEUR BERNARD: I am Inspecteur Pascal Bernard of the Paris Central Police Department. Today is June 14th and it's six thirty in the morning. This camera will record the interview with Anders Koskela, who claims to have information on the disappearances of Gretchen Eleanor Dubois and Harley Bryn Martin. Monsieur Koskela is most comfortable with Finnish, Swedish, and English, so we will be conducting the interview in English.

[Inspecteur Bernard adjusts the camera to include Anders Koskela. He is dirty, unshaven, and exhibits a number of abrasions and minor lacerations. He has a police issue blanket across his shoulders and clutches a coffee cup in front of him with shaking hands.]

INSPECTEUR BERNARD: Monsieur Koskela, I want to say again for the recording that our medical professionals believe you should be in the hospital. They say you're dehydrated, malnourished, and suffering from both emotional and physical exhaustion. Are you sure you want to stay here right now and continue this interview?

ANDERS: [growls] Did you listen to anything I said? We need to go back in there and get them.

INSPECTEUR BERNARD: I listened. You told me two people are dead and at least one of them was murdered.

Can you repeat how that happened again?

[Anders groans and takes a sip of coffee.]

ANDERS: [speaks slowly] Our guide was caught in a cave-in.

INSPECTEUR BERNARD: That was Roland Lambert?

[Inspecteur Bernard jots down notes on a pad as Anders speaks.]

ANDERS: Yes.

INSPECTEUR BERNARD: How did the cave-in happen?

ANDERS: We found a big cave with pillars made of bones. Pa- [Anders stops and drinks his coffee] Paolo pulled a couple of loose bones out of a pillar to tease his girlfriend and—

INSPECTEUR BERNARD: And you said her name was Maud [pauses]

[The Inspecteur flips through his notebook.]

INSPECTEUR BERNARD: Maud Kumas?

ANDERS: [Long pause] Is.

INSPECTEUR BERNARD: What was that?

ANDERS: [Voice muffled as he wipes his hands across his face] I said her name is Maud Kumas because she's still alive. She, Liv, Harley, James and Gretchen [pauses] they all should still be alive if we can get to them soon enough.

INSPECTEUR BERNARD: [long pause] That is our plan, I assure you. We need to be sure that the information you are giving us will be helpful before we continue.

ANDERS: [Frowns] What do you mean? I know where they were and which way they were heading. How could that not be helpful?

INSPECTEUR BERNARD: [flips to a different page of notes and clears his throat] I need you to explain again how you became separated from the rest of the group.

ANDERS: It was after we found Paolo. [voice muffled as

he looks down] They thought I did it.

[Inspecteur Bernard takes notes. He pulls a missing persons report out of a file folder and places it on the table in front of Anders.]

INSPECTEUR BERNARD: Paolo Salvetti, correct? Is this him? [long pause] Can I get a verbal agreement, M. Koskela?

ANDERS: Y-yes. That's him.

[Inspecteur Bernard returns the report to the file folder.]

INSPECTEUR BERNARD: And you are saying Monsieur Salvetti is dead?

ANDERS: [whispers] Yes.

INSPECTEUR BERNARD: And the reason you left the group is because they believed you killed him?

ANDERS: Yes.

INSPECTEUR BERNARD: And did you kill Paolo, Anders?

ANDERS: No. [pause] I didn't do it. They thought maybe I went after him because he punched me. They were wrong.

INSPECTEUR BERNARD: If you didn't kill Paolo, then who did?

ANDERS: I don't know. I wish I did, but I don't. Somebody killed him, and whoever it was, they're still down there. My friends are in even more danger than they think. [rests head on arms on table] That's why we need to go back.

INSPECTEUR BERNARD: You were lost down there for days. Are you sure you're willing to go back into the Catacombs to help us find the others?

ANDERS: They're still down there--in the dark. [pause as he clears his throat and takes another drink of coffee] If it can help you find them faster, then yes.

[Anders begins to shake. He winces and blinks his eyes slowly.]

INSPECTEUR BERNARD: Are you okay to continue?

ANDERS: [shakes head, eyes unfocused] No. I'm not

feeling well. Can we take a break for a minute, please?

INSPECTEUR BERNARD: Of course.

[Inspecteur Bernard waves to someone outside the room and the door opens. Two medical professionals enter and crouch down beside Anders asking him muffled questions. Anders Koskela slumps over. Inspecteur Bernard moves to turn off the camera and the image goes black.]

6:44 a.m. [End of recording]

■ ■ ■

Maud's eyes won't stay closed. I keep pushing the eyelids gently down, but they refuse to stay that way. It's like she wants to watch us as our frail grip on sanity withers away.

My emotions are indistinct and distant. When I let myself feel them, I want to curl into a ball. Numbness is better. This is the best I can hope for here, and I'm clinging to it as hard as I can. It only takes one thought to drive it away and let the panic permeate my entire being:

This is the fourth death—and our last flashlight.

A horrible shudder passes through me and travels straight into Gretchen beside me. She scoots closer for warmth, but my body heat seems to have been sucked out by those few steps into the lake. Even through our clothes, I can tell she's warmer than I am.

I lift my eyes and focus on Liv and Henri. I'm surprised they're still arguing. They've been going in circles since Henri's flashlight went out. I wonder how I managed to tune them out so completely.

"Why would Anders even do that?" Henri is borderline whining now. He's always been the patient and level-headed one of the group, and seeing him losing it unsettles me even more.

"We sent him away and now he's coming back for us. He's going to get us all." Liv's pitch rises with each sentence like it's trying to climb out of this God-forsaken pit. She's pacing in circles, talking to the walls, to the cave, to the lake, to the darkness, more than she's actually talking to Henri.

"Stop talking about Anders! He's not even here!" Henri shouts at Liv's back, and she spins to face him. Before she can respond, there's is a rumbling sound from nearby and both of them crouch low to the ground, covering their heads with their hands. Gretchen and I cling to each other. The ceiling is lower here. I scan my flashlight across it, searching for signs of an impending collapse.

My breath catches in my throat and I choke on it. Cracks are spreading across the ceiling above us. They leap across the stone, stretching so far out over the lake that I can't see them anymore. The cracks widen and dirt falls, followed by larger stones. My whole world is shaking and I know this is it. This is where we're all going to die.

Then I blink and it's all gone.

I rub my eyes with the palm of my hand and look again. The ceiling is solid and unmoving. My heart beats so fast it feels like a hummingbird in my chest. It seemed so real, but it wasn't. After a cloud of dust floats out of a nearby tunnel and the rumbling finally stops, I manage to breathe again.

I've gone too long without decent sleep and I'm probably in shock. My heart slowly regains a semi-normal rhythm as I try to make sense of what I saw. The cracks weren't real. They were never there. I imagined the whole thing. I can't decide if that's better or worse than the alternative.

"Stop it!" Gretchen breaks the new silence with a harsh and angry whisper directed at Liv and Henri. "Stop fighting! It isn't helping anything."

She's right and I know that, but Maud is dead. We can't ignore that fact. And once again, everyone had the opportunity to kill her. The only one I know with absolute certainty didn't do it is me.

And with the way I'm seeing things, am I even sure of that?

No. I was nowhere near Maud. I couldn't have done anything. I wasn't hallucinating then, anyway . . . was I?

There is an eerie silence in my head, and I realize I'm waiting for someone else in there to answer me.

I can't be sure of *anything*.

I suppress a shudder and climb to my feet, as much to get away from that thought as anything else. I pull Gretchen up beside me, and we walk toward Henri and Liv. "How did this happen? She didn't strangle herself and then wander into the lake."

"No. Someone did this. Just like the others." Henri gestures weakly back toward Maud without looking. "But who . . .?" He leaves the question in the air, and I'm filled with another intense urge to get away from here.

"You *know* who," Liv mutters, and the rest of us pretend she didn't speak.

"How can we stop this from happening again if we aren't sure *who* is doing it?" Gretchen asks, and her eyes flick to Liv, who fiddles with her camcorder and says nothing.

Henri nods emphatically. "There's only one thing we can do. We need to stay together."

But I don't agree with Gretchen. While I'm relieved that she seems to have moved on from suspecting Henri, it's hard to believe that Liv would kill her main ally down here. Why would she do that?

Then again, it's even harder to believe that Gretchen or Henri did it. Who else is left? Someone in hiding, hunting us from the darkness? Or some spirit, like Liv said, haunting us and killing us one by one?

I swallow, tapping the top of my flashlight with one trembling finger. "This is our last one. We still have one more set of batteries, but that's it."

Gretchen stares at me with wide eyes. "That's *all* we have?"

I nod, climbing slowly to my feet. "We can't sit here arguing. We have to get around this lake and see if we can figure out the tunnels on the other side."

"I want to bury her." Liv goes to Maud's side and bends over to grab her shoulders. When she looks back at the rest of us, her expression turns pleading. "I'll be fast. I promise."

Without answering, I move to pick up one of Maud's feet. Gretchen grabs the other and Henri moves to her shoulders to help Liv. Together, we carry her toward the unstable tunnel and use some of the fresh rubble to cover her.

We all move in silence, and I start thinking about how nice it is to work together instead of arguing . . . until I remember we are burying a friend. Nausea makes me gag and I press my hand against my mouth for a moment.

"I'm scared," Gretchen whispers.

After the silence gets awkward while I try to come up with something reassuring, I finally give up. "Me too."

"My brain is stuck in an awful loop. I can't stop wondering if it would be worse to be trapped down here forever and starve . . . or to be k–killed like her." Gretchen eyes the makeshift grave we're creating. "I keep wondering if James, Paolo, and Maud might be the lucky ones. How messed up is that?"

"We're going to get out," Henri states simply, but from his expression, I think that even he can hear how unconvincing he sounds.

"We have to get out." Liv mutters under her breath. "We have to." She stands and walks away.

"Do you . . . do you think he's dead?" Gretchen asks Henri, and it takes him a second to understand who she's talking about.

"No." Henri covers Maud's hand with a big handful of pebbles and dirt. Then he sighs. "I think we sent away our best chance to get out of here."

I stiffen like he smacked me, even though I know he didn't intend it that way.

"I'm sorry. I wasn't blaming you. We all did it." Henri reaches out and rubs a thumb across my cheek. "I should've fought harder, and the others should have known him better than that. You'd barely met him."

I don't say anything. I don't mention the movement I've seen in the shadows or the whispering and footsteps I've heard in the darkness. I don't tell him that my mind doesn't feel like it's mine anymore. I'm not sure how to say that right now I'm as scared of the cruel tricks I'm playing on myself as I am of everything else.

What if I'm the crazy one they should be sending away?

Henri places the final few stones and I check on Liv, determined not to let anyone else wander away and die. She hasn't gone far. She's got the small light from her camera on and is fiddling with her backpack in her lap. The shifting gloom closes in on her from every side and I steadfastly ignore it, afraid of what I might see this time. Liv should try that instead of talking into her camera and casting paranoid glances into every shadow, like she spends half her time doing.

I suddenly wonder if that's how I look to Henri and Gretchen: paranoid and jumping at shadows.

But then, maybe we're right to be afraid. Shadows aren't always harmless, especially when whatever hides in them is killing people.

I shiver, and beside me Gretchen does the same. And then she does it again, and again. I pivot to study her, bringing the light with me. Dark circles ring her eyes, making them look sunken. Her face is gaunt and her skin has lost its healthy glow. When she shivers again, I put my hand on her cheek. It's hot—too hot. I feel her forehead and my stomach sinks.

"Do you feel sick?" She pulls away weakly, but I grab her head and press my forehead against hers, hoping it's just my cold hands that are making her feel feverish. It's not. Her skin pulses with heat.

"Harley, what are you doing?" She pushes me away, wobbling as she steps backward. Henri steadies her.

"You have a fever, Gretchen." I glance nervously at the lake water. "Does your stomach hurt?"

"I'm fine." She turns to walk back toward Liv, but I grab her arm.

"Could it be a cold or something?" I ask, hoping desperately that this is all we're dealing with.

"I said I'm fine." She wrenches free from my grasp and goes over to sit down next to Liv. From here, it's easy to see what bad shape she's in, but when I look at Liv next to her I realize we all probably look awful. For some strange reason, that relieves a bit of my worry.

Liv stands and walks over to where we buried Maud. She takes something from her pocket and places it on the highest rock before going back to sit by Gretchen again without a word.

I check it out and see an embroidered pink flower from Liv's backpack. She must've picked it free while we finished burying her best friend. It's such a sweet gesture. My heart aches for her, for all of us. We need to stick together. The Catacombs can and will make us turn on each other if we let it.

"Do you think Gretchen's fever is from the water?" Henri interrupts my thoughts. He's transferring the few remaining supplies Maud was carrying from Paolo's backpack to his.

"I don't know." I search his eyes. "Do you feel sick?"

"I feel exhausted, hungry, and cold." Wrapping his arms around me, he pulls me against his chest. "But not sick."

"Good." I snuggle closer to him, savoring the comfort the simple hug gives me. I want to stay here, with him, but the flashlight feels like a ticking time bomb in my hand. "We need to get moving. Can I see the map again?"

He pulls it out and we study it. Tracing my fingertip along the edge of the area where I think we are, I look for anything I recognize. Then I see something familiar and feel a flutter of hope. Three tunnels next to each other, two dead ends and a bigger tunnel in the middle. I can't be certain, but it looks like the tunnel that I wandered into on my walk beside the lake.

"I think I know where that is." I point out the lines on the map and Henri squints at it.

"That looks like it could lead toward that exit we were looking for."

I point to a spot midway between the tunnel and the exit where there is a bigger area with little dashes all through it. "Right. It's hard to tell with all the smudges, and who knows what that room is supposed to be . . . but maybe."

Henri gently folds the map and tucks it back in his pocket. He takes my hand in his and puts on a determined smile. "I guess we'll see when we get there.

Chapter 16

From: Chantal Dubois (ModelLife@zmail.com)
To: Eric Martin (EMartin@zmail.com)
Subject: Re: Flight

I know you won't land for another 30 minutes, but I'm running out of the flat right now and wanted to update you. I won't be at the police station. I received a call from the inspecteur. One of Gretchen's friends came into the police station this morning. While they were trying to interview him, he collapsed and they sent him to the hospital. He said he was with the girls! He escaped from the catacombs. He's dehydrated and in bad shape. His name is Anders. I've met him once and don't think he has any family in the city, so I'm going to the hospital to wait for him to wake up. At this point, I think he's our best hope.

I'm not sure Inspecteur Bernard would want me at the hospital. I don't care. I can't wait in my flat anymore. But please don't tell him that's where I am unless you have to. Keep me updated on the police and I'll call when Anders wakes up.

I promise, Amanda. I will get them back.

Love you, Chantal

■ ■ ■

We walk through the darkness as our last remaining flash-light flickers. Every time it sputters my heart seems to stop—then when it flares back to life my pulse races again.

"Is it the bulb?" Henri whispers from beside me. When I look at him, the darkness seems to undulate around him like snakes. A tendril of shadow wraps around his throat and tightens. I know it can't be real, but I still see it. I tell myself it's only because I'm so tired and because I'm starv-ing. That's all it is. It isn't real. *It isn't real.*

Even with the terrifying hallucinations I'm having, the thing that still scares me more than anything else is the idea of losing the light. If the others knew what I was seeing, would they send me away? Would they make me leave? Would they do to me what I did to Anders?

Wouldn't I deserve that?

The guilt threatens to rip me in two, so I shove the thought to the back of my mind, focusing on Henri and not on his best friend that I probably killed. He's waiting for me to answer him. Hurry before he suspects that I'm going crazy. Hurry before he remembers I killed Anders. No! I didn't kill him. But I might as well have.

"Pro–probably the bulb, but I'm not sure." I rub my eyes, but my hands are so dirty they feel like sandpaper on my face. Or is it my face that's dirty? Every part of me aches. When did we sleep last? I can't remember. Even though I'm too terrified to sleep, my body begs for it with each step. "We've been using this one off and on the whole time. We could be getting to the end of the battery life, too."

I stop walking and drop my backpack on the floor in the middle of the cave. Gretchen and Henri follow suit. When

I hand Henri my flashlight, he lifts both eyebrows at my cousin, but neither of them say anything. I open the pocket on the front of my backpack and pull out the extra batteries. Then I stand and hold my empty hand out to Gretchen. "I need your flashlight."

She frowns at my hand before understanding dawns in her eyes. Shifting her backpack onto one shoulder, she unzips the biggest pocket and pulls out her flashlight. I take it and dump the used batteries into the unzipped backpack and slip the new ones in. I flip it on to test it and blink against the sudden brightness of two flashlights at once before turning it off again.

"Better to be prepared," Liv whispers over my shoulder, and I jump. I forgot she was standing behind me.

"Exactly," I answer, slipping the backup flashlight into the big pocket on my backpack. I wasn't lying when I told Maud my spare batteries wouldn't fit her flashlight. I've checked the other flashlights. They all use different bulbs and different size batteries. Only Gretchen's and mine are the same.

I glance up at Gretchen and fresh dread grips me. She's swaying on her feet. Henri puts one hand on her shoulder to steady her. When I take my flashlight back and shift the light toward them, my worry only gets worse. Gretchen's face is flushed with fever and the circles under her eyes are darker and have taken on a sickly greenish hue. Her cheeks have a sunken look to them that chills me to the bone.

We have to stop and rest soon, no matter what. We'll do it in darkness, conserve our light. Maybe sleep will help us all. We haven't slept since the ghost station. I'm not even sure how long ago that was anymore. It feels like an eternity. We haven't found another place that looks safe to sleep in, but it's getting to the point where it won't matter. If we all collapse from exhaustion, we won't be any safer.

And maybe when we wake up, I won't see the shadows reaching out for us anymore.

We come to an intersection that isn't marked on the map, and just to be safe we check both sides. The passage to the left quickly reaches a dead end. So we try the one to the right. This one is much longer. It curves around and the ceiling gradually lowers until we're all crouched to avoid banging our heads.

"I don't think this is going anywhere." Gretchen rests her hand on top of her head to protect it from the jagged ceiling.

"Me neither." I start to turn back, but Liv draws in a shuddering gasp and grabs the flashlight from my hand.

"Look." She points the beam farther into the tunnel. I squint, seeing some moss-covered rocks on the ground, but nothing else.

"What?" I glance at Liv warily. Maybe she's seeing things too. It wouldn't surprise me if we all were.

"Is that...?" Henri reaches to steady Liv's shaking hand and my stomach rolls. What I thought was moss is actually hair. Human hair on a skull. I fight the wave of nausea that hits me, careful not to react until the others do. I can't trust my eyes anymore.

Henri takes the flashlight from Liv and moves a bit closer.

"Henri, don't," I whisper, reaching out to tug on his jacket. My heart races and my head spins. I'm not up to this. I want to curl into a ball and cry until all these nightmares go away. Instead, I take a deep breath and hold on to what remains of my sanity.

"W–why does it still have hair?" Gretchen's lip curls up in disgust. I'm relieved that what I'm seeing is real, even if that it means we've stumbled onto dead bodies.

"It's a whole person." Henri's voice sounds hollow. He backs up quickly, grabbing my hand and pulling me toward the main tunnel. "Let's keep going."

"Wait." I shake my head. "Who is it? What happened to him?"

He stops, his wide eyes darting back into the shadows behind us. "Them. What happened to *them*."

"Them?" Liv spins back toward the body.

"There are three bodies back there." Henri swallows hard, and his eyes watch the narrow tunnel warily. "One guy and two girls. I don't know what happened. But they've only been dead a few years, I'd guess."

This is a reminder of what happens to us if we don't find a way out. My heart races and then slows. My skin gets hot and then so cold. I can't seem to move. Too many have died down here. If this isn't hell, it's the closest thing I can imagine.

Three more dead. Three more to add to the six million bones already here. Three plus M. Lambert, Paolo, James, and Maud.

These tunnels are more than just bones. Something lurks down here and it is hungry. Greedy for more souls to add to its collection.

How long before I become just one more set of bones among millions?

No.

This train of thought is the reason Maud shut down and why Liv is going downhill so quickly. The hallucinations are bad enough. I can't let myself think this way.

My palm is clammy when Henri hands me the flashlight, and I almost drop it. Shifting it to my other hand, I curse as it flickers again. I hear the others draw in a collective breath and only release it when the beam steadies.

"It shouldn't be too much farther to the mystery room on the map. We'll take a break once we get there." I fight against the overwhelming fear as I take the lead. I need to be stronger. I can't give in to it. Gretchen *needs* me.

I round the corner into the main tunnel and stumble back a step as the wall next to me begins to ooze something thick and black. It runs down and across the ground, coming for my feet, pooling around my shoes. Henri steadies me when I bump into him.

"You okay, Harley?"

The black ooze disappears as quickly as it came. I shake my head no, but then manage to say the words he needs to hear. "I'm fine. Just tired."

He nods, but the concern on his face doesn't fade.

I start walking before he can see the madness in me.

The next section is a tunnel of bones, which oddly gives me hope. We haven't seen organized bones for a while; I think we may have been too deep in the caves for that. Maybe this means we're getting closer to an exit. Maybe these grinning skulls of the dead are a sign that we might live.

The tunnel narrows as we go on and the bones creep closer around us. Soon Henri has to duck to avoid the ceiling. The skull next to my elbow starts to ooze the black

190

stuff I saw on the walls before, but this time it turns red like blood. Dark blood flowing from the vacant eye sockets and down across the bones stacked below. I cringe back and ram my elbow into the wall on the other side. I spin on instinct to make sure I didn't knock any supporting structures loose, and gasp. All the skulls on this side are flowing with the same blood. A warm yellow light flickers behind the sockets. They're looking at me, smiling and welcoming.

They want me to join them.

My arm feels damp where I banged it against the wall, and when I touch it my fingers come away sticky with blood. It could be mine or from the wall. I can't tell. Taking a shuddering breath, I close my eyes and press my hand against my eyelids.

"It's not real. None of it's real. There's *nothing* there," I whisper, and when I feel fingers on my neck my eyes fly open. I jump, spinning around. Henri's hand comes up to grab my arm when I swing the flashlight down to hit him.

His eyes sink back into his head until he has empty sockets too. Henri is like all the skulls in the walls. He's part of the Catacombs now—just like I am. Blood drips from his eye sockets and down his cheeks like tears. All I can think is how he's sad that he has to kill me.

He opens his mouth and inside is a dark pit of nothing. A voice that isn't his comes out. It calls my name, dark and raspy and endless. It repeats my name again and again before shrieking, *"You will never leave!"*

I scream, trying to pull away from Henri, but he tightens his grip.

"Harley!" he shouts in his normal voice, and I freeze. His eyes are wide and afraid. There's no blood on his face,

191

on the walls, on my elbow, on my hand. It's all gone in an instant. I step back again in horror, whimpering an apology. But instead of shoving me away like I expect, he wraps his arms around my shoulders and tugs me in against his chest. "Shh, stop. It's okay."

I hear Gretchen's weak voice filled with concern. "Is she all right?"

Henri pulls back enough to look in my eyes and I whisper, "I'm sorry."

"Yeah, she's okay," he answers Gretchen, and I wish I could drain a little of the confidence I hear in his voice and pour it into myself. Taking the flashlight gently from me, he takes the lead and wraps his warm fingers around my hand. "Come on. It's not much farther."

I let him lead me, putting what little energy I have left into looking at the ground in front of me. It reassures me to know that for at least this moment there is only one thing I need to do: not fall down.

Henri leads us around the corner, and when he stops I lean my head against his back. He lets out a low whistle. "What *is* this?"

Only when I hear the awe in his voice do I lift my head. I peer around his shoulder, and the instant my eyes focus I know what all the dashes on the map are. Chairs. There are probably fifty chairs and even a couple of musty old couches. Most of them are facing the same direction, like the cave is an auditorium just waiting for the crowds to come before the show starts.

Liv and Gretchen shuffle in around us, staring at the room. If everyone else didn't wear an expression that matched my confusion exactly, I'd wonder if I was hallucinating all of this, too. The chairs are definitely there. The jury is still out on the couches.

Liv gasps and runs out to the middle of the room.

"Liv, wait!" Henri follows her with the flashlight beam, and I know he's thinking the same thing I am. We can't lose track of anyone else. When we lose people, they die. At that thought, I grab Gretchen's hand and hold tight.

Liv stops at a large metal box behind the chairs. When Henry shines the flashlight over it, I see two big circles sticking up from box and realize what it is. If Liv wasn't currently running her hands across it, I definitely wouldn't believe what I was seeing. It's so much easier to believe I'm having another hallucination than that I'm actually looking at a movie projector sitting smack dab in the middle of the Paris Catacombs.

Chapter 17

Investigation Regarding Missing Persons – Gretchen Eleanor Dubois and Harley Bryn Martin

Update current as of June 14th at 09:43. Notable progress and new leads are as follows:

LEAD: Information found in Monsieur Roland Lambert's apartment indicates that he is likely the guide that took Mme. Dubois and Mme. Martin down into the Catacombs. Our contacts among cataphiles offered to help with search.

ACTION TAKEN: Yesterday, there was a more focused search through the Catacombs led by cataphile volunteers. They concentrated on areas of the Catacombs that M. Lambert is known to frequent. Search party was unable to locate current whereabouts of missing group, but they did find an area of obvious recent collapse and the body of an unidentified adult male.

LEAD: During the search of M. Lambert's apartment, our team found phone numbers and information that belonged to the victims in two different missing persons cold cases from several years ago: Case #'s 28944 and 73308

ACTION TAKEN: It isn't clear whether M. Lambert was involved in these cases or not, or whether this may tie into the cases of Mme. Dubois and Mme. Martin, but a team has been assigned to look into it.

LEAD: Search team returned with the body of the adult male last night. There is no current missing persons report to match his description.

ACTION TAKEN: Forensics is running prints and DNA

for identification while the coroner is collecting dental records for comparison with database.

LEAD: Cyber division was finally able to access information on Mme. Dubois's laptop last night.

ACTION TAKEN: Located virtual invitation sent by a Mme. Liv Greenwall to the off-limits section of the Catacombs. No confirmation on who the guide is, but we still believe it is likely M. Lambert.

LEAD: Invitation provided information on which Catacombs entrance was used. Also confirmed invites to five additional individuals: Maud Kumas, Anders Koskela, Henri Pelletier, Paolo Salvetti, James Evans.

ACTION TAKEN: Compared names with missing persons and other identifying databases. Connected missing persons reports for Maud Kumas, Henri Pelletier and Anders Koskela to this case. Retrieved confirmation from immigration department that Paolo Salvetti and James Evans entered France via Eurorail last July. Prints and photo identification confirmed that the body retrieved from the Catacombs is M. Salvetti.

LEAD: Monsieur Anders Koskela came in to the police department this morning.

ACTION TAKEN: Inspecteur Bernard conducted the interview (transcript is available upon request). Based on the information M. Koskela provided, we believe M. Salvetti was murdered. M. Koskela also indicated that M. Lambert is also dead, but that his death was accidental. Based on the interview, it is likely the rest of the group is still lost in the Catacombs. M. Koskela's interview was cut short for medical reasons and will be completed as soon as he is medically able to do so. M. Koskela has not been ruled out as a suspect in the murder of Paolo Salvetti.

Please direct any additional leads or new information to:
Inspecteur Bernard at the Paris Central Police Department

■ ■ ■

I stare up at the mostly flat cavern wall across from the projector and wonder how a movie would look on it. A movie . . . movies need *power*. As soon as the thought clicks, I'm moving toward Liv and the projector. She's winding the reels. I walk around to the back and find the power cord. Gretchen slumps down in one of the aluminum chairs, but Henri is behind me before I even ask.

"Please tell me that goes somewhere." He points the flashlight beam down at the cord and we follow it back toward the wall until we find the end—unplugged. And my heart sinks.

"Hey, bring the light back," Liv whines from the darkness, but Henri ignores her. He plows forward, not seeming nearly as discouraged as I feel. Liv glares at his back and pulls out her phone, using the light to keep looking at the projector.

"I read this old article once." Henri's voice is low as he moves along the wall, almost like he's talking to himself. When I turn around and see that Gretchen is following us, I'm not surprised. I wouldn't want to let the one with the flashlight get too far away from me either. Henri continues, "It was a really cool story about a group of cataphiles that set up a movie theater in the Catacombs about ten years ago."

"Well, looks like we found it," Gretchen says, and as weak as she sounds, I'm relieved to hear a bit of the familiar biting sarcasm in her tone.

"Yeah, but the article said that the cops found the theater and were planning to dismantle it and confiscate the equipment." Henri shines the light around and I see that the area on the other side of the cavern from the projector and chairs has a couple of tables and a long rectangular bar. I don't have time to comment on it before Henri goes on. "The cataphiles were too smart, though. They had some kind of alarm system set up, and by the time the cops got the paperwork done and came back down, they had cleared all of their stuff out."

"So, this must be where they moved it," Liv speaks up from behind us. I didn't hear her come up behind us, but I'm glad she's here. I always feel better when we're all together. She frowns at the chairs, and I know she's noticed the same thick layer of dust that I did. "Doesn't look like they've used it in years, though. I doubt we can count on someone popping in to find us here."

"That's not what I'm hoping for." A smile breaks out on Henri's face. In the beam of his flashlight, I spot a narrow tube, maybe two or three inches around. It's runs along the bottom of the cavern wall and has been painted the same gray as the stone around it, which made it difficult to see at first. Probably exactly as the cataphiles who put it here hoped it would.

"What is that?" I ask, and Henri and I move closer, following the tube along the wall and away from the theater. I still see things that can't be real in the darkness: the tube turns into a sharp blade and cuts Henri's hand to ribbons, then it's back to normal again. I ignore it, focusing on the possibility before us. The tube takes an abrupt turn and goes straight up through a deep crevice in the wall. Henri follows it with the flashlight. A couple of feet above my head, the beam shines on a rectangular box.

It's a junction box. It's covered in dust and grime, exactly like everything else, and it's been painted the same gray as the tube. The tube continues out the top of the box and up the crevice . . . up, up, up, and out through a small crack in the ceiling.

Henri grins over his shoulder at Gretchen, who has both hands pressed over her mouth. Then he winks at me. "I think it might be hope."

Handing me the flashlight, he reaches up to open the front panel. I point the beam with shaking hands. Inside, I see four switches forming a square. Henri places his fingers gently on the top right switch and closes his eyes, whispering, "*S'il vous plaît, Dieu.*"

Then he flips it on.

Nothing.

He moves down to the switch below it and flips that one as well, with the same result. Henri's shoulders slump as he tries the switch on the upper left, then the lower left. Nothing happens.

We stand in silence, drained of hope, and my flashlight flickers. Our situation weighs on me like an anchor, a length of chain closing around my throat. It pulls tighter and tighter as it drags me down in this hell forever.

"Wait, maybe . . ." Gretchen reaches out and takes the light from my hands. She walks unsteadily through the cavern, following the tube back toward the theater. We follow behind her, wary about getting our hopes up again. I let Liv and Henri pass me. All my energy has disappeared, replaced with despair, and I barely have the strength to keep my head up anymore. My stomach has even given up rumbling.

The shadows close in around me, and even though the flashlight doesn't give off any heat, I feel somehow colder without it in my hands. I watch the others, but my ears fill with a rushing noise and I can't hear them anymore. I fall to my knees and wait. I see movement in the darkness and know we aren't alone.

But I don't care anymore. The shadows and demons I see can all come and get me. I'm tired of fighting the inevitable.

Then I see *them*. The ghosts of the Catacombs. Haunting us for what we've done and what we haven't. Dead because of our awful choices, starting with the decision to come here at all. I see Paolo and Maud, James, Anders, even M. Lambert. They're all in the shadows, reaching for me. But I know in my soul that it's wrong. They aren't in the shadows—they *are the shadows*. They are the darkness.

They're here, watching and waiting for us to join them. They use fear to bleed the life out of us so that one by one, the rest of our lights eventually go out.

And the rushing sound changes to a hiss so loud it drowns out everything else. Is this some kind of signal that I'm the next to go? That they're coming for me? Did the others hear it before they died?

I feel Gretchen's hot hands on my face. I blink up at her as the edges of my vision fade in and out of blackness.

"You deserve to die," she snarls, her enraged voice joining the sound attacking my eardrums. Her lips curve into a menacing smile and her teeth grow into fangs, dripping blood. I try to push her away, but all my strength is gone. Tears run down my cheeks and I tell her again and again how sorry I am.

The noise fades to nothing. Normal sound returns and the first thing I hear is the panic in my cousin's voice.

"Get a granola bar," Gretchen orders Henri, and he digs quickly through his backpack to comply. He unwraps it and hands it to her. She breaks some off and puts it in my mouth. I chew on instinct at first, then hungrily, savoring the peanut butter taste as it replaces the dirty metallic tinge of the air that I've become used to down here.

After I swallow the first bite, Gretchen hands me the rest of the bar and I take a second bite. I know in my head that I have to stop, that we're supposed to be rationing these, but pure *need* overpowers any rational thought and I keep going. None of the others say a word as I eat the whole thing.

By the time I've swallowed the last bite, I feel almost too full and my stomach churns. I take a deep breath and some of the fog lifts from my brain. What have I done? That was supposed to be for all of us. The others let me have that food when I know for certain our rations are almost gone. Two granola bars left for the four of us. That won't last us long. Especially not when our bodies are already starving from rationing. I hold my sore wrist across my stomach, like somehow having it there will stop the churning inside me. There's no way in hell I'm going to waste the precious granola bar I've devoured by letting my stupid body throw it back up.

"Thank you," I whisper feebly. "I won't have any next time."

Gretchen hugs me against her shoulder as she splits another granola bar with Liv and Henri. "I'm glad you're okay. It was probably low blood sugar or something."

I don't have to check the bag to know there's only one granola bar left now. I make a silent vow not to touch it, no matter how low my blood sugar might be. No matter what madness I'm seeing. Gretchen's fever seems worse every time I touch her. She's going to need what little food we have to get through whatever is causing it.

I squeeze Gretchen closer. She hugs me back and my mind fills with a memory of the last sleepover we had together before she moved to New York. It was the middle of the night and we slipped out into our backyard after my parents went to sleep. We were lying on our backs in the grass and staring up at the sky. Gretchen was crying and I desperately wanted to make her feel better.

"Mom told me that it's only two hours to New York," I said, gripping her hand in mine.

Her crying increased. "That's on a plane. I looked it up. It's half a day in a car and a whole day on a train. You're my best friend, Harley! I'm used to biking to your house!"

"I know," I responded miserably, brushing my own tears off my face. I rolled on my side to face her and she did the same. "But we'll find a way to see each other. I don't know how, but we will. We have to."

"Promise me." Her light blond hair clung to the tears on her cheeks as I rested my forehead against hers and stared straight into her eyes.

"I promise."

I stare up at Gretchen's fever-flushed face and her edgy purple hair and know how badly I must've hurt her. We were kids and I didn't know how hard it would be to keep my promise. Still, I could've done more. I should have tried harder.

She deserves better.

She catches me watching her and gives me a half-worried, half-exhausted smile. "Stop it. You have no right to look so terrible when *I* have a fever. I get the attention right now, got it?"

"Understood. I'll save my terrible-looking-ness for later, then." I smile feebly and she laughs. Why did I think she changed? She's still Gretchen, still the same cousin I've always loved. I might have messed up and let her down, but there's still time for me to make up for it. I *will* find a way to get her out of here alive. *I have to.*

Liv shifts uncomfortably next to Henri and I lift my gaze to her. If looks could kill, the one she's giving me right now would be more lethal than any collapsing cave. I can't blame her after scarfing down one third of our remaining food, but I still don't want to give her time to dwell on being mad. I turn back to my cousin. "Did you find anything helpful?"

Gretchen shakes her head. "Not yet, but let me show you what I'm thinking."

Henri helps Gretchen to her feet first then bends down to help me. "You sure you're okay?"

I nod, ignoring the way the shadows seem to crawl across the wall behind him. "Still need to sleep soon, but the food helped. Thank you."

Gretchen walks me over to a place where the tube ends. She lifts it up from the ground a bit and I see a bunch of dusty wires tucked inside with electrical safety caps on them. "It looks like they never finished setting this up."

Henri nudges something in the dirt. It's an old electrical outlet. It's not connected to anything and every speck of exposed metal is coated with rust. "Is there any way this can help us?"

"That?" Gretchen frowns and lifts one eyebrow. "That's more Harley's department than mine."

I pick it up, blowing some of the dust off. "I'm not sure. Everything I know about wiring I learned from reading DIY renovation books. Plus, I think American wiring is different from European. I'd be more likely to get us electrocuted than be helpful." The others nod, but I'm still thinking it over. If it comes down to being stuck in the dark or risking electrocution, I might have to re-evaluate my position—but not yet. Thank God, we're not that desperate yet.

Liv leans her forehead against the wall, kicking it with the toe of her shoe. "I just want to get the hell out of here."

"Well, maybe the other end might help us." Gretchen bites her lip and inclines her head toward the junction box.

"How?" I may not understand what she's talking about, but I've learned not to doubt my cousin's technical prowess. If she has an idea, I'm already all in. I start moving toward the box before the others even turn in that direction.

"Well, I'm not sure yet." Gretchen grabs one of the folding chairs. When Henri immediately takes it from her and carries it for her, I think again how lucky we are to have him here. He's been calm when everyone else has panicked. Plus, having a hot guy around is really never a bad idea.

I stop him as he passes and place a quick kiss on his cheek, whispering, "*Merci beaucoup.*"

He rewards me with a wide grin. "*De rien, ma belle.*"

It's all I can do not to swoon at his accent, and fresh determination fills me to get out of this endless maze and back up to the city so famous for romance. I hurry to catch up with Gretchen.

She climbs up on the chair and starts pointing out things I didn't see the first time we opened the box. "See these wires back here? Notice the green and blue ones? How neither of them actually go into any fuses but instead pass behind them?"

"So, they aren't power lines?" Henri asks the question before I get it out.

"I don't think so. And if they aren't, I may be able to use them to send out a message." Gretchen bites her lip before climbing down and sitting in the chair. She looks utterly drained as her eyes turn to me. "But I need your phone. Yours has the most battery life left and I'll need as much as I can get. And you won't get it back in one piece."

I don't even hesitate. Digging it out of my backpack, I power it on. The wallpaper is a picture of Gretchen and me from back when she still lived in Chicago. I saved it as my home screen right before I got on the plane to Paris. I grip it tight, promising myself that we'll take a new picture once we both get out of here alive. Then I place it in her hand. "Done. What else?"

"I'll need something sharp to cut open the wires. I'm not sure what else until I start working on it. Maybe a small piece of metal or tin foil." She drapes her arm on the back of the chair and rests her head against it.

"Okay. We'll search and see what we can find. You rest." I know it's better than dragging her around with us when she's sick, but I don't want to leave her alone in the dark. And I'm not ready to pull out her flashlight with the new batteries until we have absolutely no other choice.

Henri seems to have the same concern, and within a few seconds he is rummaging through his pack and pulling out his phone. He turns it on and hands it to Gretchen. "There is less than five percent left on the battery, but it will give you some light so you can still see us. And we can see you."

"Thanks, Henri." Gretchen holds the phone in her palms like it's encrusted in diamonds. Liv, Henri, and I start moving through the cave. We start on the theater side, but don't find anything new there that we didn't already see. Liv does manage to find a piece of thin, bendable metal to break off the bottom of the projector. It's part of what Gretchen needs, so it's worth the trouble, even if Liv mutters constantly about it being a travesty the whole time she's prying it loose.

"The Gods of Film will understand." I pat her on the shoulder, but the withering glare she shoots back at me tells me that she's not on board with my sense of humor. I resume holding the flashlight for her in silence.

The chair next to me starts moving. It wobbles before spinning to face me. It's like someone invisible is sitting in it. Then it jumps toward me an inch at a time. I hear the wooden feet bump across the stone floor as it moves closer, and I take a step back.

"I can't see without the light," Liv snaps, and suddenly the chair is back to normal again. I realign the light for her while I wait for my pulse to slow down.

I was hoping the hallucinations would stop now that I've eaten. Apparently not.

We move toward the other side of the cavern with the tables. Henri notices me glancing over to check on Gretchen and says, "She's okay."

I nod. It looks like she might be sleeping. As I watch, the darkness around her ripples. I say a silent prayer that the hallucination stops there. Then Gretchen stands up on her chair and steps off. Her feet jerk to a stop, dangling a few inches from the floor. Her body shudders and she claws at an invisible rope around her neck.

"Gretchen!" I choke out her name, taking two steps toward her. But with my next blink, she's sleeping in the chair again. A slow whimper escapes me and I want to claw my stupid, cruel brain out of my head.

"She's okay." Henri is back in front of me again, turning my chin until I look into his eyes. He repeats himself until I relax. "She's okay."

I nod and hand him the flashlight. It's better if someone in their right mind has it. He holds my hand as he shines the beam across the tables. We come up empty until we move to the bar.

The first drawer I check has a box of old silverware, including several knives. "Got it."

The next has a handful of old glow sticks in a foil packet. It's not the kind of foil Gretchen needs, but Liv and I take a couple sticks each and stick them in our pockets to test later.

Liv tugs open the lower cabinet half-heartedly, but when she looks inside her eyes go wide. "Is—is that—?" She lets out a small squeal.

Henri and I crowd behind her to look inside. And then I smell it. Opening the cabinet released a puff of sweetness into the air, and suddenly my stomach remembers how to rumble. Marshmallows, chocolate, cakes, sugar, and—

thank the God of Unhealthy Life Choices—every wonderful preservative that mankind could come up with.

This theater comes complete with a snack bar.

Liv dives in with both arms, dragging out box after box and placing them on top of the bar. Rice Krispy Treats and some kind of chocolate bar I don't recognize, followed by a box of what I think are French granola bars. And they're all full. They stocked this place and then never used it. Liv giggles as she works. When she drags out a box of Twinkies a vivid memory of my dad pops into my head and my eyes fill with tears.

I locked myself in my room during one epically bad fight between my parents. An hour after things quieted down, a knock sounded on my door. It was Dad, with his dress shirt and hair all rumpled. He handed me a Twinkie. When I asked what it was for, he gave me a sad smile and said, "I heard a joke that the only things left after an apocalypse would be Twinkies and cockroaches. I figured you'd rather have one of these."

When I laughed, he pulled me in for a hug and whispered, "I know things are difficult right now, Sweetie, but it will get better. We're tough enough to see the hard times through. I think you are, too."

It turns out their marriage wasn't tough enough to survive the hard times, but I hope I am. It doesn't get harder than what we've been through the last few days in the Catacombs.

Picking up the box of Twinkies, I tear it open, deliberately not looking at the expiration date. If they still look decent, I'm in. It isn't like we have a lot of options anymore anyway, and these may buy us some more time to get out.

"Is that . . .?" Gretchen says from behind me, and I spin around, pulling the first individually wrapped cake out of the box and presenting it to her with a flourish.

"Yes." I grin so widely my cheeks actually ache. "It's a miracle."

She gapes down at the yellow cake that somehow still looks almost exactly like the ones we would find in a store today. "I don't think anyone's been in here for at least five years. Is it safe?"

"Safer than starvation." Henri checks the expiration date before pulling another Twinkie out of the box. He taps it against Gretchen's like he's clinking a glass during a toast. She holds out his phone to him and he stuffs it in his pocket without looking at it, completely focused on tearing the wrapping off his Twinkie.

I shrug. "I think if it doesn't taste bad, then it's probably better than not eating anything at this point."

Gretchen carefully unwraps hers, takes a small nibble, and then moans. "It's a little stale, but still *sooo* good."

Henri is devouring his before she even finishes her sentence.

I hold back. After eating that whole granola bar, I should probably wait. We may have replenished our stock of food, but we still have no idea how to get out of here. The flashlight flickers again. The others are so busy eating, I'm not sure they even notice.

Gretchen holds out a Twinkie to me. When I shake my head, she takes my hand and places the cake in it. "Stop. You need this. We all do."

Henri shoots me a look that is as close to threatening as I think he gets. And Liv is too busy eating a Rice Krispy

Treat with her eyes closed to object. I peel the plastic wrapper off the Twinkie and wave it like a white flag of surrender. "I know when I'm beaten."

"Good." Gretchen moans again as she takes another bite of her Twinkie, and soon I'm making the same happy noises. Her assessment was spot on. It doesn't taste bad, but it's a different texture than I expected.

And right here, right now, it's more delicious than any of the food we had at Sacrée Fleur before coming into the Catacombs.

Once we've finished, I pull a knife out of the silverware box and link my good arm through Gretchen's. "Let's go figure out how to send that message."

Chapter 18

Text from Chantal to Amanda sent on June 14 at 12:22 p.m. –

Anders is awake and he asked to see me. He wants to help! Tell Inspecteur Bernard to come to the hospital right away! The doctor said he isn't well enough to leave yet.

Text from Amanda to Chantal sent on June 14 at 12:26 p.m. –

Bernard is organizing another group to go search the catacombs. He said he'll come straight over as soon as he can. Should Eric and I come to the hospital?

Text from Amanda to Chantal sent on June 14 at 12:43 p.m. –

Hello? Did you get my last text?

Text from Chantal to Amanda sent on June 14 at 1:03 p.m. –

Sorry. I was talking to Anders and they made me silence my phone in his room. Oh my God, Amanda. I can't believe what these kids have been through. We have to get them out of there. No, don't come here. I need you at the station. The only way you can help is to get Bernard to come here as soon as he can. I really think Anders can help us find them. And pray, if you do that anymore. Mom would pray if she were here. I miss her. I miss you.

Text from Chantal to Amanda sent on June 14 at 1:05 p.m. –

Love you.

■ ■ ■

By the time I slump back into a chair and let Gretchen take over, my arms ache from holding them over my head for so long. She walked me through the first few steps to get the wires ready. Under her instructions, I cut the blue and green wires below the fuse box, pulled them out from the top so we had a longer length of wire to work with, and stripped the last inch of insulation off each wire. It was hard work and took longer than I expected. Of course, it doesn't help that I feel so weak. I had to take breaks and sit down or risk passing out.

I had to convince Gretchen to let me take care of the grunt work, and watching the way she wobbles as Henri steadies her on the chair, I know it was the right choice. She spent the time taking apart my phone, so it isn't like she got to rest much, but letting me do most of the physical stuff is better than doing the whole thing herself.

I didn't lie when I told her letting me help would save us precious time, but I left out the part about how terrified I am about her fever. I wonder if something in the lake water made her sick, but then wouldn't the rest of us be getting fevers as well? My cousin looks worse by the hour, and nothing we try is helping. Gretchen took the last of the ibuprofen about an hour ago, but since I've been taking it for my wrist, we only had one tablet left and it doesn't seem to be doing much. I wish more than anything I'd just sucked it up instead of wasting pills. Gretchen needs the ibuprofen so much more right now.

I stretch my arms, trying to work the kinks out. It's hard to believe how much more comfortable this old aluminum chair is than the floor. I don't even bother to rub away the layer of dust and grime that coats everything. I'm so filthy anyway, so it doesn't bother me like it would have a few days ago. Those few days feel like a lifetime. I feel older. My body is weaker—much weaker.

I glance back toward the cavern wall across from the projector. It's shrouded in darkness, and I try again to picture a movie flickering over the uneven stone.

What would they even watch down here? After being stuck in the Catacombs, it's hard to imagine that I would ever choose to come down here in the first place. It sounded so cool and adventurous before. Now I would give anything to go back in time and say no, to beg the others not to do it at all, to keep them all safe and alive and warm and fed.

"Movie night?" Liv slumps down in a chair next to me and gives me a feeble smile. I hope finding the food in the snack bar made her forget how angry she was at me for eating that entire granola bar. "I'd tell you what our little theater is showing, but the label is too faded to read."

"Doesn't matter. I have plans." I spread my hands out in front of my inert body. "Can't you see how very busy I am?"

"Me too. I forgot." Liv sighs. She holds the flashlight in her hand, pointed at where Gretchen is working. It looks like my cousin has finished rigging up the wires. Now she's frowning as she fiddles with my phone.

The flashlight in Liv's hand flickers again and she bangs it lightly against her wrist until it stops. Gretchen barely seems to notice. She's completely focused on the phone's backlit screen. "At least we saved the glitchy one for last." Liv taps the flashlight's power switch twice.

"Yeah, we should've brought more flashlights."

"More batteries." She nods, and I notice her eyes are taking longer to open each time she blinks. Since Maud's death, she's been muttering to herself a lot. It's good to see her looking more coherent, for now at least. Maybe eating helped her as much as it's helped me. The hallucinations linger at the edges of my vision now. I hope it stays that way.

"Yep, more batteries." I yawn. "More water, more everything."

"I'm sorry, by the way." Liv doesn't look at me. Her eyes stay on Gretchen's back, but her head angles slightly in my direction.

"Sorry for what?"

"For inviting all of you. This was my idea, my plan. I'm the reason we're all stuck here." She looks at me, and I see guilt and fear in her eyes. It gives her a haunted look. I want to help her feel better, to reassure her somehow. Especially when she says with her voice cracking, "I'm the reason they're dead."

I put one arm around her and her head flops onto my shoulder when I squeeze her gently against my side. "No one could know this would happen. No one blames you."

She nods and her blond hair brushes my nose. Beneath the topcoat of dirt, I smell a hint of coconut shampoo. The thought of a hot shower nearly makes me moan. I release Liv, getting back to my feet. I move closer to Gretchen. Seeing my beloved phone with all the circuitry exposed and wires sticking out brings on a surprising wave of sadness. Oh well, at least it was butchered for a good cause.

"How's it going?"

Gretchen gently places the phone on top of the junction box, careful not to knock the wires loose. "I think I'm done."

"Did anyone answer?" Henri asks immediately.

Gretchen lets us help her down and slumps into the chair. "It doesn't work that way."

"How does it work?" I place my hand on the back of her head and am able to tell her fever hasn't come down at all before she lightly pushes me away.

"It's old wiring and I think it's only set up as a one-way system." Gretchen leans forward, putting her hands on her knees. "I think the line I'm hooked up to is another alarm like the one Henri read about in the article."

"The one that tipped the cataphiles off that the police had found their theater?" Henri pulls one of the other chairs forward. He sits on it backward, facing Gretchen.

"Right. This one never got installed, but the wiring is in place. So imagine it like a bank alarm to warn police if there is a robbery or something. Pushing the panic button notifies the police, but they can't send back a message. It only goes out, not back in." Gretchen rolls her head from side to side, stretching her neck.

"But you got a message to go out, though?" Liv's eyes scan the shadows around us again.

"I hope so." Gretchen wraps both arms around herself and suddenly looks very small and nervous. "Like I said, it's old equipment and I have no idea what kind of system could be receiving it on the other end. For all we know, it could be disconnected. Or it could still be connected, but to equipment so old that it doesn't know how to interpret something as sophisticated as a smart phone. So I sent a basic message in binary. If they still have a system in place to get the message, they should already know *where* it's coming from. All we can do now is hope the message will go through and that they'll understand what it means."

I open my mouth to ask another question, but then the flashlight goes out. Henri whips out his phone, but as soon as he turns it on, it beeps twice and shuts down.

"And there goes my battery," he mutters.

"It's fine. This is why I set up the other flashlight before." I try not to freak out. I've never really liked the dark, but now I'm not sure if I'll ever be able to stand it again. Of course, normal darkness above ground has nothing on this. This is cold, suffocating, eclipsing.

Feeling my way in total blackness, I find my backpack on the ground by the wall. My fingers fumble on the zipper. Liv moves closer and I can feel her whole body trembling. "D–did you find it? My phone died when I was looking at the projector, but I can get my camera out of my backpack for light if you need help."

"No. Save that for—" I stop, not wanting to talk about what happens after the replacement flashlight goes out. "One sec, I've almost got it."

A hand on my back makes me stiffen until I realize it's Liv. "Okay."

Once I get the right pocket open, my fingers close on the barrel of the flashlight. I hear everyone breathing in the silence as I pull it out of the backpack and flip the switch. The light blinds us at first, and then there's a united sigh of relief and Gretchen whispers, "Let there be light," with a half-smile.

"We should get some rest," Henri says, and no one argues.

I know we need to get moving again soon, but not before we sort through the snack bar and decide what is worth taking with us. Plus, we all need sleep, and we can turn off the light while we're resting—as much as that scares me—so we won't waste any battery life. I turn toward the couches on the other side of the theater and wonder if they're still useable.

"Before we sleep, though, I need to show you something," Henri says from behind me, and I pivot to face him. His tone doesn't make it sound like good news, and I really don't think I can take any more bad. He leads the way across the theater to a couple of caves on the other side.

"I checked the map while you three were working on the junction box. This is the tunnel we're supposed to take to go to the exit." He nudges my flashlight up until it illuminates the tunnel. About ten feet past the entrance, the cave is blocked by a collapse. A snap of cracking stone makes us all scramble back, but it's coming from a tunnel to the left. I shine my light into it and am amazed it's still standing. Tiny cracks and crumbling rock covers the entire ceiling. When the other tunnel collapsed, it obviously weakened this one. A single rotting piece of wood props everything up. I take another wary step back as falling dust from the freshly cracked rock settles.

I guess we won't be heading toward any exit on this side of the cave. Somehow I'm numb to this. I know I should be discouraged, but maybe I'm past feeling that now.

I glance at Gretchen, and she looks back at me. She seems to be feeling the same thing I am: nothing. Liv starts muttering to herself and rubbing her face as she turns toward the couches. We all follow in silence.

"I do think that this one over here might end up leading us back to the passage we want, hopefully past the collapsed section." Henri's tone is deeply apologetic, like he alone is responsible for this new obstacle in our path. "I can't be sure, though, until we check it out." He indicates a large tunnel in one corner of the room then lifts the map to show me. I see immediately what he's saying. The corner tunnel goes in for a bit before branching off in two directions. The left branch seems to head straight back toward the tunnel that's barely standing. The right branch looks like it meets up eventually with the exit tunnel, but there are several *X's* through it, and who knows what that could mean.

"Think that's where they buried the treasure?" I try to cheer him up with a wink and he rewards me with a smile.

"Cataphile by night, pirate by day?"

"Hey, don't knock it until you've tried it." I stop and wrap my arms around him in a tight hug. He doesn't respond or laugh this time, and I can feel hope seeping out of him with every breath.

"Thanks for trying to find another way," I say simply. That's all we can do now. Keep trying. An alternate route is the best we can hope for.

His arms close around me. Henri's voice breaks as he whispers against my hair, "I want to go home."

"Me too." I pull slowly out of his arms and cling to his hand as I lead him toward the cushions. "But for now, let's sleep."

The couches aren't in terrible shape, even if the springs seem to be hell-bent on poking us in all the worst possible ways. Instead of sleeping on them, we take the cushions off and lay them on the floor in a big square. Henri helps me set up chairs in a big circle around the cushions. If someone tries to approach while we're asleep, they'll have to move them or risk knocking them over. It's by no means a fool-proof system, but at least we have something between us and the rest of the cave.

All of our feet hang off the edges of the cushions when we lie down, especially Henri's, but at least the rest of our bodies are off the floor for a little while.

I lie in the middle, between Henri and Gretchen, and we flip off the flashlight. Liv, who has the spot on the other side of Henri, sits near the edge of our chair circle, whispering into her camera. Every few seconds, I'm able to pick out one or two words like *dark*, *die*, and *scared*.

I'm honestly amazed the camera is still working, but I guess when you only use the battery for a couple of minutes at a time, it lasts awhile. If we get to the point where we are out of all other options, that little spotlight is all we'll have to help us find our way out of here.

I reach out to check Gretchen's fever again. Instead of feeling her forehead, I bump her nose and she swats me away.

"What are you doing?" she mumbles. She's already half asleep.

"Just checking," I whisper back. "Are you okay?"

"It's probably just a cold or something," she answers, and I notice for the first time that she does sound a little congested, which is kind of a relief. No fever is good down here, but a cold is at least something I know what to do with. "I'll be fine, Harley. I promise."

"Okay, sorry. Go to sleep." Exhaustion settles over me like a heavy blanket. I'm still cold and hungry, but nothing can keep me awake when I'm *this* tired. Even the lumpy cushions feel like the softest bed compared to the stone floor. One more thought occurs to me before I completely drift off. "Gretchen?"

"Mmm?"

"What did you send with my phone?" I whisper into the darkness.

"I set a message to repeat over and over until the phone dies. It seems like our best bet to make someone notice."

"Yeah, but what does it say?"

"*Aidez nous.*" When she doesn't add anything else, I wonder if she's fallen asleep. Then she whispers the translation, but it doesn't sound like she's talking to me. It sounds more like a prayer.

"*Help us.*"

Chapter 19

VIDEO CLIP #3 Recovered from Liv Greenwall's camera for use in criminal case #41773/The Paris Catacombs/Time stamp: June 14th

2:13 p.m. [Beginning of recording]

[Liv Greenwall is holding the camera pointed at herself.]

LIV: (whispers) I'm so scared. Nothing down here makes sense. People keep dying and our lights are going out one-by-one. I know, I know we're going to be left down here in the dark. I think we're all going to die.

[Liv turns to look over her shoulder and the camera catches a glimpse of three people lying on cushions on the floor and a circle of chairs around them.]

LIV: Some of my friends are (voice cracks) dead. I invited them down here and now they're dead. I [long pause] I'm afraid to go to sleep because when I sleep I see them. I see their bodies. I feel their blood on me. It's awful. I don't know if it's my fault, but I think [pause] I think it might be.

[Liv jumps, looking around her before turning back to the camera.]

LIV: (whispers) I never believed any of the stories. I don't believe in ghosts or evil. [looks down](mutters) Didn't. I didn't believe in them. [looks back up into camera again] Now, I don't know. How am I supposed to know whether something is real or not? How do I know what to be afraid of? Should I be more scared of what I see moving in the dark—or of what I hear it say? What it tells me to do? [long pause] Or more afraid that there could actually be nothing in the darkness at all?

[Liv looks up suddenly and squints over the top of the camera. She shakes her head, rubbing her fist against her temple. Then she knocks her hand hard against her head.]

LIV: Stop. Just *stop*. [closes her eyes](whispers) It's not real. None of it's real. He is *not* real.

[Liv hits her fist against her head again, harder this time. Then she fumbles with the camera.]

2:19 p.m. [End of recording]

■ ■ ■

The walls crumble around me. I feel dust in my hair, on my skin, in my mouth. The air is heavy with the metallic smell and taste of blood, but I don't know whose. I run through rapidly narrowing tunnels. My breath burns in jagged bursts. If they catch me, I'm dead.

Dead like all the rest of them.

My flashlight flickers as I come to a bigger tunnel. Something in a pile of bones catches my attention. Instead of skulls looking up at me, it's the severed heads of M. Lambert, Paolo, James, and Maud. Their mouths stretch wide in endless screams of horror. I cover my mouth, crying.

I keep running.

My light flickers again. Someone falls against me in the darkness, pinning me to the rock wall with their weight. I cry out, fighting to free myself. When the light steadies, I'm released. I spin to see Anders slump down the wall. Blood spreads out in circles across his dirty shirt. In my hands, I have a sharpened bone covered in his blood. His cheeks are sunken and his skin is gray. He looks up at me then down at all the blood pooling in a circle on the ground around him. I want to stop it, to save him, but my body locks in place

"You killed me," he growls. A final shudder passes through him and he lies still.

I collapse to my knees beside him, but there's nothing I can do to save him. He's dead and it's my fault. Footsteps echo behind me again and I'm on my feet, my skin flaring hot and cold. I put all my remaining strength into my escape.

Turn after turn, I run while darkness gives chase. I crawl across bones and wade through puddles of blood, but I keep going. My muscles burn with fire and my lungs struggle with each breath.

I stumble, head spinning. I'm too weak. I crash into a dead end and scream in frustration. This battle is pointless.

I'm going to die down here.

My flashlight beam lands on someone curled up in the corner. Dread breeds within me like moss in a forest and threatens to suffocate me.

Then I see purple hair and my heart stops beating.

Gretchen.

Sprinting to her, I roll her onto her back and her eyes flutter open. On the other side of her Henri appears, and an intense wave of nausea hits me. His gorgeous brown eyes stare vacantly up toward the city above us. His head is split open like Paolo's. As I watch, his skin melts away until all that remains is another skull for the Catacombs to claim as its own. There's nothing I can do for him.

He's one of them.

I sob as I clutch Gretchen's jacket and shake her. "Wake up. We have to get out of here."

Her gaze is distant, like she can't see me. When she speaks, the voice isn't hers. "This is the Empire of the Dead."

I scramble back. The voice is made of all the worst sounds in the world combined into one. It's squealing tires and fingers on a chalkboard. It's howling cats and groans of pain and screams of terror. Pure fear drenches me, soaking deep as my bones as she sits up. Then Gretchen's lips curve into an eerie smile.

"You belong to us now."

■ ■ ■

I sit bolt upright, panting, eyes wide in the blackness. My heart races in a staccato gallop. I need to touch something, to use one of my other senses to reassure myself that I'm okay.

"Harley?" Henri's muffled voice whispers beside me, and my mind fills with the horrifying image of his face melting away all over again. My whole body quakes with a violent shudder. Then his arms are around me and he's pulling me against his warm chest.

He whispers, "Shh . . . it's only a nightmare. It's okay," again and again until I relax into him. I press my hands against his abdomen, drawing reassurance from the movement of each breath, the beating of his heart. He leans back until we're lying down and I have my head on his shoulder, holding tight to him. The mingled warmth of our bodies comforts me. It's a tiny spark of life in the face of all the death that surrounds us.

"Do you want to talk about it?" His voice is so soft I can barely hear him.

I shake my head fervently. Talking about it won't help me forget the nightmare images seared into my brain. Being close to him helps, though. "Do you think we're going to die down here?"

He doesn't answer right away. I feel his breath stir my hair before he kisses the top of my head. "I hope not. I'd hate for our one and only date to be in a place like this."

I chuckle softly. "Which part of this was a date?"

His shoulder moves slightly beneath my head as he shrugs. "All of it, obviously. If you didn't know that, it's probably a misunderstanding because of our vastly different cultural backgrounds."

"The massive cultural differences between the US and Canada?" My lips curve into a smile. I nuzzle his neck and a small groan comes from deep in his chest. I whisper, "I agree. It's a problem. How are we ever going to overcome this barrier?"

"It's not going to be easy." Rolling to face me, he wraps both arms around me and places soft kisses on my forehead and cheeks as he talks. "But I'm willing to put in the work."

I lift one finger and put it against his lips to stop him before he can move his mouth to mine. "All right, then. Are you ready for the first cultural difference we'll have to work past?"

I can feel his lips curve up beneath my fingers. "Yes?"

"Americans don't kiss on the first date."

He laughs louder than he should and immediately drops his voice back to a whisper. "*Now* you tell me? And are you sure this is all Americans?"

I smile, running my fingers lightly over his lips, across his jaw, and up into his hair. I scratch my nails gently across the back of his neck. His groan is a little louder this time. I whisper, "This American, but I guess it's too late to take it back at this point."

"I have good news." He moves his lips to my ear and nibbles on it, sending ripples of pleasure through my whole body. "In Canada, if a date lasts for more than twenty-four hours, then it counts as two dates."

I laugh softly and shake my head. "Is that a strict rule for all Canadians?"

"It's my rule now," he murmurs, and then his mouth is on mine and I wrap my arms around him, kissing him back. Henri is a magician. He uses his lips and hands to make all lingering thoughts of the nightmare disappear. My mind empties of all my fears and fills with Henri. For those few minutes in his arms, even the cold, pitch-black tomb we are trapped in seems to fade away, replaced by warmth and light.

■ ■ ■

I'm shivering when I wake up to Gretchen muttering curses under her breath. Henri is gone from my side, and when I reach out all I find is a few feet of cushion with no one on it. Liv is gone too.

A couple of *whap* noises make me sit up and turn toward Gretchen. "What is going on?"

"It's this flashlight. When I flipped the switch there was a popping sound and now it won't turn on."

I hear the *whap-whap* sound again and recognize it as Gretchen hitting the flashlight. I rub my eyes, trying to make my brain catch up. "But those are brand new batteries."

"I know," Gretchen snaps. "So why isn't it turning on?"

"Let me see." I reach for the flashlight and my hand collides with Gretchen's shoulder instead. She grabs my fingers and presses the flashlight into my hand. I dump out the batteries and put them back in again, making sure everything is secure and lined up correctly. I flip the switch.

Nothing.

A whimpering sound comes from our left and there is the scrape of a chair moving across the floor. Both Gretchen and I shift toward it.

"Liv?" Gretchen calls.

"No. I knew it. The light is out and we're all going to die." Liv's voice echoes in the darkness.

"No, it's going to be okay," I answer. The pure despair and fear in Liv's tone sends a chill through me, but I keep my voice calm and level. "It must be the bulb that went out. These batteries will fit my flashlight. Let me find it. Until then, maybe try one of those glow sticks?"

Crawling carefully across the cushions toward the backpacks, I can feel Gretchen moving beside me. When we get there, we both pull all four bags up onto the cushions. In the darkness they all feel the same. There's a momentary flare of light from across the room as Liv breaks one of her glow sticks and shakes it, but it's obviously past its expiration date. The light fades to a dim glow, and she tosses it toward the middle of the room where it barely illuminates anything.

"Well that helps no one," Gretchen mutters.

"Liv, I'm coming to you," Henri says. I hear him bumping into chairs and shoving them aside as he moves through the makeshift restaurant toward where Liv is still crying.

Maybe she'll feel better with him near her. "Everything is okay."

"No. It's not! We're all going to die!" she yells at Henri, and I jerk my head up in surprise.

My hands race over the first backpack, searching for the outer pocket. It's empty.

"You need to calm down, Liv. This isn't helping." Henri's tone is firm now, and it sounds like he's closing in on Liv.

"No!" Liv screams at him. "Nothing is helping any of us anymore! We're going to die. Stop! Everyone just stop!"

Gretchen starts to scoot toward Liv until I nudge her. "Find it."

"No!" The pure panic in Liv's voice seeps into me. My hands start to shake and I lose my grip on the next zipper. The tiny pool of light only seems to make the shadows in the rest of the room seem thicker. The air churns with motion that makes it harder to focus. Every part of me is alive with apprehension. I get the zipper open and my fingers close around the barrel of my flashlight.

"Liv?" Henri asks. My heart pounds harder. He sounds genuinely scared. A massive thud echoes and I hear all the air rush out of Henri.

"Henri?" I yell. My whole body tenses.

"Stop. Stop! What are you doing?" Henri shouts, and I fly back into motion.

I screw the top off the flashlight with shaking hands. "Got it. Gretchen, give me the new batteries. Hurry."

Liv is sobbing. "It's not real! Stop! No! *We'll* stop. We shouldn't have lived." Nothing she's saying makes sense. Every cell in my body shouts in a frightened cacophony:

We need light!

Gretchen presses the batteries into my hands. "What's she doing?"

"I don't know. I need to see." I slide the first battery into the barrel, but the other falls through my fingers. I feel the slight impact as it bounces across the cushion next to me, and curse.

"Should I go help?" Gretchen clutches my arm so tight her fingernails feel like they're drawing blood. It's easy to tell even amid the chaos that her fever hasn't gone down at all.

"No, stay here. She sounds crazy. Wait until we have light." I feel frantically across the cushion for the battery.

Henri releases a long moan followed by the unmistakable sound of a person collapsing to the ground. My stomach clenches in fear.

"Henri!" I yell as my fingers close around the battery.

"No. NO!" Liv screams, and I hear running footsteps.

My body's basic instincts seem to shut down. My heart is unwilling to beat, my lungs unwilling to breathe, until I know he's okay. I screw the flashlight top on, flip the switch, and am blinded by the beam of light. I point it in Henri's direction.

He's slumped down in front of the bar. When the light shines in his eyes, he flinches and my body starts functioning again. Half of our chair barrier is gone. Some are knocked over while others have been shoved aside. Scrambling across the room toward Henri, I'm careful not to trip over any of them. I fall to my knees on one side of him, Gretchen on the other.

"What happened? Did she tackle you?" Gretchen asks, checking his head for signs of injury.

"No. She got me too quick. I never even touched her." Henri moans and his voice sounds weak. "She was swinging a knife. I couldn't get hold of her. I couldn't see."

"What do you mean she got you?" I ask, followed immediately by, "What knife?"

He winces in pain. Blood wells from cuts on his left palm and forearm. "She must've taken one from the bar."

Gretchen growls under her breath. "She's totally lost it."

"She g–got me." The moment his horrified eyes meet mine, I know we missed something. I look down and see the dark, wet spot spreading across his gray shirt. Dark red blood drips down the fingers of the hand he has pressed tight against his stomach.

And my flashlight flickers.

Chapter 20

(For use in criminal case #41773)

112 Operator:

Please state the exact nature of your emergency.

Eva Moreau:

I need to talk to Inspecteur Bernard. I already called his desk and he's not there right now.

112 Operator:

Is this an emergency? If not, then I suggest you—

Eva Moreau:

Oh, it is. I think I know where his missing teens might be.

112 Operator:

[pause] Please hold while I get him on the line. [long pause]

112 Operator:

I'm transferring you now.

Inspecteur Bernard:

This is Bernard.

Eva Moreau:

This is Eva Moreau. I think [pause] a friend might have received a message from that Catacombs group you've been looking for.

Inspecteur Bernard:

How did they send a message—Never mind, it doesn't matter.

Can you tell me where they are?

Eva Moreau:

I know exactly where they are, but I can do better. I can take you there [pause] if you agree to my terms.

Inspecteur Bernard:

[pause] What terms?

Eva Moreau:

My friend might have some items stored in the place I'm leading you to. If I take you, I need assurances that you'll only get the kids out. You won't touch my friend's belongings.

Inspecteur Bernard:

[pause] Are we talking about drugs or weapons of any kind? Stolen goods? Anything like that?

Eva Moreau:

No, only personal property that was stored somewhere it's not supposed to be.

Inspecteur Bernard:

Then, I agree to your terms. My first priority is saving these kids. When and where can my team meet you?

■ ■ ■

"Oh my God, Henri." I squeeze his free hand, wishing he would tell me that he's going to be okay. His eyes are closed now. A stab wound to the stomach—people survive that sort of thing in the movies all the time, right? He'll be okay. He has to be.

Gretchen picks the flashlight up from where I dropped it. She backs up against the bar and shines the light around frantically. "Where did she go? Where's Liv?"

Henri's eyes flutter open again and the tight clamp on my chest eases slightly. I start to pull off my jacket, but his weak voice stops me. "Don't. You need that."

I shake my head fiercely. "Not as much as you do right now." I make a dash for Gretchen's bag and grab her workout T-shirt. Scrambling back to Henri's side, I move his hand out of the way. The blood flows faster and dread courses through me when I see the growing puddle beneath his right side. I look away. The blood makes me think of Paolo and James and Maud, and I don't want to picture Henri joining them. When I press the shirt tight against his wound, Henri groans.

"Sorry. Hold that for a second." I pass my jacket around him and tie it tight, securing the shirt in place. It's soaking through already, but it's better than nothing. I just hope it's enough. Henri's jaw is clenched and his face is losing even more color.

"There. You're going to be fine now, okay?" I whisper, kissing his forehead. I say it at least as much for me as for him.

He grabs my hand and his eyes are barely able to focus on my face. I go cold as a Chicago winter, inside and out. "You need to g–get out of here."

A small choking laugh escapes me. "We're *not* leaving you."

His eyes close again, and I have to lean even closer to hear his words. "Someone n–needs to get out. Tell my parents—tell them I love them and I'm sorry."

"You'll tell them, Henri." I kiss his forehead again. His skin is even colder than mine. "You owe me a date, remember? Will this one be the third or fourth? I can't keep up with your Canadian customs."

"I'm glad—" He coughs, and when I see blood at the corner of his mouth I can't hold back my tears anymore. "I'm glad you were my last date, Harley—my best d–date."

"Not your last date. You've made too many promises about your music to back out on me now." I force a smile over my terror and he smiles back, but he doesn't answer. "*Promise me.*"

"I promise." Henri sighs, closing his eyes, and I grip his wrist tightly in both hands. I feel his pulse beneath my fingers, but it's weaker now and the pool of his blood still grows.

"Henri?" I whisper his name. No response. I cling tighter to his wrist. Feeling his heartbeat reassures me that I haven't lost him yet, that I can still save him somehow. Gretchen sits frozen on the other side of him, her hand pressed tight over her mouth. I find myself counting his heartbeats, the way he taught me to do with Maud. I sit by his side, holding his hand and counting. Counting and ignoring the way his skin beneath my fingers is growing colder, counting the moments of light and life we have left, counting because it's the only thing keeping me from losing my sanity completely.

Until his pulse fades to nothing.

No ... please, no.

I shift and tighten my grip. I think a feel a flutter, but then nothing. I check for a pulse at his throat.

Nothing.

Am I doing it wrong? I never did this before yesterday. I check on both sides of his neck with no luck. I shift into survival mode, doing exactly as he taught me. Drawing in deep breaths and focusing on the motions, I place my hands on his chest and start compressions, the throbbing pain in my sprained wrist helping me keep the rhythm.

Pump, pump, pump—

Memories flood my mind as I move. Memories of watching Henri doing the exact same thing to Maud. I feel dizzy.

How could Henri die now? After all of this? I won't let him. I can't. I wouldn't have made it through the last few days without him. None of us would have.

He's the reason I'm still alive. He's the reason I'm still sane—mostly.

I bend over, tilting his head back and blowing into his mouth. I remember his lips on mine, his arms around me. Only a few hours ago he was so alive. My tears fall on his face as I breathe for him, then I go back to compressions.

I keep going, relying on the rhythm of the movements to keep my heart beating—to keep it from having to feel anything else.

Gretchen's hand is shockingly hot when it closes over my arm. "Harley, stop."

I look over at her, blinking in confusion. I forgot everything but the motions for a moment. Her fingers are pressed against Henri's throat and she's crying. He's gone. We both know he's gone and there isn't one damn thing we can do to save him. The pain of losing him threatens to crush me. I only knew him for a few days, but he was *everything* for those days. He was hope, humor, and life. Only Gretchen keeps me from crumbling now. She still needs me, and that's all that keeps me from giving up.

"Please, I'm so scared," she whispers. She's still got her back pressed against the bar and is keeping her eyes on the room around us. Watching for danger as I fight a losing battle.

Watching for Liv.

Liv killed Henri. She must've killed all of them.

Gretchen drops her fingers from Henri's throat, picks something up off the ground, and moves around to my other side. I see what's in her hand. It's a rusty knife dripping with blood. I feel sick. "Where did you get that?"

"It was on the g–ground next to him." The flashlight flickers again. I hear Gretchen suck in a breath, holding it until the light stabilizes.

I swallow back the wave of nausea and reach for the knife. Gretchen presses the handle into my hand and I grip it tight.

"She's *not* going to hurt anyone else," I whisper through clenched teeth.

Gretchen's eyes widen, but she doesn't say anything. I hear Liv whimper in the shadows, and everything in me wants to hurt her—to make sure she will *never* hurt anyone else again.

"Go behind the bar and get all the knives out of the box of silverware," I say, fighting to keep fear and panic from my voice even as they rampage through my body. "There were probably five or six in there before."

With a shaky nod, Gretchen stands and moves around the bar, leaving me in darkness with Henri's body. Holding the knife out in front of me with my trembling right hand, I watch the shadows and wait.

I hear the scratch of metal bumping against metal and know Gretchen is digging through the silverware box. Then the alarm in her voice when she says, "They're all gone, Harley. Liv took them all."

My heart plummets to my feet. When the flashlight flickers again, Gretchen scrambles back around the bar to me. She sits beside me and shakes her head. "How could she do this? What is she thinking?"

"If she's capable of doing all this, I'm not sure she was ever who we thought she was."

A table crashes to the ground in front of us. Gretchen whips the flashlight toward the sound, but we can't see anyone there. A soft sobbing comes from the shadows, and when Gretchen shines the beam toward it, I see Liv crouching near the projector.

"This—place—is—hell," Liv shouts savagely in between sobs.

"Why did you attack Henri, Liv?" Anger bubbles up inside me and my hands clench tighter. She didn't just attack him. She *murdered* him. But thinking about it hurts so much that I can't bring myself to say it yet. She killed James, and Paolo, and Maud. Why should she get out of here alive when four of her friends won't?

"We're in the Catacombs, the land of the dead. I'm not dead. *I don't belong here!*" She screams the last part, and Gretchen presses closer against my side.

"Stop, Liv," Gretchen yells. "Please, don't hurt anyone else."

Liv's eerie laugh echoes through the cave, followed immediately by soft crying. "This isn't me."

The light flickers and Gretchen shakes it. When it steadies, Liv isn't behind the projector anymore. "Stupid flashlight. Do we have any others that would fit these batteries?"

"No." I squint into the darkness, clutching the bloody knife in my shaking hand as I search for Liv.

"Well, I guess if it goes out, I can always use the flashlight as a weapon." She gives me a grim smile and swings it through the air like a club. Then she stops, raising her fingers to her temple. She looks a bit unsteady. "Whoa." She lowers the flashlight to her lap and leans back against the bar, her eyes closed tight.

"Gretchen?" My sheer panic must be obvious in my voice because she opens her eyes immediately.

"Sorry. I'm dizzy." She leaves the flashlight on her lap and presses both hands against her forehead. "I really don't feel well."

Gretchen closes her eyes again and my heart tightens. "You stay with me. I *can't do this by myself.*"

She opens her eyes again, but they're a little glassy. "I'm not leaving, but I'm so tired."

"Close your eyes and lean on my shoulder," I whisper. Resting might actually help her get better.

She isn't hurt like Henri. This is different.

"No, I'm helping you." Gretchen forces her eyes open and shines the flashlight beam across the room, looking for Liv. We hear movement in the darkness here and there, but when she shines the beam toward it, we see nothing. I take the flashlight from her, and this time she doesn't object. Her hand falls limply to her lap and she closes her eyes.

"What do we do now?" Gretchen asks as a shiver runs through her.

My heart aches and I bite my lip to stop myself from dissolving into a puddle of tears. I want to have the answers, but I don't. I'm terrified and I'm not sure how much longer I can keep this up. "I don't know. Our best bet for now is to stay here and hope your message got through."

I watch the cave around us in a daze of paranoia, trying to ignore the moving shadows and dripping blood that's starting to haunt the edges of my vision again.

I will not end up like Liv. *I won't.*

Gretchen scoots closer against me and I gasp. It's worse than I thought. She's actually radiating heat, her whole body constantly shivering. "Gretchen—"

She cuts me off, her voice sounding sleepy. "You've changed."

"What do you mean?"

"You're stronger than you used to be. Remember when we used to have sleepovers and you would wake me up when you had to go to the bathroom? You were afraid of everything back then."

I chuckle uncomfortably as I scan the flashlight beam across the room again. "Sometimes I still am."

"No, you're stronger now." Gretchen tilts her head to look up at me. "You control your fear."

I have serious doubts about that, but maybe she sees me clearer than I see myself.

"You aren't coughing or anything." I lean my head against hers, worry pushing away everything else. She shivers so violently it shakes my body. "Do you still think it's just a cold?"

She doesn't answer right away, and that tells me everything I need to know.

When she finally answers, she sounds reluctant. "I have a stomachache. Everything's cramping up and it really hurts."

"How long have you had it? Do you think it could be from the water? Or maybe the food is older than we thought?" I think about the Twinkie I ate. It was a little dry, but other than that it didn't seem too bad.

"It started after I got the fever, so before the food but after the water. Maybe a stomach flu or something." Gretchen changes the subject, her voice soft and vulnerable. "I always thought we would be college roommates."

A surprised laugh escapes me. "You did?"

"Yeah, and date twins." Her words are slurring now. "You were my sister."

It's been so long since I thought about how things were between us back then, but she's right. That's exactly how we grew up, like sisters. And I let her down. But I will never do that again. "I'm still your sister."

The silence gets heavier the longer she takes to answer me.

"Gretchen?" I whisper. She doesn't respond, but her body still shivers every few seconds. She must've passed out—never a good sign. Gretchen needs medicine. She needs help.

I consider our options again. We can't stay here forever, but Gretchen can't go anywhere right now. And there's no way I can leave her with someone hunting us in the darkness. I can't even make myself really consider leaving Henri here, not now, not yet. At least in the theater we have boxes and boxes of food on the bar above us. Here we have water . . . *water*.

I aim Gretchen's flashlight over at the couch cushions. It's halfway across the room from us, but I can see that our backpacks are still where we left them. Hopefully, they still hold all of our refilled water bottles. Even if the water is what made Gretchen sick, it didn't hurt the rest of us, and being sick still isn't worse than dying of dehydration. I glance down at Gretchen before shifting her back against the bar and slipping away.

Gripping the knife tight in one hand and the flashlight in the other, I inch my way slowly across the room. My shaky breath seems impossibly loud. Each footstep crunches on the ground and then echoes. More than once, I consider going back and cowering next to Gretchen, but I know I can't.

Our only chance to survive here is if *we* have the water.

As I reach the cushions, a chair gets knocked over to my right and I swing the flashlight beam in that direction. Liv races toward me faster than I knew she could move. She barrels across the room with a snarl on her face and a wild look in her eyes.

"Liv, stop!" I shout. Her momentum propels us both backward onto the cushions. The knife flies out of my hand and the wind gets knocked from my lungs. My head slams back into the cushions hard enough that I see stars. Adrenaline courses through my body, but I can't lift my head right away. I can't make my eyes focus. I can't imagine the damage that tackle would've done if the cushions weren't here. It definitely would've knocked me out, maybe worse.

Liv kicks me in the abdomen as she scrambles over me toward the backpacks. Pain explodes in my side and I curl up out of instinct. As soon as I realize that she's after the same thing I am, I wrap my arms around her foot and she falls on her stomach before she can reach the bags.

Shifting my position, I pin her legs down with my body, crawling over her. I swing the flashlight at her head, but she slams her elbow into my forearm. Numbing vibrations shoot up my arm and I lose my grip. The flashlight falls onto the cushion beside us, shining back toward the bar where Gretchen and Henri slump, looking more like ragdolls than people. Rage floods my veins. The sparkling rhinestones on Liv's camera catch my eye only a couple feet away and I climb off Liv to grab it.

Liv gets on her knees and swings her arms wildly, knocking me in the side of the head and scratching up my arm. I bring my hands up to defend myself and drive my shoulder into her stomach.

She claws at my back, but I pull away enough to free my arm and swing the camera with all my might. It connects hard with her head. She collapses instantly, and I think of Henri and hit her once more before I can stop myself. I kneel there in the sudden silence, trying to catch my breath.

I look down at Liv, lowering my quaking arms, but still terrified she'll open her eyes and attack me again. She's unconscious and there's a big gash above her left temple. Blood flows freely into her hair.

My eyes go to the camera in my hand. I gasp when I see how badly it's been damaged. The lens is shattered and one whole side of the camera is smashed. Did I really hit her that hard? Liv's blood drips from it. Red drops seep behind the rhinestones, discoloring them. I drop the camera in horror, suddenly desperate to get it away from me. It falls onto the cushions beside Liv.

I pick up the flashlight, and it flickers one final time before going out. I swallow hard, hitting it several times against my palm, but nothing happens. The old glow stick had long since gone out. Reaching into Liv's pocket, I dig out her remaining glow stick and break it. The tiny pool of light it provides is truly pathetic. I kneel in the smothering darkness, shoving back a wave of nausea as I realize that Liv's unconscious and bleeding body might be one of the last things I ever see.

As much as I don't want to touch the bloody camera again, I know it's the only real light I have access to right now. I draw in a slow, deep breath and reassure myself that Liv is still unconscious, that she can't hurt me anymore, that I don't have to be afraid. It takes a minute to find the power button. The viewfinder lights up and I open the fold-out screen, hoping to find the button to turn on the camera's spotlight. Instead, the camera starts playing back a video.

Even though the screen is dark at first, I can hear the sound. My whole body locks up in horror. I don't want to see this again, but I can't make it stop.

It's the last video Liv recorded—a video of the attack on Henri.

Chapter 21

Case Update Addendum to Missing Persons Reports

Filed June 12th at 13:29 at Paris Central Police Dept.

(For use in criminal case #41773)

Investigation Regarding Missing Persons –

Gretchen Eleanor Dubois and Harley Bryn Martin

Update current as of June 14th at 17:32. Notable progress and new leads are as follows:

LEAD: Further information provided by M. Anders Koskela regarding their supplies has lead us to believe that our window for rescuing the remaining members of this group alive may be closing.

ACTION TAKEN: Additional units have been requested to join the search team. This will allow us to cover more ground quicker and safer and hopefully return a positive result.

LEAD: Emergency call received from Mme. Eva Moreau with information on possible whereabouts of missing tour group.

ACTION TAKEN: Search team will meet Mme. Moreau and some cataphiles at the left bank entrance to the Catacombs at 18:00. They will lead us to the area where they believe we may be able to locate the group.

Please direct any additional leads or new information to:
Inspecteur Bernard at the Paris Central Police Department

■ ■ ■

I stare at the tiny screen, immediately gripped by what I saw there. I hear our voices repeating the things we said only minutes ago: Liv panicking, the rest of us trying to reassure her. It's all the same, but it feels different from her point of view. When she cracks the glow stick and tosses it into the middle of the room, I start to realize just how different.

The screen flashes green and a thin line of text appears in the bottom left corner reading *Night Vision*. The glow stick wasn't enough to illuminate much more than a tiny area, but with the camera's settings amplifying that light, much more of the cave is visible on the small screen.

Liv isn't stupid . . . but that just might make her even more dangerous.

I watch the distant forms of Gretchen and myself hunting through backpacks as Henri starts moving toward Liv. My heart aches and my muscles tense. I want to stop him, but I can't. I don't want to watch, but I know I need to see it. I need to know exactly what happened.

He's making his way toward her slowly, mostly by feel, trying to reassure her. "Everything is okay."

"No! It's not! We're all going to die!" she yells, and suddenly everything she said takes on an entirely different meaning.

I see a large figure moving behind a table to Henri's right and suddenly I can't breathe. It appears to be limping, but Liv can't seem to keep it in frame. I hear her breathing speed up as she pans around trying desperately to get a better look.

"It's not real. It's not real," Liv whispers, and the image wobbles as she stumbles backward trying to get a better view. The figure is still there, but it's moving closer to the ground now, on the other side of the tables, and getting a clear shot is nearly impossible.

Liv screams. She's yelling about how we're all going to die, and I want to scream right back at her for not just telling us about the figure moving toward Henri. Her hand comes into view as she reaches for Henri. It's like she wishes she could just grab him and move him to safety. Henri is still walking toward her, getting closer and closer to the figure behind the tables. My heart goes into my throat as Liv's hand drops out of frame.

"Stop! Everyone just stop!" Her voice is pleading, desperate.

The figure stands up from behind the table, limping forward. He's taller than Henri and his back is to the camera, but I see the knife in his hand. My fingers grip the camera tighter and I shake my head, but I can't drag my eyes from the screen.

Liv screams, "No!"

"Liv?" Henri freezes in place, which might be the worst possible thing he can do.

The man slashes at him and Henri backs away, tripping and falling down. Liv takes a halting step forward and stumbles. The man turns to face her, and my heart feels like it just stops, leaving a sucking black hole in my chest that rips my breath away once more.

It's Monsieur Lambert.

The right side of his head is gashed open, swollen, misshapen, and bloody. He has his high-tech goggles on and

I realize they must be like Liv's camera—night vision. Liv backs up with a horrified gasp until she runs into something and stops with a jolt. The frame fills with static and cuts in and out. It clears up just enough for me to see M. Lambert lift his finger to his lips and smile before turning to Henri again.

"No. No. No." Liv whispers and then there are several low thuds and the image shakes. I realize Liv is hitting herself in the head with her camera. "He's dead. Lambert is dead."

I hear myself calling out Henri's name, and then his voice rings out. "Stop. Stop! What are you doing?"

Liv focuses the camera back on him. M. Lambert is slashing at him again and again, backing Henri up toward the bar. She moves toward them.

"It's not real! Stop! No!" Her words come out between terrified sobs. "*We'll* stop. We shouldn't have lived."

The image continues to cut in and out, but I can still make out enough to know that Henri is now backed up against the bar with his hands out in front of him. Liv breaks into a run. M. Lambert turns and looks straight at her. For just a moment, the image clears just as he turns and stabs Henri in the stomach.

Liv skids to an abrupt stop. "No."

Monsieur Lambert rounds on her. The image spins as Liv sprints away, yelling, "NO!"

The recording ends and a single battery warning flashes in red across the screen, and then it's gone and the camera dies. The glow stick has faded to a thin line of dying light. I drop it on the cushion beside Liv. I need to slow my racing heart, try to process what I just saw.

I'm afraid to trust anything strange that I see anymore, but can you hallucinate a video recording? That all had to be real, right? Or was it? The way the image flickered ... my mind goes back to all of Paolo's spooky ghost stories and I shudder.

No.

I have to hold on to reality. I have to be brave and deal with what I have in front of me. Starting with the most important question: what do I feel sure of?

Liv didn't kill Henri.

According to what I just saw, she didn't kill any of them, M. Lambert did. He survived the cave-in. I don't know how, because his head was smashed, but somehow he's still alive. Apparently taking someone's pulse on their foot is even more unreliable than we thought. M. Lambert has been stalking us this whole time with his night vision goggles and picking us off, one by one.

And now I'm the only one left standing for him to hunt in the dark.

Dread sweeps through me and I reach out with a trembling hand, feeling around until I wrap my fingers around the knife handle. I consider breaking one of the remaining glow sticks, but after watching that video I know that will help him far more than it will help me. The night vision shouldn't work without at least a little light. For right now, he should be as blind as me. I listen, but the only thing I can hear is my own ridiculously loud body—my racing pulse, each gasping breath. My first thought is of Gretchen. How can I protect her from this monster in the dark?

Now that I'm on my own, all my nightmares come to life. The darkness churns with movement and patches of light that I know can't be real. They aren't in front of me, always flashing at the edges of my vision. My body tingles with fear no matter how hard I fight to stay calm. I hear faint voices, whispers, words, but then they're gone and I don't know what they said. Footsteps come from my right, then my left. I whip back and forth, holding the knife out before me. I try to face the direction of the sounds, but I can't tell if they're real or not.

My breathing is too loud, but I can't make it slow down or be quiet. When I hold my breath, my head spins and I know I'll pass out if I keep that up. I count, slowly and deliberately, like Henri taught me. It helps me focus, and my lungs slow down with it, but then my skin rebels. My nerves tingle and I feel things crawling on me. I jerk around to brush the creeping things off, but nothing's there.

A voice deep inside me tells me I have to get control of myself or any chance for Gretchen to survive is gone. Liv, too. Liv, who isn't guilty, but is now unconscious and completely vulnerable because of me.

Someway, somehow . . . I *have* to protect them both.

This thought douses my panic like water on fire. I distract myself with music. Beautiful buildings always remind me of songs, the way each individual piece builds on others to create something amazing and unique. One more thing that I wish I had time to share with Henri. I picture my favorite buildings, using songs to put me back there. Gretchen said that I can control my fear. She thinks I'm braver than I used to be.

This is my chance to prove that she's right.

"I know it's you, Monsieur L–Lambert." I stumble over the words, but they're clear enough that I know he understands me. "*Please*, stop this."

Footsteps approach from ahead and I gasp, holding out my knife. I'm not certain if they're real this time, but I want to be prepared in case they are.

I hear the slight whistle of something cutting through the air and my left arm burns with pain. I jerk back with a scream. The cut isn't deep, but it stings. Hot blood drips down my arm. M. Lambert took all the knives. I have the one he used to kill Henri, but he has the rest. I thrust my knife out toward where I think he is and I hit something, but I can't tell what.

Footsteps stumble backward.

"Leave. Us. Alone," I growl as fiercely as I can manage.

I remember the goggles he was wearing in the video and pick up the nearly spent glow stick, tossing it as far across the room as I can. It was stupid of me to forget about it. Even that pathetically feeble light could be enough for his night vision to work.

My pulse pounds so loudly in my ears that I can't hear, and that's the only one of my senses that can help me right now. I can't protect Gretchen and Liv like this. I can't move them together without exposing myself, and them, even more. My only choice is to keep M. Lambert's focus on me. I'm the only one who has *any* chance against him now. But how can I hope to stay alive like this? How can I even out this playing field? What can I do to survive against someone so hell-bent on killing us all?

He can see in the dark, for God's sake.

And then the answer is as obvious as it was when the first flashlight went out: light. I need light—a lot of it. It's the only thing that can help me in a world soaked in darkness.

And right now, it's worth the risk.

Another quick movement in the dark and I feel a burning sensation on my forehead. I flinch back, and warm blood drips toward my eyes. I close them. Sight can't help me yet anyway.

"Monsieur Lambert, please, *please* stop!" I beg, but again no response. I wonder if the cave-in broke his jaw or something. Maybe he *can't* answer me.

I listen closer for any sound or movement. I hear the slight crunch of pebbles against stone to my left, not a footstep, but maybe a shifting of weight. I duck my head to protect it and slash wildly toward the sound. It feels like I hit something more solidly this time. Footsteps stagger back. Then I move.

My heart jolts into my throat as I scramble on all fours toward the edge of the cushions. I grip my knife tight as I move, trying to picture the room in my head the best I can.

The stone floor is shockingly cold and rough against my hands as I feel my way across it to the cave wall. I manage to avoid running into anything. Staying low as I'm winding my way around the tables and chairs also gives me a bit of cover. I find the wiring tube and follow it along the base of the wall until it curves up to the junction box. The limping footsteps aren't far behind me, but I think I have time. My plan is working for now, as terrifying as it is. He isn't going after Liv or Gretchen. I rub the blood out of my eyes.

Grabbing the nearest chair I can find, I pull it in front of the junction box.

"Please, please . . ." I whisper to myself as I climb on the chair. My fingers fumble over the box as I search for my phone. Once I've got it, I hit the home button. The screen lights up.

"Thank God." Hoping that this works the way it does back home, I flip every fuse in the junction box to the off position. I hesitate for an instant before disconnecting the wires Gretchen hooked up to my phone. If they didn't get her message by now, I guess they aren't going to.

M. Lambert's getting closer. Jumping back down, I hold the phone screen up for what little bit of light it can give me and slash at him with the knife. He's still a few feet away and eerily silent as he recoils. The room around us turns a creepy monochrome in my meager light. Goose bumps blanket my arms and I shiver. I didn't hit him this time, but he doesn't come any closer. I skirt around the tables, grabbing every chair I can and knocking them over in M. Lambert's path. My heart pounds and my lungs burn, but I ignore them. Every second that I keep his attention is another second that Gretchen and Liv stay alive. I grab the rolling cart with the projector and move it over against the wall.

An echoing growl comes from halfway across the room and I hear a chair slide across the floor. Crouching down next to the wall, I look at my phone. The battery is at two percent. A whimper slips from my lips, but I refuse to think about it going out on me. I can't afford to right now. I don't have time.

I pick up the rusted outlet and brush the loose wires roughly against my jeans. Shining the meager light of the phone screen into the end of the gray wiring tube, I pull out the electrical wires. The wooden knife handle digs slivers into my hand, but I grip it tighter and release a breath as I rip the blade through the rubber protecting the wires. No spark, so either the fuse box works or the lines are dead . . . I push the thought away. Dropping the blade, I pull the wires apart. It's hard to tell what color they are. Air gushes out of my lungs. I can't get this wrong. The rubber on one wire definitely looks lighter than the other, so I cross my fingers it's the neutral. I connect it to the left, connecting the darker wire to the right. Then I plug in the projector.

By the time I'm back on my feet. M. Lambert is almost on me.

"No!" I whip the phone around and hit the flashlight button, getting the most bang for my remaining battery life. I shine the bright light straight into M. Lambert's night vision goggles. He makes an enraged shrieking sound, stumbling back. I clamber toward the projector, catching one clear glimpse of it before my phone beeps and turns off.

Everything is silent in the darkness until I hear M. Lambert release a low, wheezing laugh. I turn in the direction of the noise and hurl the phone as hard as I can. There's a disappointingly small thud before it hits the floor. I feel around for the red button I saw on the projector and press it. Almost there. Now I just need to get back to the fuses.

I keep my hands on the wall for guidance and hurry to the junction box. I stub my toe hard against a rock and pain shoots through my foot, but I don't even miss a step. M. Lambert comes after me faster, and he isn't even trying to be quiet anymore. The sound of him limping toward me creates a horrible rhythm.

Step-drag, step-drag, step-drag.

I almost trip over the chair below the junction box. Cold sweat beads on my back as I climb up on it and start flipping all the switches. Hoping I wired it right. Hoping it all still works. Hoping it can help me survive at least a few more minutes.

First switch—nothing.

Step-drag.

Second switch—nothing. I bite my lip, almost more afraid to flip more switches and find that all my effort was for nothing than to sit still in the deadly darkness. Almost.

Step-drag.

Third switch—a whirring noise starts and my heart soars. The cavern is bathed in gray light from the projector. It's more light than I've seen in days. M. Lambert shrieks again and rips the goggles off his face, cowering down to cover his eyes. I flinch, falling back against the wall and tumbling off the chair. My elbow throbs, but panic pushes me back onto my feet. Using my sleeve, I wipe more blood out of my eyes and off my forehead. My eyes adjust relatively quickly, but M. Lambert is having more trouble.

Stars flash across my vision. I grit my teeth, drawing out all the strength I have left. Then I take off. Darting past M. Lambert, I grab the goggles in his hand and yank as hard as I can. The strap snaps and I've got them. I bolt toward the nearest couch and duck down behind it, fighting to catch my breath.

I have no idea what to do now. I never thought I'd get this far.

I never thought past this moment.

Never.

Clutching the goggles to my chest, I try to figure out what to do next. The projector shines the opening credits of a movie onto the stone wall above me in black and white. It's like I'm in the haunted remains of an old theater in hell. When the title card comes up, I cringe. *The City of the Dead.* Someone has a seriously sick sense of humor.

Step-drag.

M. Lambert is on the move again. I need a plan. I have the tiniest advantage now and I can't afford to waste it. I have to figure something out for Gretchen and Liv, for Henri, for me.

Then I remember Henri's map and I know what to do. I pop up as soon as M. Lambert gets close and he startles, wildly swinging his knife at me. He obviously had no idea I was here. I head straight for the tunnel in the corner and he follows behind me. I glance toward Gretchen, slowing as I pass, but there's no time to check on her. M. Lambert slashes at my back and I speed up again. We don't get far into the tunnel before the blackness swallows us and pure darkness returns.

But this time I have his goggles.

I take one of my glow sticks out of my pocket, break it, and drop it in the tunnel halfway through. I take the next and get ready to drop it after I get to the fork in the path and head left. Pressing the goggles to my face, I slow down. Even with the meager light from the glow sticks I can see the tunnel well enough that I could make my way silently without any problem, but I don't. As I walk, I pull my thin leather belt free from my jeans. Then I stumble and shuffle, making noise any time M. Lambert's *step-drag* falters.

"You win, okay? Please, I'm scared and I'm sorry," I whimper. I don't have to fake the fear in my voice.

As soon as I know M. Lambert has made the turn after me, I hurry to the end. Through the goggles, the unstable tunnel looks even worse than I remember. I feel like I'm on a tightrope for the last few feet. I move carefully, not daring to touch either wall as I edge my way around the rotted support beam. I don't even dare breathe on it.

As soon as I'm back to the theater, I turn the projector off. The room plunges into darkness again, but now the advantage is mine. Using the goggles, I look back into the unstable tunnel. M. Lambert is halfway in, but he isn't moving. He's holding completely still. Turning off the projector must have made him suspicious.

I crawl into the tunnel on my stomach and encircle the wooden beam with my belt. I cinch it as tight as I can without actually letting the belt touch the beam.

M. Lambert hears me and turns toward me. His smashed face looks like a nightmare through the goggles, but I don't dare turn away.

"Please. I fell. Don't hurt me," I whisper into the darkness. "I wasn't the one who hurt you. You saw. I tried to stop them."

The normal half of his face twists into a sneer and he takes one step forward, then another. I don't think he cares about guilt or innocence. He plans to kill me either way. I think of the three skeletal bodies we found on the way here and wonder if he's the one who put them there. Could he have been planning to kill us all along? Smashing his head obviously messed up more than just his face, but maybe he was already a murderer before that. Maybe we were dead the moment we hired him as our guide.

I shake the thoughts away. It doesn't matter right now. The only thing that matters is this: only one of us is getting out of this alive.

Every muscle in my body tenses. If I can't get out of the way quick enough, I may end up killing myself. I don't want to do this. I'd much rather he give up and go away. But if it will keep Gretchen and Liv safe from this monster then I'll do whatever it takes.

M. Lambert is close to the edge of the most unstable area when he stops.

"Please, stop this," I whimper, and I mean it. I'm freezing and on fire and oh so nauseous. *Please, just stop.* I *do not* want to be a killer.

But he comes forward again, more confident now. My weakness only makes him bolder. A strange stillness settles over me and I know what I have to do. He takes another step, and I get to my feet, my trembling hand gripping the belt. At his next step, I drop the goggles and grab the belt with both hands, pulling as hard as I can. At first, the wooden beam doesn't budge, only making a strained creaking noise. I swallow back the nausea and pull again. This time, the wood cracks and then splinters and I release the belt, scrambling backward. I hear M. Lambert's terrible scream as the tunnel crashes in on him. I'm left coughing in a cloud of dust, his scream echoing around me, on and on forever.

Chapter 22

■ ■ ■

I don't know how long I sit alone in the darkness. M. Lambert's scream goes on and on. I hear it long after I'm sure it must've stopped. I want to turn the projector back on for light, but I don't dare. What if M. Lambert isn't dead, just like last time? I haven't heard a sound from Gretchen or Liv but I keep thinking I hear the scrape of his foot dragging across the floor on one side of the room and then the other. If I turn on the light and he comes back after us again, they'll be exposed, defenseless. I'm the only one who can fight back. I crawl along the wall to the projector and feel around until I find the knife I dropped. When I hear distant voices again, I press my hands over my ears and cry.

But this time they don't go away.

The world behind my closed eyelids turns red and I jerk back in confusion.

"*Ils sont ici!*" I hear a female voice and my eyes snap open. Crusted blood coats the right side of my face and it makes it hard to open that eye, but I don't care. I see outlines of people—a lot of people, rushing toward me. This can't be real. Where did they all come from? Were they real? I cower, ducking my head behind my left arm and holding my rusty blade out to ward them away.

The people speak to each other and gesture at me. They're speaking French. A man and woman approach me slowly and the man speaks in English. "You are Harley? I'm Inspecteur Bernard from the Paris Police Department. This is Eva. She got your message. I need you to put down the knife. None of us will hurt you."

"He was trying to kill me," I whimper, my voice raw and frail.

Inspecteur Bernard crouches down until his eyes are level with mine. "You're safe now, Harley. Put down the knife."

My arms fall limp to my sides. I refuse to blink. I'm too afraid they will all disappear. I'm still not convinced that this is real and not some new cruel hallucination.

And if it isn't real, I'll still embrace it. Maybe I can die happy believing it's real. I prefer a joyful illusion to the reality of my last few days down here.

Inspecteur Bernard pulls the knife from my numb fingers, handing it to another officer who puts it into a plastic bag. Inspecteur Bernard continues to whisper calming words. "It's okay now. You're safe."

Somehow, I doubt I'll be capable of feeling *safe* again for a very long time, but my safety isn't what matters. "Please. They need help."

I point to the bar where Gretchen sleeps next to Henri's blood-drenched body. Then I point to Liv, still unconscious on the cushions. Inspecteur Bernard shouts to the others in French. I can't make it all out, but I recognize the French words for *medical* and *now* and that's enough to fill me with relief.

"What happened?" he asks me. His question is simple, but the answer is anything but.

"M–monsieur Lambert."

"I was under the impression he was buried in a cave-in. Is that not the case?"

I shake my head, wrapping my arms around myself. I try to think of a way to explain what happened with M. Lambert, but I don't know how many of the things I've seen weren't real.

"Did you use your knife on anyone?" He squints over his shoulder at Henri and Gretchen.

"N–no!" It's almost a shout. "Just to keep M. Lambert away from me."

He nods, flipping open a notepad and jotting something down. "And where is M. Lambert now?"

"He killed them and it . . . and I had to . . ." I gesture back toward the tunnel I collapsed and then my throat closes up and I have to try again.

His eyes widen and he watches me closer now. "He was in there when it came down?"

A nod is the only response I can give. A shudder goes through me from head to toe and the Inspecteur gives me a look of concern.

"That's enough for us to get started. We'll need to have a longer conversation, but that can wait until later at the hospital. For now, Marie will take care of you." He pats my hand and then gets back on his feet, pointing to the cave-in and speaking in French that is too fast for me to even attempt to understand.

Everything from the last few days falls on me like a weight. I just want to sink into the rocky ground as a medic—Marie, I guess—rushes up and puts a blanket around my shoulders and starts examining the cuts on my forehead and arms.

It's too much of everything after so much nothing—too much light, too many people who are too clean, too loud, and too aware. I have to force myself not to pull away and curl into a protective ball.

Someone prepares a stretcher for Gretchen while another woman bends down to check for Henri's pulse. When she frowns, fresh misery washes over me. But then she moves closer, bending down to place a stethoscope on his chest. She says a few words in too-fast French, and Marie rushes to her side, pulling a syringe and a small clear vial from her pack. My hands fly up to my mouth and I lock my heart up against the hope that threatens to burst it. Marie jabs the needle into his arm while the other woman pounds his chest once with her fist. A moment later I hear Henri take a rasping breath. Relief explodes inside me. The cavern walls seem to spin around me as I scramble to his side.

"Henri?" I whisper his name, still afraid to believe, but his eyes flutter open and land on me. A choked-off sob catches in my throat. "You're okay?"

He gives me a weak smile with blue-tinged lips before closing his eyes again. "I k–keep my promises."

I laugh and press my lips to his cheek before Marie gently nudges me out of the way. "We're taking him out first. He's in the worst shape and his heart rhythm is irregular. But it doesn't appear that any vital organs are damaged. He's lucky. The bandage on his stomach slowed the bleeding and saved his life."

I watch them move him onto a stretcher and hurry away.

Every part of me seems to tremble with emotion. If I don't sit I'm going to pass out. Stumbling to the nearest table, I collapse into one of the chairs. My pulse beats hard with one staccato thought.

He's alive!

Gretchen and Henri are both alive. I kept them and Liv safe even after I thought I'd lost Henri. It seems impossible, but I did it.

Before I get too proud of myself, guilt forces me to acknowledge something a little less heroic and a lot closer to the truth: I knocked Liv out and put her at greater risk before eventually keeping her safe, but at least she's not dead.

Shouting comes from behind me. When I turn to look, I see Liv on another stretcher, struggling to sit up. The medics are trying to strap her down.

"Stop! What happened? I don't understand!" she yells as another medic hurries over with a needle in her hand. Liv sees me and her eyes go wide.

I stand and walk unsteadily toward the group. "Stop!"

The medic with the needle freezes, glancing over her shoulder at me. An officer with a worried expression moves to steady me as I weave my way toward Liv. She goes still as the stone walls around us, warily watching me approach. As soon as she stops fighting them, the medics release her.

I start with the thing I need her to hear first. "I'm sorry that I knocked you out." I don't miss it when Inspecteur Bernard flips to a page in his notebook and jots that information down.

Liv frowns, but says nothing.

"I saw your video. I didn't understand before. I thought it was you."

Liv wraps her arms around herself. "I was afraid you were taking all the water."

"Oh." My brain is too exhausted to provide a better response. After all, I *was* trying to take all the water. "I stopped M. Lambert."

"He's not real." She shakes her head and lifts her hand in a fist. One of the medics grabs her wrist, barely preventing her from hitting herself.

The medic with the needle steps closer again, ready to intervene. I reach out a hand and press Liv's fist gently back down. "He won't hurt us anymore."

Liv's eyes fill with tears. "How can you be so sure?" Dread drips from her voice.

When she looks behind me, I spin on instinct, afraid she's right, afraid that he's not gone and never will be.

There is nothing behind me but shadows and darkness at the edge of the room. But that's where M. Lambert lives. In the shadows.

That's where he watches us, *hunts* us—and I'm not sure that feeling will ever be truly gone.

Liv breaks down. She tries to hit herself again, and when the medics restrain her she cries out in agony. I don't get a chance to calm her this time. They slip the needle into her arm, and in seconds she relaxes and then she's out. She looks so peaceful I almost hope they brought along a needle like that for me.

I retake my seat at the table, squinting over at the medics with Gretchen. My eyes keep tearing up in the bright light. There are so many flashlights in the room now, far more than I've become used to. All together, they're even brighter than the light from the projector.

Every second that passes makes me more anxious that Gretchen isn't waking up. I know she's sick, but there are so many people, so much light, and they're making so much noise. I watch as they place an oxygen mask over my cousin's face. The fear of losing her is like a boulder that I've been trying to hold back. I don't have the strength to fight it anymore and it's going to crush me. We've seen so much death, I'm afraid to hope that it's over.

"Harley?" The murmur is so soft that I'm not sure I heard right, but I'm still on my feet instantly. Her head swivels toward me, and when the medics start to roll her away, I see her eyes widen with panic.

I grab her hand and lean over her. She relaxes as soon as I'm close.

"It's okay, Gretchen. They're here to help. They got your message. They're going to take you out of here." I lean over and give her my bravest smile. "We're leaving the Catacombs."

She nods, closing her eyes. Tears wash streaks through the dirt on her cheeks. The medics carry her toward a tunnel behind the bar, and I'm relieved we never left this makeshift theater. It isn't the tunnel Henri and I thought might lead us out. Once again, we would've gone the wrong way.

The weight of everything hits me again. Hands guide me onto a stretcher of my own and I close my eyes. I don't move a muscle as someone places an oxygen mask over my face. I don't flinch as they bandage my forehead and my arms. My body feels like a heavy statue, weighed down by all I've seen, by all we've lost. I don't feel like a person anymore. I'm something else hiding deep inside this beaten and bruised body. I retreat from the light, from the awful truths that it brings. I cower and hide in a far corner of my mind, humming songs to keep me sane in the darkness.

■ ■ ■

"Harley!" Mom and Dad, the sound of their frantic voices, their warm hands on my head, my fingers, my shoulders—these are the only things that pull me back to the world. I blink up at the stars above and feel overheated in the warm summer air. The medics have just brought me out of the Catacombs and into a massive group of people—police, medical crews, reporters, and spectators—crowded along the bank of the Seine. They move my stretcher next to Gretchen's and leave me to get the ambulances ready to transport us. I see two sets of parents crying as they talk with police officers nearby, and I look away. Wondering which of our dead friends they might belong to brings on a fresh agony that threatens to drive me back into my personal darkness.

Not yet. I'm not ready yet.

My parents pull me up to a sitting position and enfold me gently into a jumble of arms. It's like they can't hold on to me tight enough and yet they're terrified they might break me. It's confusingly wonderful. Their tears fall on my head, on my face. Something inside me wishes they could wash away the horror of the Catacombs. But I know there aren't enough tears in the world to accomplish a feat like that.

I can't find any words to speak yet, so I just let them hold me, listening to Gretchen and Chantal next to us.

"I'm so, so sorry, Mom." Gretchen is crying hard, and when Chantal responds, I know she's doing the same.

"Me too, honey. Don't worry. The only thing that matters is that you're okay."

Their words fill me, healing cracks and crevices deep in my soul. I did it. I kept Gretchen safe from M. Lambert. I fought him off for her, and now I have to keep fighting for myself. Mom's face is so worried as she looks at my father. They can both see my battered shell. I can't let myself become only that . . . not after everything I did to stay alive.

In my mind, I see M. Lambert being crushed by the rocks in an endless loop. I have to get away from it before it consumes even more of me. He can't have that power. I won't let him. I force my arms to move, wrapping them around both my parents. It's feeble and my arms feel weak, but it's a start. Tears finally fall down my cheeks as I whisper, "I'm so glad you're both here. I'm so sorry for what I said, Mom."

She cups my face in one hand and kisses my cheek. "Honey, it's okay. Don't even worry about that."

They both hug me tighter. Their relief flows into me. Someday, this might all be behind us. Someday, we might be okay. It isn't today, and it probably won't be for a long time, but I *need* to believe it's possible.

And I know now that I'm strong enough to make it happen.

From the comfort of my parents' arms, I see Anders coming to stand next to Gretchen and Chantal. Gretchen reaches out and slides her hand into his. When he smiles, a pang of bittersweet emotion hits me and I suddenly doubt whether that moment with Henri really happened. Is he really alive or was that just one more impossibly cruel trick of my mind?

I pull free from my parents, suddenly desperate to ask Anders even though I'm afraid of his answer. "Did you see him? Did you see them bring Henri out?"

He nods and his face breaks into a tired smile. "He gave me a message for you."

I blink in surprise. "What?"

"He said to tell you that he'll have his flugelhorn sent to the hospital." Anders looks confused as he adds, "And something about a giant backpack?"

And then I'm laughing through my tears.

Gretchen rolls her eyes. "He doesn't even own a flugelhorn, does he?"

Anders chuckles and shrugs. "Who knows?"

"He can probably play anything he touches." I smile softly, thinking of all the instruments he talked about.

"I'm really glad you're all okay." Anders holds Gretchen's hand in both of his and gives me a look so full of gratitude I instantly want to make him stop.

"You too." I answer as I flush with guilt. I hesitate before adding, "I'm really sorry for agreeing with the others. I was scared and we—"

"No need to say anything more. I understand." He waves my apology away and helps Gretchen as she struggles to sit up. He kisses her lightly on the cheek and almost looks shy as he turns away. "I'm going to see if Inspecteur Bernard has any other questions for me."

"Tell him to get Liv's camera. It should explain a lot," I say, and he nods.

Marie pops her head out of the nearest ambulance. "We're almost set up. Just a couple more minutes and we'll load you into the ambulances."

"Thank you," I say, and she disappears again.

I lean over to Gretchen and pull her into the tightest hug I can manage. The only thing that keeps me from accidentally pulling down her IV bag is Chantal moving quickly enough to grab it. I don't know what's in it, but her fever already seems a little better.

"I'm so relieved that you're okay," I whisper, my tears making her hair wet.

"I'm so sorry this all happened. I heard the Inspecteur talking . . ." Gretchen pulls back to look at me with wide, haunted eyes and her whole body is rigid. "M. Lambert was alive?"

I nod, pressing my lips together and looking away. I don't want to talk about everything that happened—not yet.

"Why didn't you run or something when I passed out? I'm sorry you had to face him alone, Harley. That must have been—" She stops because there isn't a word to describe it, and I'm glad she doesn't try.

I hug her tight, my tears mingling with hers as I tell her the only thing she needs to know. "I would never leave you down there. Besides, you *did* help me. The only reason I even tried to face him was to save you. I had to prove you were right about me being strong."

"You're strong all right . . . and crazy." She laughs and shakes her head. "I can't believe you did that."

"It was selfish, really." I smile. Pushing aside the pain of losing so many, I let the relief that Liv, Gretchen, Henri, and I are all out of the Catacombs and still alive wash over me. "I can't believe I let you move away and forgot how much I needed you around. I promise not to let that happen again—ever."

Gretchen squeezes me tighter. My gaze lands on Chantal and I realize she's crying again. She mouths a "thank you" and I smile in response. "You'll have to get used to the idea of seeing me more, Gretchen. Whether you like it or not."

"Good." My cousin laughs. I finally release her as Anders returns and helps her lie back down. Gretchen looks weak and exhausted. She can barely keep her eyes open as she clasps my hand in hers. "This time I'm going to hold you to it."

"This time you won't have to." I squeeze her hand in mine and relax onto my stretcher under the stars that I wondered if I would ever see again.

I feel the warm pressure of Dad's thumb on my wrist, then gentle strokes of Mom's lighter touch as she rubs her finger over the back of my hand. I watch them as they watch me. Worry fills Mom's eyes as she glances at Dad, and he returns her look. And with that image in my mind, I finally let my eyes close, giving in to the exhaustion that permeates every cell in my body.

I still don't know what's going to happen when we go back home. I don't know who I'm going to live with, where we'll be, or what I'll do about school. The point is I don't need to know right now. No matter what happens, I will never push them away again. They need me and I need them. Nothing will change that. Divorced or not, they will be here to help me figure out my future.

No matter what.

I wear that thought like armor, using it to defend against the nightmares. Instead, I embrace dreams of courage to face an unknown future. I will hold tight to hope and continue the fight I started in the Catacombs. For now and for always, I'll find my way back out of the darkness—back into the City of Light.

Epilogue

Investigation Regarding Case #41773

Update current as of **June 24th** at **11:17 a.m.** Notable progress and new leads are as follows:

LEAD: Recorded statement from Harley Martin and Liv Greenwall regarding Roland Lambert's role in the deaths of Paolo Salvetti, Maud Kumas, and James Evans, and the assault on Henri Pelletier.

> **ACTION TAKEN:** Excavated cave-in section that Harley Martin believes crushed M. Lambert. We were unable to recover a body or any conclusive DNA evidence in the section she indicated. A pair of crushed night vision goggles was recovered from the rubble. The camera memory card is corrupted and we haven't yet recovered the final recording the witnesses say Liv Greenwall made in the theater. The statements from the surviving witnesses are consistent, so we are working from them. But as of right now, after a week of searching, we have been unable to determine the whereabouts of Roland Lambert.

Case #41773 is still open, pending further information and/or the location and arrest of M. Lambert.

Please direct any additional leads or new information to:
Inspecteur Bernard at the Paris Central Police Department

HERE WE WORSHIP A DIVINE MONSTER
CALLED DEATH.

IT HAS NO REASON.

IT IS BLIND.

AND ITS CRUEL EMPIRE TAKES OVER EVERY
BREATHING SOUL.

Acknowledgments

A few years ago, thanks to a dear friend (Love you, Bree Despain!) I was invited to join a large group of authors for an incredible adventure. We did a signing in Paris and then went for a writing retreat at an artists' commune in the French countryside. It was magical. As a part of our visit, we went to the Ossuary—and the spark for this story was born. Thank you to Amy Plum for making that trip happen and to Gilles Thomas for making sure I knew exactly what I was talking about firsthand when discussing what it is like in the off-limits sections of the catacombs . . . and for not allowing me to become lost down there just like Harley.

To my mom, Wendy and my sister, Krista—thank you for being my best friends and for always being there for me. Love you! A big thank you to Bill, Eric, Amanda, Matt, Mike and Emily for always acting excited whenever I share new book news. I didn't get to choose my family, but if I could have done that, you are the ones I would've chosen. Love you!

To Cameron and Parker: you are too tall. Just stop it already. I feel so lucky to get to share your lives and see what absolutely magical people you have become. You are my everything. To Ande, thank you for trying to help me through the scariest times and standing by me in the darkness.

I've been lucky enough to have the same brilliant agent by my side for the last nine years of this adventure I call a career. She has helped me through struggles and celebrated triumphs and I'm grateful for her—thank you, Kathleen Rushall!

To Georgina Dritsos, Gala Boccazzi, and Melisa Corbetto—thank you for being champions of my books and helping get them into the hands of readers. Your editorial team has all made me feel so welcome and I've truly loved working with you. To Leo Teti, thank you for believing in me since Insomnia and for building a relationship with me from a continent away—it's hard to explain how much that meant to me. Thank you so sincerely.

I've been blessed with some of the best people in the world as my friends. They keep me grounded and help remind me what is really important and I'm certain I wouldn't still be writing without them. To Kasie West, Renee Collins and Bree Despain—you are my crew. You carry me. I love you more than words can express. And LS Entertainment is going to be a thing someday, mark my words! To the rest of our merry band of rabble-rousers: Candi Kennington, Natalie Whipple, Michelle Argyle and Sara Raasch. Thank you for the friendships that manage to always exist even when we don't get to see each other as often as I would like. Love you!

For my other beloved author-friends both nearby and around the world who make a big world feel a little smaller and more manageable—Jennifer Wolfe, Jessica Brody, Marie Lu, Brody Ashton, Morgan Matson, Jessica Khoury, Emmy Laybourne, Frank Cole, Leigh Bardugo, Lisa Mangum, Gretchen McNeil, Kathryn Purdie, Shannon Messenger, Ally Condie, Andrea Cremer, and so many others, thank you for making my life infinitely more magical just by being in it.

Some friends you see often and others you may only see every year or two—I want to give some love to my BWB friends who always make me look forward to every next gathering with eager anticipation. To Nichole Giles, Julia McCracken and Andi Galusha—Vegas may never recover from our shenanigans.

To my Axe Fam over at Urban Axes. I love you all. When I took a breather from publishing you welcomed me with open arms and gave me a new home that was more loving and wonderful than I ever could've anticipated. You made it SO HARD to leave! Now as I dive back into my writing career, you've given me the strength of knowing you've all got my back. Thank you for the late night axe throwing, 3am burger orders, the boat parties, the wine tastings, karaoke nights, outdoor flipcup adventures and all the fun this girl could handle. Big love to my Corporate Events Team. And I'll be around to cheer on Team UA as often as I can. We'll always have the Urban After Party and Axe Prom!

And saving the best for last, thank you to my wonderful readers! I love hearing from you. Each time you reach out (whether in person or online) to tell me how much my stories mean to you, it makes me want to keep doing what I do. Thank you for taking time out of your busy lives for my books. I am lucky to have such amazing fans.

J.R. JOHANSSON is the author of the Night Walkers Series (*Insomnia*, *Paranoia* and *Mania*) as well as stand-alone novels, *Cut Me Free* and *The Row*. Her books have been published in over a dozen languages and more than twenty countries worldwide. She is the creator and host of the Riveting Reads podcast and the AuthorGamerGirl channel on Twitch. She has a B.S. degree in public relations and a background in marketing. She credits her abnormal psychology minor with inspiring many of her characters. She lives in a valley where the sun shines 300+ days per year with her family and her hot tub named Valentino. Visit her online at www.jrjohansson.com.